SAMBISA ESCAPE

A NOVEL

IFEANYI ESIMAI

CIPARUM
PRESS

ISBN: 978-1-63589-702-9

This is a work of fiction. Certain long-standing institutions, agencies, and public offices are mentioned, but the characters involved are wholly imaginary. Time has been rearranged to suit the convenience of the book, and except for public figures, any resemblance to persons living or dead is coincidental.

In memory of my mother.

PROLOGUE

Dr. Lambert Muzo almost jumped out of his chair when the door to his consulting room clicked shut. He had been so engrossed in his thoughts he had not heard it open. He stared at the man who had walked in. Had he agreed to an appointment and forgot?

"Good evening, Dr. Muzo," said the man in English, with a slight Hausa accent.

"Don't you know you should knock first?" said Muzo, annoyed. "Yes, how can I help you?"

The man, dressed in a faded blue kaftan, walked forward. He was huge with a shaggy beard and uncombed hair. Three scarification marks fanned out from the corners of his lips like dark drool.

Muzo's mind raced. He never saw patients on Sunday unless by private arrangement. Was this a robbery? He was about to yell at the man to leave at once but reconsidered. It was Sunday night. There was no one else in the office, maybe the whole building. He didn't recall seeing the security man when he walked in earlier. The guard was useless anyway, more like furniture. "How did you get in?"

The man turned and looked at the door. "I turned the handle to the door and it opened."

Muzo knew not to dismiss people on appearance alone. Here in Abuja, Nigeria, people wore their wealth on them. Expensive watches, shoes, sandals, eyeglasses. On this guy, there was nothing. But still, Muzo was cautious. "Okay, so, how can I help you?" he asked, his tone sharp, eyebrows raised.

"I don't want to waste your time," said the man. "But I believe you have information you want to share with the highest bidder. I am your highest bidder."

A knot tightened in Muzo's stomach. "What information?" He willed himself not to look at his briefcase with the package.

The man smiled, looked down, and exhaled. "It seems like the person you went to see at the presidential villa was not there." The man chuckled. "If you can hand over the package, we both can have a good night. Like you, I'm looking forward to a good night's sleep. It's been a long day."

Muzo's comfortable leather chair felt like concrete under him. The man must have followed him to Aso Rock. Maybe he should have waited at the Aso Rock clinic for his colleague to get back from his emergency.

"Dr. Muzo?"

Beads of sweat tickled Muzo's forehead as if he was eating a bowl of spicy-hot goat pepper soup. "I don't have any package," Muzo said in a strangled voice.

"In that case, you can tell me the information you have," said the big man. "I am a good listener. I understand it can make or break political aspirations."

"Who are you?" blurted Muzo as sweat poured down his forehead like liquid fire. The information he had could, no, would impact the outcome of the coming presidential primary election.

"Doctor, my name is Gambo. I've come a long way to see you, and I've been following you all day. Every good thing must come to an end. The choice is yours. Tell me what I need to know and I'll go away. Refuse to tell me and I'll beat you until you do, then the EFCC gets what's left of you."

Dr. Muzo looked up. Gambo had him cornered.

The Economic and Financial Crimes Commission— EFCC—was a Nigerian law enforcement agency established in 2003 to investigate financial crimes and money laundering. The EFCC was like a chopping block and lived up to its unofficial motto: "WE WILL GET YOU".

Muzo didn't need an evangelical pastor to tell him that the bank officials would never swap his head for theirs at the EFCC chopping block. The bank would have no choice but to inform the EFCC unless Muzo came up with the cash.

Muzo had gone into debt to build his multimillion-naira clinic in the wrong location. His checks to cover the loans bounced. Bouncing checks was a crime in Nigeria. He had greased the bank officials for years to misplace his files, but now he had run out of grease, and the bank officials had run out of hiding places. The loan was overdue. Then there was also the gambling debt to that loan shark. Muzo was in a desert without a camel. The information would solve all his problems.

"Were you thinking?" asked the man called Gambo. "Thinking is good for you."

"I . . . I have nothing to tell you," said Muzo. At sixty-five, and overweight, Muzo was aware he had no chance if things got physical. "Please . . . don't harm me; I'll give you money."

The man shook his head. "No. But you can tell me what I came for."

Muzo reached out and grabbed his briefcase. His whole body shook. His heart pounded as if it would burst out of his chest.

"Oh, so, it's in there," said the man.

Muzo's breath caught as Gambo reached into his trousers pocket. He brought out a phone, pressed the screen, and it lit up.

"It's getting past my bedtime, sir," said Gambo as he put the phone back in his pocket. He reached into his other pocket and brought out a black nylon rope and wound it around his palms.

Muzo had seen a lot of people strangled in movies. *I must get out of here.* Muzo sprang to his feet, pushing his chair back.

Gambo was faster, and before he could get his large frame away from the desk, Gambo was upon him, winding the rope around Muzo's neck.

Pain exploded in Muzo's throat. He reached for his neck, but the rope was too tight. The light in his office dimmed just as it became almost impossible to breathe.

"Are you going to tell me?" asked the man.

Muzo tried to speak, but only managed a choking sound. He would tell this man whatever he wanted to know, if he stopped. He nodded repeatedly.

"You've had enough?"

Muzo nodded, and the pressure left his neck. He gulped in air and went into a coughing fit. Tears stung his eyes. With the tightness in his throat gone, he inhaled deeply and the light got brighter. He wanted to live.

CHAPTER ONE

I entered the living room. It was quiet, as I'd expected this early in the morning. I thought I'd catch the news before I settled down to read. I had the TV volume just loud enough to hear it. As I flipped through the pages to the dog ear I'd made, the newscaster caught my interest.

"In the early hours of today, a gruesome discovery was made at one of the exclusive medical facilities in Maitama Abuja. Dr. Lambert Muzo, a prominent doctor and personal physician to presidential aspirant, Dr. Hamza Tarbari, was found dead in his private clinic. Dr. Muzo's body was discovered by his cleaning lady. He is predeceased by his wife and daughter who perished in a car crash a few years ago on their way to visit him. Dr. Muzo, dead at sixty-five."

Sad. Dr. Tarbari must find himself another physician. But why did he need a doctor anyway. Isn't he one? I shook my head—politics. Another piece of news interrupted my thoughts.

The female newscaster continued:

"This morning, St. Peter's Church in northeastern Nigeria in the city of Lamija was attacked by a suicide

bomber who drove in on a motorbike. According to eyewit-nesses, the young man pretended to be one of the parishioners and blew himself up. The casualty count so far is one hundred souls dead."

Again, in Lamija, I thought. *When are these people going to stop?*

"Six days ago in Nyanya, Nasarawa State, eight kilome-ters southwest of the capital, Abuja, at least two hundred people were injured and eighty-eight killed when two bombs detonated in a crowded bus terminal. There has been a—"

The TV went dead. Power failure. I hissed. What else is constant in this country? Strange, the refrigerator next door at the dining room was still humming.

I glanced around, and my pulse shot up. Maryam lowered herself on the couch and placed the TV remote control on her lap, her cell phone pressed to her ear. Not a glance in my direction, she continued her conversation as if nothing had happened. She must be talking to one of her numerous boyfriends.

"Really," said Maryam and nodded.

I looked at my cousin, oval face, round eyes, too much makeup. We could pass as sisters on looks alone, but our hearts are like day and night. I looked back at the blank TV, amazed at how people seek out trouble. I gave her a few more seconds to turn the TV back on, but she kept on yapping on the phone.

"Don't waste your time with her," said Maryam. "Cousin? Who told you that? Not true. She's more of a servant. Mommy said she was even adopted."

I'd heard enough. I knew Maryam was talking about me. I jumped to my feet and marched toward her.

Maryam ran her fingers through her long braids and looked up as I approached. She clasped her palm over the remote. I had an excellent idea in my mind to rip her braids off one by one.

Maryam looked at me, nostrils flaring. "What do you want?"

I ripped the remote control out of her hands. "Give me that!"

Maryam's eyes widened. "What are you doing?"

"What are you doing?" I said back to her in a whiny voice, mimicking her. "Who are you talking to about me? Spreading rumors again?" I pointed the remote control at the TV and turned it back on.

"How . . . how do you know I was talking about you?" asked Maryam.

My eyes were on the TV. The newscaster kept on talking while the camera panned to the victims of the bombing. Men and women lay on the ground, dead or injured, their possessions scattered all over.

"The terrorist group Boko Haram claimed responsibility for the Nyanya attack."

The newscaster went on to say that Boko Haram was a terrorist group that was founded in 2002 by Mohamed Yusuf and operated in northeastern Nigeria, Chad, Cameroon, and Niger. Their message: Western education was a sin. The primary mission of the group was to purify Islam in northern Nigeria.

"You're in trouble," said Maryam. "I'm going to tell Mommy."

"Mommy's girl. Tell your mommy what?"

"I don't know why you like to pretend you are one of us. You are not!" said Maryam. "I can come down and relax in the morning because this is my father's house. Your place is in the kitchen!"

I stared at her. If only looks could kill. Her words stung

me because she was right, Auntie had turned me into a servant. Maryam and I were both sixteen, but sometimes she talked and acted like a five-year-old. Over the years I'd lived with them, I'd learned the hard way not to give an inch. If you kept quiet, you became a foot mat or a punching bag, depending on the person you were dealing with and their mood. If it were her brother Peter, my response would have been different. At eighteen, he packed a powerful punch.

"Why are you looking at me like a *Mumu*?" asked Maryam. "You've lost your sharp tongue?"

"You are the idiot. Would you tell your mom the full story?" I asked. "That I was minding my business, and you came in and turned the TV off? Would you tell her that you're also spreading rumors about me?"

"Mommy!" shouted Maryam.

I heard a clatter of footsteps upstairs and I froze, controlling an incredible urge to flee. Auntie Halima was on her way down, and her children were always right.

The door to the kitchen creaked open and the cook, Fatima, poked her head in. She opened the door wider and shuffled in, wiping her hands on her apron. She must have heard the commotion long before Maryam called for her mom, but preferred not to take sides. But now her madam was coming, and she must do eye service.

"What is wrong with both of you girls?" asked Auntie Hamila. "You two cannot stay in one room in peace." She stepped off the last step and walked into the living room.

Auntie Halima, my late uncle's wife and technically my guardian, tolerated me until my uncle died five years ago in a road traffic accident. Now she cared less of what became of me. She wore a black embroidered *buba*, and panted from the exertion of running down the stairs.

"Ngozi, what happened this time?" asked Auntie.

"Emmm . . . I stammered. She'd surprised me. Usually she was only interested in her daughter's version of events.

"Speak," said Auntie. "I don't have all day."

"I was here listening to the news, and Maryam came and—"

"Who told you to watch TV?" Auntie barked. "There are many things to be done in this house. You can't just sit back and watch TV, you lazy good-for-nothing nonsense."

I'd swallowed the bait, hook, line, and sinker. By mentioning TV, I'd given her the opportunity to label me lazy.

I wanted to say, "What about Maryam?" She would spend the whole morning on the phone, but I bit my tongue. I hoped I wouldn't say anything that would get me into more trouble. Across me, Fatima's eyes widened, pleading with me to keep my mouth shut.

"She's spreading rumors about me," I said.

"What rumors?" asked Auntie, her eyes narrowing. She glanced at Maryam and then back at me.

"She told somebody on the phone that I was adopted."

Auntie looked at Maryam sharply. That confirmed to me that Maryam must have heard that from her.

"How do you know it's a lie?" asked Auntie. "Were you there?"

Fatima cleared her throat, her eyes as big as tennis balls now pleading with me to keep my mouth shut.

"She wasn't there either," I said.

"Enough!" said Auntie, finality in her voice. "Ngozi, no more watching TV. You must go to the market to buy fish. Peter is coming home today and I want Fatima to make his favorite meal."

"Hello, sorry for the interruption," said Maryam, her

phone pressed to her ear. She lowered herself back on the couch. "So, what were we talking about?"

"As I was saying, everybody that lives here has to do something, not just sit down, eat food, and watch TV."

I glanced at Maryam who was now sitting, twirling her braids, and doing a lot of nothing.

Auntie pushed some naira notes toward me. "Here, buy good fish, catfish, and come back to help Fatima. Make suya too, the way you always make them, very spicy."

I took the money from her, counted it in front of everybody, placed it in my purse, and slipped it into the front pocket of my jeans. I turned to Fatima. "Could you please tell the driver to get ready to take me to the market?"

"I need the driver," blurted Maryam from the couch.

"Where are you going?" asked Auntie Halima, her eyes on her daughter.

"To the market."

"When?" asked Auntie.

"I don't know when," said Maryam. "Ngozi can take the bus."

Auntie shrugged, turned around, and headed toward the stairs. "Ngozi, use any change that comes out for your bus fare."

CHAPTER TWO

Gambo drove the red pickup truck all night away from the federal government capital territory. He wanted to be as far away as possible from Abuja. The capital city could be efficient, and the police might be onto him sooner rather than later.

The plan had gone without a hitch. A slow smile parted Gambo's lips. "*Allahu akbar*, God is great," he said in a low voice. He was always thankful to God. Even the best-laid plans sometimes failed.

It was early in the morning, and he'd already passed several night buses heading in the opposite direction toward Abuja. He continued driving, looking for a rest stop that had a lot of activity, at least two luxurious buses or a few minibuses parked in front. This way he would blend in and be another traveler that had stopped to get some hot food and use the bathroom.

"Vegetable soup with pounded yam," said Gambo to the young girl who came to take his order.

The girl scribbled on her paper. "What type of meat?

We have goat meat, cow leg, chicken, guinea fowl, fried snails, fish, and bushmeat—"

"Bushmeat."

"Cold Guinness to wash it down, sir?"

"Pure water."

"Fufu and bushmeat coming soon," said the girl and walked away.

Gambo studied the crowd of travelers while he waited for his food. Most of the travelers were still groggy, having slept away from their beds. The girl reappeared with a tray and put down two sachets of pure water. She cut off the edge with a razor blade. He gulped down the first one and tried to push from his mind the source of the water and where the razor blade had been.

Gambo finished his food and went to his truck. With a full stomach, he felt better. Not that he was complaining before, but he felt good that he accomplished the task. For the first time, he felt he was paying back his debt. He unlocked the pigeonhole and brought out the mobile phone with its thick antenna. He punched some numbers into the phone and waited.

"*As-salāmu ʿalaykum,*" answered the voice on the other side, deep and deliberate.

"*Wa alaykumu as-salam,*" said Gambo, completing the greeting and the response. Peace be unto you and unto you peace.

"How did it go?"

"It went well. The doctor is of no use to society anymore."

"I presume you got the information?" The voice on the other end was cautious though expectant.

"Yes." Gambo took his time in explaining what had happened that night. When he mentioned the trip to Aso

Rock, there was a sharp intake of air on the other end. Gambo understood the concern.

Aso Rock is a four-hundred-meter-high monolith rock in the metropolis of Abuja. In 1976 the military government of Murtala Mohammed decided to move the federal capital from Lagos to the middle of the country in Abuja. They completed the residence of the head of state in 1991. Since 1992 Aso Rock Villa, or Aso Rock, has been the workplace and official residence of the President of Nigeria. The current occupant of Aso Rock would, in a few months, be in the fight of his life to keep his job. Any information to get an upper hand before the election was good news.

"Do you believe him?" the deep voice asked.

"I wasn't sure at first," said Gambo. "He said he put the information in envelops which had not been delivered. But pain is an excellent motivator. Muzo had sealed envelopes in his briefcase which concurred with what he'd said under duress. He wanted to drop them off with a colleague who had the ear of the president."

"In that case, we could still win the game," the voice said. "No. We will win." There was a pause. "We have to move as fast as possible. From what transpired today, you can see that the stakes are high. We must take this to the next level. You have done well, my subject."

The compliment filled Gambo's heart with delight. He could hear the excitement in Malam; in the teacher's voice. For the first time, Gambo felt like he was beginning to pay the debt he owed. "Listen carefully," said Malam, and he told Gambo what he needed him to do next.

Gambo had another five to six hours to drive before he got to his destination. But things couldn't wait. Setting the satellite phone aside, he picked up his regular mobile phone. Gambo would have preferred to do things himself, but time was of the essence. His subordinate would have to carry it out.

Next were the envelopes retrieved from the doctor. Malam wanted them mailed to him. Gambo weighed them in his hands and fought the urge to open them. Trust was important in his line of work. He placed the envelope in the pigeonhole. He would DHL them once he got to Akko.

CHAPTER THREE

I sat on the bus sweating. The conductor had packed us as tight as sliced bread. It was only 9:00 a.m., but it was hot. The sun blazed in all its glory. The bus smelled of petrol, exhaust fumes, cassava, and body odor.

My mind went back to the argument this morning. Maryam's reaction was overboard. But each time I turned the other cheek, she would want my head. I must do something drastic. In the book I was reading, Chinua Achebe's *Things Fall Apart*, Eneke, the bird, had stopped perching when hunters became expert shots.

I wished there was somewhere else I could go, somewhere without Maryam, Auntie, or Peter. A shudder went through me. My mom and uncle should never have died.

I looked around to distract myself and caught my reflection in the driver's side-view mirror. My two-week-old cornrows still looked good. My big round eyes looked isolated on my oval face. My nose was still as broad as ever. I remember when I moved here when I was five. Other kids would make fun of me in elementary school. "You suck up all the air with your big nose."

A pair of eyes in the mirror winked at me. I hissed and drew back, removing myself from the field of vision.

The bus driver adjusted the mirror, and I knew the eyes belonged to him. I lowered my head to avoid conveying the wrong impression. I didn't raise my head again until we got to the market and the bus stopped moving.

Hawkers shouted out their wares at the top of their lungs. Cars and motorbikes tooted their horns. The market was organized chaos. I checked my purse and exited the bus.

"How much is this one?" I asked the fishmonger's apprentice in Hausa. I pointed at a catfish, half the length of my arm.

"This is a beautiful fish," said the apprentice. "I'll give it to you for one thousand!"

"Six hundred," I countered.

Loud hysterical laughter broke out close to the store. The apprentice turned and looked.

"What is it?" I asked. I clutched my purse tighter, ready to flee. Rioters, armed robbers, religious fanatics, terrorists—anything could disrupt the peace.

"*Dabbobin daji!*" said the apprentice—a broad smile on his lips.

"Wild animals?" I whispered and looked in the direction the noise was coming from. "Okay, because it's you," said the apprentice. "Eight hundred naira only."

"Because it's me? What does that mean? I'll give you seven fifty. That's all I have."

He glanced toward the noise again and the gathering crowd. "Give me the money."

I raised my eyebrows. "Seven fifty?"

He nodded in rapid succession. "Hurry before the animals move on!"

I brought out my purse and counted the money. With no warning, the apprentice dashed off.

"Where are you going?" I asked, eyes wide.

"Wait, wait. I'll be right back. I must see."

I stood there with the money in my hand and watched him disappear into the crowd. "God." I exhaled. I put the money back in my purse. Curiosity got the better of me, and I followed. I might as well see the wild animals.

Ahead of me, a man carried a young boy in a white kaftan and hat on his shoulders. The boy giggled with delight as they made their way toward the commotion.

A crowd had formed around a buff twenty-something-year-old man. Sweat trickled down his shirtless torso. A skirt of dried palm leaves secured around his waist hung over his black trousers. His face was half smile, half grimace. Big taut biceps strained as he held on to a leash fabricated from thick coconut fiber rope. Something aggressive was at the other end. I couldn't see what it was, but I knew it was an animal.

"What animal is that, Papa?" asked the boy in Hausa.

I glanced up at the smiling face. The lad had the best seat in the arena. Without warning, the smile disappeared, the boy's eyes grew wide, and his jaw dropped.

Out of character, I pushed and shoved through the crowd to the front. The animal had a large head with big, mouse-like ears. Its thick neck sloped down its back to its hind limbs, covered with patchy, shaggy brown fur with black dots. There was no rhyme, rhythm, or symmetry to the dots. It looked like a dog, but bigger and uglier than any dog I'd ever seen.

The animal paced around in circles: one lap, two laps. It stopped and looked at the crowd, repeated the lap, and stopped again. It seemed bored. Without warning, it lunged toward the crowd right where I stood.

I froze while people around me took to their heels. In a flash, I was alone. The handler yanked at the rope and drew the animal back. He stared at me and shook his head. My knees felt like jelly.

The crowd came back, all smiles. Some looked at me, shrugged, and continued to watch the spectacle.

"You are not afraid?" asked the man next to me in Pidgin English. "That's a hyena. It can crush your bones and eat you while you're still screaming!"

The handler and the hyena repeated the routine in another section of the crowd, driving the people wild. A baboon appeared from nowhere. It wore shorts, a T-shirt, and a New York Yankees baseball cap. The handler held on to the rope attached to its waist. The crowd roared its approval and held out money. The baboon walked to them, collected the money, and gave it to its handler.

My heart had stopped racing. The fear was gone, replaced by amazement. "Who are these people?" I asked the man beside me.

"*Gadawan Kura*, hyena handlers," said the man.

"How come the hyenas don't attack them?" I asked.

"Trust," said the man. "The hyenas know their handlers will always feed them. In the wild, they can't be so sure of the next meal, especially now that farmers had encroached and turned their habitats into farms.

The show was over. The hyena handlers were busy counting their money, and the crowd started to disperse. The man with his son on his shoulders walked away. The son turned back for one more glimpse at the hyena.

I smiled and wondered how it would feel to have parents who loved you. I remember after Mama died and

Uncle Thomas took me to live with them. Even though my uncle treated me like his daughter, I dreamed that my father was a prominent businessman or government official and one day would come and take me away with him. I watched the boy's face dissolve in laughter, and I knew that sight was the closest I would ever come to experiencing being on my father's shoulder. I went back to the fishmonger's stall.

The apprentice waved his hand impatiently. "Bring the money, quick quick." He sliced the fish and wrapped the pieces in old newspapers and put them in a black plastic bag.

I dug into the front pocket of my jeans. My stomach tightened. I patted my back pockets and confirmed what I already knew.

At first, I'd thought the fishmonger's apprentice had played a trick on me. After I realized he was laughing at me, not with me, I left and wandered the market confused. All I got for that effort was a painful knee and ankle.

I thought of Auntie Halima. It is one thing to argue when you've been wronged, but a whole different ball game when you are in the wrong. My friend Zainab lived fifteen minutes away. My best bet was to walk to her house. As I walked to Zainab's house, my mind drifted back to the market for the one thousandth time. What could I have done to prevent the robbery? I prayed Zainab was home.

CHAPTER FOUR

D r. Hamza Aminu Tarbari got out of the shower and hurried to get dressed. He had the choice of wearing a suit and tie or the traditional *sokoto*. He preferred suit and tie. His cell phone peeped on the counter.

"Always peeping," he muttered to himself and picked it up. Hamza wondered what his agenda for the day was. He had tons of messages, emails, texts, and missed calls, and his voice-mail was full. The first time he had seen that many messages on his phone, right after he officially announced his candidacy, he'd thought his phone was faulty.

Nowadays, that was the norm. He scrolled through and selected the messages he considered necessary. He had fought the request by seasoned politicians and other hangers-on who had insisted he get a personal assistant, and that they had the right person for the job. He didn't want to lose control. *There must be a better way*, he thought.

Hamza switched screens to his schedule for the day. It was packed solid. There was no breathing room. He looked for what he could cut. His finger hovered over an appointment with an old family friend. He was too busy and would have canceled it, but old friends could never be replaced; new friends took a while to fit like old jeans. He put on his suit jacket and went downstairs.

"Good morning, sir," said the steward as Hamza came down the stairs. "Breakfast, sir?" The steward pointed toward the dining table.

Dressed in an Armani suit that was probably worth the steward's lifetime salary, Hamza flashed his signature smile at the steward and directed his six-feet-one frame toward the table.

Aliyah, his wife, a fellow physician, was almost done with her food, scrambled eggs and slices of fresh tomatoes. She had worked with him at their family-owned medical facility until six months ago when he took a leave of absence to pursue politics.

"Good morning, sweetie, you already look like a president," said Aliyah, a big smile on her face.

"Ali!" Hamza walked over and kissed her on the cheek and sniffed. "Hmmm, you smell good. I was looking forward to cuddling." He sat at the head of the table beside her.

"I scheduled an early morning surgery. I want to have enough time to meet you at the fundraiser. A wife has to support her husband, you know."

Hamza smiled. He knew she was his most significant cheerleader. Even bigger than he was. Not just because she would be the first lady but because she wanted him to be happy. He couldn't even muster enough enthusiasm to be his own biggest cheerleader. He never assumed he would quickly become the party's presidential candidate, but it was highly likely.

"And you are as radiant as ever," said Hamza.

"I have to go. I'll meet you at the fundraiser in the afternoon."

Hamza watched his wife leave and wished that their prayers would be answered soon. "I love you."

Aliyah turned, blew him a kiss, and disappeared through the door.

Hamza made an egg sandwich, took a generous bite, and as he chewed reached for the newspaper. He liked to look at the headlines and read interesting ones, a habit he picked up from his father as a kid. Every day, all the major newspapers were bought by the driver and presented to the older Tarbari. On Sundays, it was almost double the number of papers delivered on a single day.

Hamza wished he could run after Ali and ride with her to the hospital as they used to. He missed being with her and practicing medicine. The thrill when a new patient showed up in his consulting room. Like a seasoned detective, a medical Sherlock Holmes, he would pay attention to the signs and symptoms. Narrow the diagnosis down to a few differentials, and then start the process of elimination.

One by one he would order laboratory tests and other diagnostic procedures, witnesses to the defense, he called them. The results would come in to validate or disprove his differentials and guide treatment.

Since he was in a wishing state, he wished he had not agreed to this bid for the presidency. But he couldn't have refused. The event that put him in the spotlight that had started it all flashed through his mind, and sadness overtook him. He tried to think of something else, but it was of no use. His supporters advised him to embrace his calling; it was from Allah.

Hamza felt he would be like Janus, the two-faced Roman deity that looked at the past and the future. The god of transition. If he somehow found his way into Aso Rock, he would clean up a system that he had benefited from, and ruffle a lot of feathers. That's the only way this country can move forward.

Corruption had eaten into the very fabric of the public sector in Nigeria. *It was unfortunate*, thought Hamza, *but the private sector is held hostage by civil servants and politicians. Nothing happens without the exchange of money.*

The well connected grease the wheels of their progress with bribes called different names depending on the nation. Payoffs, kickbacks, lobbying, *vzyatki*, Roger me, or campaign contributions. *No country is immune to the misuse of money, but in my country, it has become a culture, a way of life.*

"It's a good system," he had heard his father say many times. "You know what it would cost you to get what you want."

"What about the man who does not have what it takes?" I'd asked.

"If he doesn't have the means, he does not deserve it," replied his father.

The common man doesn't deserve good roads, schools, hospitals, and decent housing, yet he paid his taxes. Hamza pushed the thought of his father away and the many problems out of his mind.

He sighed and poured himself a steaming cup of coffee. He took a sip and read the headlines.

Two of them screamed at him. The first headline was damning but not specific: "Oil Pipeline Explosions and Kidnapping of Expats Linked to the Opposition Party".

The second said: "Prominent Physician Dr. Muzo Dead".

CHAPTER FIVE

"Sweetheart, you fell for the oldest trick in the book," said Zainab in her singsong voice. "That's what happens when you are poor and live with rich people. It robs you of your street smarts."

Zainab was petite with a pretty face, despite a single horizontal scar on each cheek. Men always did a double take. We'd met in elementary school many years ago. One day she forgot her snack, and I shared mine with her; that day and every other day. We grew to become terrific friends. She always got a lot of attention. Now in secondary school, men were becoming interested in her.

Her mom ran a small kiosk where she sold anything you could think of. When Zainab was younger, she used to hawk oranges and bananas to help her mom. I'd always wanted to hawk with her. From individual sticks of cigarettes, to two or three spoons of washing detergent wrapped in clear waterproof plastic bags, to tiny pieces of meat on sticks.

Her father was a trailer driver and never home.

"Ngozi, the hyenas, monkeys, and sometimes a man

trying to slice his stomach with a sharp knife are there to distract onlookers. While everyone is watching, waiting for the man's stomach to split open, their team of pickpockets steals from the crowd."

Zainab opened a plastic bottle of Coke, raised it to her lips, and drank a quarter of it. She broke the tamper-proof seal on a cough syrup bottle and emptied the contents into her Coke bottle. She twirled it around, took a sip, and then replaced the cap.

"You know, all your problems started after your uncle died in that car accident," said Zainab in a matter-of-fact tone. "Mrs. Bashiru doesn't care for you at all. Her own kids go to a private school while she sends you to Akarika Girls Government Secondary School. Popularly known as Akarika Gals." She burst out laughing and took a sip of her elixir.

I rolled my eyes and giggled. "Foolishness. But at least that kept us in the same school."

Zainab waved a finger at me. "But you, sometimes you should hold your tongue. You mustn't always have the last word . . . and have hope too. Hope for a better tomorrow." Zainab giggled. "Without hope, there's no way you can make it to the next day."

I looked at her and leaned forward, expecting more.

"That's not me. Those are my mother's words."

I wrinkled my face. "Hope? What type of vain hope? In my case, there is no light at the end of the tunnel."

"Tunnel?" Zainab snorted. "You read too many books. I've never seen a tunnel in Nigeria. I mean the type of hope that you know is possible. For example, when you go to a wedding reception, you know that if you stay until the end, you'll eat jollof rice. There's no guarantee, but you stay; why? Because each time they open and close the kitchen door, you get a whiff. You know it's there, just a matter of time."

"Well, we're saying the same thing," I said. "There's nothing to be hopeful for, light or jollof rice. My situation is hopeless. Sometimes I wish I could run away to a place where the grass is greener, where I won't have any problems."

"You can't always run away from your problems. They'll still be there waiting for you when you get back. Look at my papa. He complains the apartment is too cramped. He jumps into his trailer and drives away for months. When he comes back, we're still here in the same crowded apartment waiting for him."

Zainab and her tirades. How am I going to get the money for Auntie for the fish? Maybe I should ask Fatima.

"Bunky, are you listening to me at all?"

"Sure, sure," I said. "What did your dad do again?"

"Listen, you have only one home, just make the best of it. If you want your grass to be greener on your own side, you must water it. Here, take a sip, it will calm you down."

Zainab passed her bottle to me. *It's funny how we get along,* I thought. *We are complete opposites socially.* I shook my head. "No, Zainab, my life is already tough as it is. I don't need to complicate it. You should stop drinking this stuff; it's not good for you."

"Your life is tough? I wish I had your brains and also lived in a big mansion," said Zainab. "At least I wouldn't have to go to school tomorrow to take these nonsense exams. You still won't come with me?"

I shook my head. Zainab had asked me to come with her to school for the remedial exam. I'm not expected.

Zainab sighed. "Any other crap I could take. Insults, abuse, jealous cousins, sharing a room with the house help.

Can you imagine, spending two whole weeks in school? I wish I'd studied hard and passed the exams the first time as you, instead of coming for this remedial session." Zainab burst out laughing. "It would be something taking another remedial session to support a weak remedial session."

I looked at my friend and wanted to tell her that she was a good student until she started taking cough syrup. But instead, I remembered why I was there. "Any chance of getting money from you?"

"I just spent my last kobo on the syrup. Thank God you came when you came, it would have been a tough decision. You or the syrup."

I knew she would have ended up giving me the money if I'd come earlier and she would have had to go get it from a boyfriend or somewhere. I glanced at Zainab, and the concentration on her face told me she was thinking of a way out.

Zainab snapped her fingers after a minute. "I have two options. One, what about your mother's friend in Yankee? The one who used to send you clothes and things. Then your Auntie would take the clothes and give them to Maryam?" Zainab snapped her fingers. "The one that wanted you to visit her in the US?"

I nodded. "My godmother, Auntie Nkechi, what about her?"

"You can write to her and ask for money!" said Zainab, widening her eyes.

"I don't know. It's been years since I wrote to Auntie Nkechi last, and it would take time."

"No," said Zainab. "She can wire it straight to your account."

"You know I don't have an account," I said and tried to laugh it off. "Where would I get money from to put in it?"

"She can send it to my account, then I'll give it to you. Dan always sends me money."

"Who's Dan?" I asked.

"Hello? My new boyfriend."

Boyfriend or boyfriends? I thought. I guess I get along with Zainab because she never pressured me to go out with her and her friends; she protected me from unwanted attention. "Sweetheart, I'm already rotten," she would say. "It doesn't make sense for both of us to go down the same road."

"Anyway, those people in America, I don't trust them," said Zainab. "Maybe they want to use you for juju or make you a servant when you come over there. It's better you stick to the devil you know and stay here in Nigeria."

"So, that means no money from you," I said.

"Nope. Option two is tomorrow. Dan went to the business center. He'll give me money to go back to school with. But by then it would be too late."

I nodded. "When are you leaving for school?"

Zainab frowned. "Around 8:30 a.m. I wish I didn't have to go. You're so lucky."

I sighed. "So no money for me?"

"Nope. Do I look like Dangote's daughter?"

CHAPTER SIX

I said good-bye to Zainab and left for home. My uncle's house—or now my auntie's house—was a good thirty-minute walk from Zainab's parents' home. All I needed to do was walk through a shortcut, a narrow undeveloped plot covered with bushes. That was all that separated the homes of rich people from the crowded street that was Zainab's neighborhood.

It was now midday, and the city of Lamija was bustling with activities. I'm sure Fatima would be wondering what had become of me. I wouldn't hear the last of it if I got home without the fish. Zainab had been my one and only hope. There was no way I could wait until tomorrow and get money from her before she leaves for school. After all the running around I'm doing trying to get fish for the pepper soup, Peter might not even eat.

"Sister, get out of the way!" a voice screamed beside me.

I turned and was just able to jump out of the path of a fast-moving taxi motorbike. I wasn't the only person that had to move out of the way.

A woman in a skirt suit cursed out the motorbike

driver's mother in Pidgin English and walked into a business center. I remembered my late mother's friend, Auntie Nkechi, in the U.S. and what Zainab had suggested. I hadn't contacted her or heard from her in over two years. Right now I was desperate.

I walked into the business center, and my fears were realized. Its four computer terminals were occupied; I would have to wait. Two ceiling fans circulated the hot air in the room, and the vibration of the generator outside was constant. That was the least of my problems. I could wait until someone was done.

On a large poster on the wall were the prices for the different services they provided. Charging your mobile phone, sending or receiving faxes, making phone calls, photocopying, laminating, and computer use. I had no money.

I looked around for the man that ran the place. He was friendly with Zainab the times I'd been in with her, and moreover, he knows I'm a Bashiru; he'd let me use the computer and pay later. All I wanted to do was send an e-mail. That would be fine with him.

"Can I help you?" asked a young girl of about twenty as she walked up to me, sizing me up.

"Where is Ali?" I asked.

"He's not here today. I'm covering the store for him."

I nodded. *Assistant clerk*, I said to myself, and tried to hide my disappointment. "I want to use a computer."

"You'll have to wait," said the girl.

She looked like the overzealous type. "Let me wait for a little and see if anyone finishes."

"But its pay before service," said the girl. "You pay first so that I can give you a number."

I nodded. The clerk walked away after I made no move

to pay. I looked at the people using the computers. On the first terminal, a man in a shirt and tie like an office worker sat there watching a Nollywood movie. His volume was turned up high as if he was in his house. From where I stood, I could see the screen and enjoy the video if I wanted to. The next terminal was the lady I had walked in with. She was typing furiously on the keyboard. The third computer was another young man in a kaftan. He looked like he was doing research. Consulting and writing into a notebook now and then. *Which of these people would leave early?* I wondered.

"Are you sure you know what you're doing?" said a voice on the third terminal.

I sat down on the single chair propped up against the wall and watched. Three young men, probably in their late teens or early twenties, were on the fourth monitor. One was sitting while the others stood around him, more or less blocking the screen.

"Give me the video," said the one wearing a dashiki. If Zainab were here, it would have been a different story.

"Which video?" replied the one wearing a white T-shirt.

"That thing I gave you," said Mr. Cute.

"That thing is the video!" said the white T-shirt in a loud whisper. "I left it in the truck."

Mr. Cute gave him the eye, then got up and started walking toward the door. The others followed. All of a sudden, the fourth computer terminal was free. I looked around for the lady I'd spoken to earlier, but she wasn't there. My heart hammered in my chest. I got up, glanced toward the door, and headed for the chair. They had been on a video-sharing site. My hands shook as I grabbed the chair. I glanced around again and looked toward the door.

No sign of the men or the manager. *What would Zainab do?* I asked myself. I felt like I was being unfair, but I had no choice. I pulled the chair back and sat down.

I opened a new tab and went to my e-mail website. My fingers trembled so much that it took several tries before I got my password right and logged into my account. It was full of junk mail. Whenever I surfed the web, I always gave my e-mail address whenever it was asked for. What was my auntie's e-mail address? I scrolled down looking for an e-mail she had sent before. I remembered it was her first name, Nkechi, her last name, and then a profession. Oh, God.

"Ole, thief!" A voice yelled.

I almost flew out of the chair. It was the man watching a movie shouting at the monitor. He was really enjoying the movie. Nobody looked at me. Pulse racing, I continued with my message, search and stab style with a finger. It took forever. All my senses were heightened, and I expected to be tapped on the shoulder at any time. The message was done, now back to the address. It had come back to me. It was her first name, middle initial, last name, and the abbreviation "MD" at the same dot com. Now to click send.

"What are you doing?" a voice shrieked.

I ignored the voice and focused on clicking send. I tried to move the cursor back to the send tab. Suddenly a hand appeared, and both my hand and the mouse were yanked off the mouse pad.

CHAPTER SEVEN

I jerked back, mouth open. The angry face of the store manager was so close to mine I could smell the remnants of her lunch, bitter leaf soup and cassava. I let out a slow moan, relieved it was her and not the young men that had returned to their computer.

"You didn't give me any money," yelled the store manager.

A few heads turned to look at us. But when no punches were thrown within the first few seconds, they went back to what they were doing. I wished the ground would open up and swallow me.

"I . . . I didn't see you," I stammered.

The lady—that thing was no lady—placed the mouse back on the table. "If you want to use it, you'll have to pay." She jabbed a finger at the wall. "The prices are up there." She extended her right hand forward, palms up to collect money from me.

I glanced at the wall, wracking my brain for what to say, how to disengage and just leave. I heard footsteps approaching and pulled my eyes away from the wall. The lads were back.

"We haven't finished, you can't give away the computer!" said the man in the dashiki.

"No . . . I didn't see anyone here," said the manager. "I thought—"

"You thought what? Get out of the way," said the dashiki guy in Pidgin English. "We have things to do."

I scurried away and tried not to think of what Mr. Dashiki would have done if he had found me on their computer.

I might as well go home, I thought, and left the business center. This could have easily gotten out of hand. The girl could have raised the alarm, shouted "thief" and within seconds a flash mob would have gathered; and before I could say "petrol" I would have either been beaten to death or given a burning necklace, a tire placed on my shoulders and set on fire.

Outside, the traffic had increased as more people were going home from the market or closing for the day. The sound of someone speaking over a loud speaker with music in the background signaled the arrival of campaigners for the presidential primary election. Posters of the smiling candidates in suits or traditional outfits were taped onto trucks and minibuses. A large banner of one of the candidates was secured on a vehicle and young men in white T-shirts with the face of their candidate printed on it milled around distributing fliers.

I walked past the truck and shook my head politely when I was offered a poster. I contemplated walking back to Zainab's house. Must I run to her each time a dog barks? Anger washed over me like a bucket of hot water dumped over my head. I was robbed. It wasn't like I took the money and did something with it.

"Enough is enough!" blasted from the loudspeakers. "Vote for Dr. Hamza Tarbari. Vote for new ideas! Vote for change!"

Then the speaker went on, lambasting the current president for having done nothing after four years in office. *Isn't this the primaries?* I wondered. Why are they focusing on the president?

I saw more posters of this doctor posted on electric poles, walls of buildings, and vehicles. The name sounded familiar, but I couldn't place it. People started to gather around the parked truck. I decided to go home and face Auntie Halima. I wouldn't want to be hanging around when the opposition showed up. Like other rallies, it would become a shouting match and then descend into a fight; a free-for-all with some heads cracked and bones broken.

I turned around and walked past the truck. The crowd was indeed getting larger. I passed the business center with my head kept straight ahead. Ahead of me was a lorry, and just as I'd predicted, the opposition. I turned off and took the road that would lead me to the undeveloped plot and the footpath to our street.

I remembered the fiasco at the business center; my problem was still weighing heavily on my shoulders. I hadn't sent the e-mail. There was nothing to hang my hopes on now. I could not smell the jollof rice. I smiled as I thought about my friend, thankful for having her in my life. If it weren't for her, I would be completely alone.

Maybe I should find a job to earn some money. But I needed money right now, not at the end of the month. I got angry at whoever it was that stole the money and wished the wrath of God upon them. Let them get into trouble as they've gotten me into trouble, or maybe even worse.

If only my mother were still here, life would be different. Apart from when I see her in pictures, I couldn't recall her face as I used to. Most of the time I only remember her when I've been mistreated. She was the only mother figure I'd ever known since I'd moved in with them when I was five. Maybe I would have forgotten about Mother by now.

I should tell Auntie what happened. What's the worse she'll do. She'll get mad, say some nasty things, and eventually would cool down. The same up-and-down cycle we've been having since Uncle died six years ago. I could never do anything right. It could be worse; Auntie could have kicked me out once Uncle Thomas died. I wonder why she hadn't just come straight out and told me to move out of the house.

I passed a few people on the footpath going the opposite way. I wondered what would happen when the owner of the plot finally finished his building and put up a fence. That would be the end of the shortcut. I stepped onto our street and started to walk. On both sides of me were mansions secured by high walls, iron gates, security guards, and vicious dogs. The plan was to keep intruders and robbers from breaking in, but it looked like the owners of the houses were prisoners inside their own homes.

As I got closer, my pulse started to beat faster. This would not be easy. Was Auntie at home? What was she going to say or do? I wondered if Peter had reached home and demanded his fish pepper soup. That would really put the spotlight on my absence. My stomach churned as worst case scenarios raced through my mind. I stopped in front of the small pedestrian gate beside the main entrance to my auntie's compound.

CHAPTER EIGHT

Hamza felt a chill trickle down his spine. His mouth fell open. *Dr. Muzo is dead.* He grabbed the newspaper with both hands and started to read. His eyes bounced over the text at top speed until he got to the end of the article. Nothing was incriminating. Hamza let out a deep breath he hadn't even realized he was holding.

"This is exactly why I'm not a great fan of politics," he muttered and took another sip of coffee.

Hamza read on. The sixty-five-year-old physician was found dead that morning by his clinic manager when he arrived at 5:00 a.m. Dr. Muzo was predeceased by his wife and two children and had no known immediate family.

What happened to Dr. Muzo, wondered Hamza. He reread the paper, this time more slowly, looking for words that alluded to a coronary. The man was a little overweight, but he seemed to carry it well. Why had he asked for the meeting? It sounded like he wanted to discuss something. But that wasn't out of the ordinary.

Hamza inhaled and shook his head. May his soul rest in

peace. When things like this happened, Hamza always wondered why bad things happen to good people.

His appetite gone, Hamza took the paper with him and left for the exit where his car should be waiting in front of the house. The steward opened the door as he approached.

The startled driver jumped out of the car. "Good morning, sir!" He opened the back door of the four-wheel drive, and Hamza got in.

For a few seconds, Hamza wasn't sure what to do. Maybe he should have stayed in the house and arranged his thoughts before coming out. He was still reeling from the shock of the news. He wanted to extend his condolences to the family, but there was nobody. He never remarried. Hamza shook his head. It was like trouble roamed around looking for someone to tag onto.

The driver looked uncomfortable and started to talk. "Sir . . . emmm . . . emmm . . . where—"

"Oh, to the office," said Hamza.

"Yes, sir."

Hamza looked ahead and saw the gate man throw open the gates. He turned around and nodded as two four-wheel-drive trucks similar to the one he was in drove up behind him. As they got closer to the gate of the sprawling estate, Hamza's driver pulled to the side to let one of the trucks get ahead. Even though Hamza preferred a low-key life, he was advised to have some security.

His father had said, "Heaven helps those who help themselves," and recounted heads of states whose decision to move without security had cost them dearly, such as Olof Palme of Sweden and their very own Murtala Mohammed.

Hamza got the message. He didn't point out to his father that other heads of state had been sought out and murdered despite their top-notch security. He refused to use any siren escorts. They exited the compound and traveled the streets of Abuja.

Hamza did not want to bring his work home and preferred to meet his campaign manager and others involved in the campaign at his campaign office. Right now his mind was devoid of any plans. The news of Dr. Muzo's death brought back memories he would have preferred remained buried.

He looked out of the window as the convoy passed the Abuja central mosque in the central business district of the capital city, its massive dome surrounded by four towering minarets. Dr. Muzo had been his support pillar.

Hamza fondly remembered many years ago when he had seen Dr. Muzo almost every other week when Hamza was a medical student and the doctor was a lecturer in his school. Hamza's father had instructed Muzo to be his son's mentor.

The more Hamza tried to move Dr. Muzo away from his mind, the more he thought about him. Dr. Muzo was the personal friend that he was supposed to meet. He couldn't help but wonder why he had wanted to meet with him. He probably would never know. Maybe he would distract himself with work when he got to the office.

CHAPTER NINE

I reached for the gate handle to pull it open.

"Ngozi," a voice yelled.

Despite the heat, I felt a coldness hit my core. I knew that voice. I whirled around. In the kiosk opposite the gate was Auntie Beatrice, Auntie Halima's younger sister. She was rough around the edges and on a perpetual search for a husband.

"Where have you been?" said Auntie Beatrice in her deep hoarse voice that reminded me of a man's.

"Good . . . good evening, Auntie." Her over-made-up face stared at me. She had removed her eyebrows and replaced them with hand-drawn dark lines, leaving her with a surprised look on one side of her face.

"There's nothing good about the evening," said Auntie Beatrice. "You're lucky I'm on my way out. I've been waiting for you all morning so I can eat fish. Come on, go inside and help Fatima before I slap your face."

I pulled open the gate and went in. I loathed Auntie Beatrice. Good thing she was not staying. She must have come to beg for money. Once, when I was a kid and she had come to visit us, Auntie Halima sent me on an errand to the kiosk down the road to buy matches and a gallon of kerosene. In my haste, I'd forgotten to take a gallon jug and had to come back to get it. I overheard Beatrice telling Auntie Halima that she should get rid of me because I was not even family and was a drain on her resources. "Get rid of her!" Auntie Beatrice had yelled.

I entered the house through the kitchen. A pot simmered on the gas stove, the aroma of cooking goat meat enveloped the house. I should tell Auntie what happened as soon as possible before I lost my nerve. There was no sign of anybody, not even Fatima. I walked down the small corridor to the dining room. Still, there was nobody.

I looked around, hoping to see Fatima. *I should tell her first*, I thought, *she might have ideas. She's the only one who has been nice since I moved into the house. She would side with me or come to my rescue sometimes.* But as a servant, Fatima's loyalty was to her mistress and her job.

Peter is all right sometimes and other times hostile.

I stopped in my tracks. On the dining table was Maryam's phone, and on the floor was her backpack. I glanced around—nobody. I grabbed her phone. It asked for a password. I smiled and typed in the month and day of Maryam's birthday. I was in.

I heard sounds upstairs, but I didn't stop. Then the toilet close to the living room flushed. My fingers moved faster. I went to the text app on the phone and tapped it. I went to the search and started typing my godmother's name. It came up on Maryam's phone. I didn't hesitate. I typed, "Please send me money to buy fish, Ngozi," and hit send. I heard a whoosh sound, and the message went. I exhaled, mission accomplished. Just then the bathroom door opened and out came Maryam.

"Where have you been?" asked Maryam.

"Here." I extended her phone toward her.

Maryam looked at me, then at the phone, eyebrows narrowed. She snatched it from me. "Don't touch my mobile."

"This girl! Where have you been?" asked Fatima in Hausa as she shuffled into the dining room.

I turned and let out a huge breath. My knees felt weak. A car honked its horn outside.

"Fatima, tell Mommy I went to Aisha's house," said Maryam as she picked up her backpack. "I'll be back tomorrow morning." She headed toward the front door.

"Okay," said Fatima. She turned to me. "Come, come, we have work to do!" She frowned and brushed past me as she headed for the kitchen.

Fatima looked around the kitchen. "Where's the fish?"

I told her everything that happened and how I went to get money from Zainab, but no luck.

Fatima rolled her eyes. "*Yeye*, foolish girl. Now you've gotten yourself into real trouble. Why did you watch those Hyena people? Pickpockets are there to take advantage of distracted shoppers." She sighed, grabbed a drying cloth, and busied herself wiping plates on the kitchen rack.

I knew Fatima was thinking, but there was no time. "What should I do? I don't know where to get money from."

Fatima looked toward the dining room and lowered her voice. "It's not about money. Oga left plenty of money for Madam when he died." She hissed and shook her head. "Madam just doesn't like you."

Fatima made a face that I interpreted as, *Can you believe that crap?* "Madam felt Oga loved you more than

Peter or Maryam," said Fatima. She poked a finger in the air for emphasis.

"That's not true. Uncle loved us all," I said.

"Shut up. What do you know? It was your mother, Matron, who trained Oga Thomas in school and helped him get his first job at the local government, from where he started to rise."

"But they're his own children," I protested.

"Yes, but Madam doesn't see it like that." Fatima's eyes lingered on mine, then she let out a heavy sigh. "Keep an eye on the goat meat. I'll rush to the corner store. I hope they have fish. Madam is already in a bad mood. Peter came back, entered the garage, and drove away with the big car."

"The Mercedes Benz?" I asked.

Fatima nodded. "Madam went to look for him."

Fatima left for the corner store and I opened the pot to check the meat. I poked a piece with a fork; it wasn't soft enough. I hoped Fatima would succeed. I looked at the table clock in the kitchen; it had been only ten minutes since Fatima left.

I cocked my head. Did I hear a noise in the living room?

"Fatima! Fatima!" Auntie bellowed from the living room.

I threw my hands up in an "I give up" gesture. Just like every good-intentioned plan that involved me, this one was already unraveling even before it had started. Shrouded with a feeling of dread, I stepped into the dining room and walked across to the living room where Auntie Halima sat on a couch, head thrown back as if exhausted.

"Has Fatima gone deaf? Where is she?"

"I . . . I don't know," I stammered.

Auntie jerked her head to face me, eyes narrowed,

nostrils flared. "What nonsense is that? Isn't she there in the kitchen with you?"

"I . . . I'm already back from the market." Just then I heard the kitchen door open and then close. Auntie turned toward the kitchen; she must have heard it too.

"Fatima, is that you?" asked Auntie.

"Yes, Ma."

"Come, I've been looking for you."

Fatima appeared in the living room, a pleasant smile on her face. She didn't look at me, only straight at Auntie. "Welcome, Ma, did you find Oga Peter?"

"That boy! I didn't find him. Wait until I get my hands on him!" Auntie lowered her voice. "Where did you go?"

Fatima let out a long exhale and sighed. "I went to buy fish."

"Fish! But I sent Ngozi." Auntie's eyes landed on me.

Fatima threw her hands up in resignation and sighed. "Ngozi, tell her what happened."

I glanced at Fatima, then back at Auntie. My pulse raced.

"Talk now!" said Auntie.

I swallowed and started my narration for the third time today. As I told the story, Auntie's face transformed as if she had bitten into fresh bitter leaf and lime. When I finished, she looked like she would explode.

Auntie's eyes were on me. "Fatima, prepare the fish."

My eyes were on Auntie. Her breathing was ragged, her lips pursed in a thin line and her nostrils flaring. She didn't speak but waited as Fatima walked toward the kitchen door. I would get it this time.

"I took you in, fed you, clothed you, and this is how you pay me back. By stealing from me!"

"Auntie, it was stolen. I didn't—"

"Shut up! You don't speak when I'm talking to you!" Auntie sat up and poked a finger at me. "You are a little thief. That's how it starts! Take some here, take some there. Before you know it you're stealing cars. You've spent my money on boys. You and that low-life friend . . . emmm . . . emmm, Zainab. Now get out of my sight, you lazy good-for-nothing rubbish."

CHAPTER TEN

My head felt heavy. My hands, my legs felt like bags of rice as I walked toward the kitchen door. Auntie's words echoed in my mind. It hurt like a fresh wound with salt rubbed on it. Resentment fermented inside me. My whole body trembled as I tried to hold my tongue and not speak back.

I was at the kitchen door. All I had to do was reach for the doorknob, turn it, and walk into the kitchen. Auntie had said things that were not true. But I couldn't help myself. I turned and walked back to the living room.

Auntie Halima sat reclined on the couch. Eyes closed, hands beside her, palms up. I watched her for a few seconds, struggling with myself to walk away, but my feet refused to obey. She took a deep breath and exhaled. Then her eyes flew open and she saw me staring at her. For a second, fear flashed through her eyes.

"What do you want?" Auntie barked.

I couldn't hold my tongue. "I'm not a thief. You throw words around as if they don't mean anything. You judge others as if you are a saint. You call yourself a good woman, but it's all hypocrisy. If you look up the word 'hypocrite' in the dictionary, there'll be a picture of you beside it. The only person who qualifies as a thief in this house is Peter. Didn't he steal your car and drive away with it? You call my friend names and me lazy, when you have a sloth and a slut in Maryam."

Auntie sat up, eyes as cold as ice. She drew in air loudly. "What else do you have to say?"

Her voice, calm and controlled. That voice, that stare annoyed me the more. It shifted something inside me. I felt a fresh wave of words rush up from inside me. I couldn't stop it. It spewed out. "I am glad you are not my blood relative. If anybody asks me how you've treated me, I'll tell them with it was abject cruelty! You are not a good woman."

"How dare you say that, Ngozi!"

"Before God and man, I'm telling the truth!" I shot back. "You think I don't feel. My uncle entrusted my care in your hands, but you have no pity. You treat me as if it's my fault I'm an orphan. Peter hits me, Maryam tells lies about me, and you pretend they do no wrong. Do you know how it feels to be alone? The only people you consider family would rather have nothing to do with you, and they remind you of that every day?"

Auntie stared at me. Her lips trembled.

"Since Uncle died, you've treated me like an outcast. Even people with leprosy are treated better. It seemed like you were waiting for him to die so you could show your true colors."

"Ngozi, you can't say that," said Auntie with a whimper. "My late husband loved you like a daughter, and so do I." Auntie shook her head. "Everything I do . . . I'm only trying to correct you. To correct your faults. I do the same with Maryam and Peter."

"No, you do not! You called me a thief. I am not a thief!" My voice was loud and climactic, as if signaling the end of my tirade. My eyes fixed on Auntie.

"Oh," gasped Auntie Halima. She raised her shaking fingers to her lips. Every part of her trembled. She got up and, shaking all over, walked upstairs.

I stood there inhaling and exhaling as the sound of Auntie's steps faded. It was the hardest battle I'd fought and my first win. I raised my head, turned, and headed toward the kitchen. I opened the door and saw Fatima. She looked at me, and when our eyes met, she looked away. I knew she'd heard everything and didn't approve.

"Rest," said Fatima in a whisper. "I'll finish up."

I nodded and went to the room we shared with two beds placed side by side with a space between them. I threw myself on my bed. My pulse had stopped racing. My heartbeat had come back to normal, and reality descended on me like taking a cold shower in a harmattan morning. *What have you done?* A dependent cannot quarrel with her benefactor as I'd done. Nor speak her mind unhindered. I'd gone too far.

I lay there on the bed, sleep eluding me. The elation I'd felt faded. The thing that I hated when done to me, I had done to Auntie. A feeling of remorse over my outburst covered me like a suffocating blanket. Outside, the sound of crickets, the croaking of frogs, and the occasional sound of a car showed how late it was. At a point, Fatima came into the room and got ready for bed.

"We'll talk tomorrow," said Fatima. "Good night."

Within minutes her breathing became regular; she was fast asleep. *Ngozi, you've done it this time.* I was afraid. I should go to my auntie, apologize, and beg her for forgiveness. Say it was the work of the devil. But I knew from experience and instinct that that would make her resent me more. I opened my copy of my favorite book, *Things Fall Apart*, and let my subconscious deal with the problem. After thirty minutes, I realized I'd been reading and rereading the same sentence over and over again. I couldn't concentrate.

I heard the security guard open the gate and a car driving in. Keys jingled as someone tried to unlock the door. Would it take three attempts? Three times I heard a curse, then the door creaked open. Peter was back, and he was drunk. God help me if he finds out from his mother what I said. When Peter was younger, he would trap ten or more wall geckos in a wire mesh and put them in the sun. Catch lizards, cut them open, remove everything in their stomachs, and set them free. When angry, he would cut holes in his mother's clothes hanging on the laundry line. Yes, he was her darling.

My pulse raced. All my senses became heightened. I monitored Peter's footsteps as he stumbled around the house. Within minutes I could smell his perfume mixed with the smell of sweat and beer. I glanced at Fatima and appreciated she was there. I stopped hearing Peter's footsteps. Either he had gone to his room upstairs or crashed on the living room couch.

Drenched in cold sweat, sleep was far from my mind. I listened to the sound of the night, my mind made up on how to respond to my predicament.

CHAPTER ELEVEN

I didn't want to take any chances. Fatima had a routine: she woke up by 5:00 a.m. every day, took her shower, and before six was preparing breakfast or tidying the house. I watched the table clock with the luminous dials all night. As soon as it struck five, I got up took a shower and dressed in jeans and a T-shirt. I packed my school backpack, then slipped back under the cover and waited. My plan was simple: run away. I'd meet up with Zainab and go back to school with her.

"Ngozi?" asked Fatima.

I opened my eyes to see Fatima leaning over me, shaking my shoulder.

"This one, you're still sleeping. Are you all right?"

"Good morning," I said, my voice still groggy from sleep. "What time is it?"

"Seven forty-five. I have to—"

"Seven forty-five!" I bolted up.

"What now?" asked Fatima, her eyes wide.

"No . . . no, nothing. I never oversleep." I tried to remain calm. I didn't want to give myself away. But my inside was in turmoil.

"Peter vomited all over the living room," said Fatima. "And he's sleeping in it. Help me boil water for tea and put some eggs in the pot. I want to clean up the living room before Madam comes down."

Fatima left the room, and I dashed out of bed. I put on my shoes, grabbed my backpack, and headed to the kitchen. I'd slip out of the kitchen door. I didn't want to see Auntie or Peter. I glanced at the clock in the kitchen. It was already 7:50. A knot tightened in my stomach.

I placed my bag outside the kitchen door, grabbed the kettle, filled it with water, and set it on the gas stove. Next were eggs. Three eggs each for Auntie, Maryam, and Peter. Fatima and I usually would eat leftovers from dinner for breakfast. That made it easier. I looked at the clock again and my pulse shot up. I moved faster and nearly dropped the saucepan with the eggs. "Calm down," I muttered to myself.

Fatima rushed into the kitchen. The acrid smell of vomit and stale alcohol followed her like a shadow. "Ngozi, buy sugar from Mama Musa." Sweat dotted her forehead.

Now I'd definitely be late. All this extra activity this morning. "Okay."

"Just buy that small sachet of ten cubes," said Fatima. "We'll buy a packet later." She pushed some money into my hands. "Go right now. Madam wants to drink tea."

The mention of the word "Madam" sent a chill down my spine. The thought of facing her after last night terrified me. "I . . . I've put the kettle and the eggs on the—"

"Just go, *sauri*, hurry."

I ran out of the kitchen. Fatima must have been impressed by my speed. If only she knew why. With my backpack slung over my shoulder, I ran to the gate. I didn't see any vehicles and dashed across to the kiosk.

"Good morning," I said in Hausa.

Mama Musa beamed at me; she knew money was coming. She always charged us a little higher because we only came to her when it was urgent.

"Sugar!" Sweat poured down my face. She started to rummage and I heard the sound of a motorbike. I turned and looked. It was a motorbike, and it had no passenger. There was no way to tell whether it was a motorbike used as a taxi or not, but I flagged it down.

"Here," said Mama Musa.

"Where are you going?" asked the motorbike driver in Pidgin English as his bike stopped beside me.

Mama Musa had handed me a whole pack. "No, no! I only want small cubes. The sachet."

"It's all right, pay me later," said Mama Musa.

I grabbed the blue box of sugar cubes, glanced at the house gate, then at the bike.

"Are you in a hurry?" asked Mama Musa. She glanced toward the back of her kiosk. "Musa! Musa!"

Musa, her six-year-old, appeared. He had on a dirty used-to-be-white cap on his head and a filthy kaftan that reached his ankles like a dress.

"Yes, Ma!" said Musa.

Mama Musa took the sugar from me. "Take this to Auntie Fatima." She gave Musa the sugar, then turned to me. "Go, go, go."

For a moment I was confused. Then I understood. I mounted the bike, gave the bike driver Zainab's street address, and we took off.

I gripped the frame of the seat on each side of me. The driver weaved in and out of traffic with expert ease, but my heart was still in my throat. He seemed to know just the right time, down to the last second, to swerve to avoid a collision. I wanted to ask the driver what time it was. Then I changed my mind. He would dutifully drive with one hand to glance at his watch, and that would be pushing our luck.

The bike came to a stop in front of Zainab's building. The rows of stores on the ground floor were already open for business. The busy scene was the exact opposite of where I'd just come from. I realized I had another problem —I didn't have money.

"We've arrived," announced the driver.

This was a polite way of asking for his money. "Give me a minute, let me go inside the house and collect money from my friend."

The driver threw his head back and laughed. "*Kyakkyawa yarinya*, pretty girl," he said in Hausa. "I wasn't born yesterday."

I glanced around. Maybe I would see Zainab or somebody. I was late, there was no doubt. The phrase "out of the frying pan, into the fire" stuck in my head. Sweat poured down my T-shirt.

Still gripping the seat frame with my right hand, I rubbed my sweaty left palms down my jeans. I wanted to do the same with my right palm when I realized that within my grip of death was a single crumbled and sweaty naira note, the money Fatima had given me for sugar.

"I don't have change," said the driver, looking cross when I offered him the money. "You rich girls, you wanted to ride for free. You were my first customer. Go break the money in there." He pointed at a restaurant under Zainab's building.

I felt like a sack of *garri* had been lifted off my shoulders. I bought a bottle of Coke, and when they gave me back the change, not only did I have enough for the bike man but also enough to pay my fare to Akarika Girls. My relief soon turned to grief. It was Fatima's money, probably my Auntie's. Now I'd actually stolen money.

"Bunky! What are you doing here?"

Only one person called me that because we once shared a bunk bed. I turned around to see a very surprised Zainab.

"I was about to go to your place," she said.

"I decided to go to school with you."

"No way," said Zainab.

"I thought you'd already left." Zainab looked like she was going for a party and not back to school.

"Would have. I was waiting for this." Zainab brandished a bottle of cough syrup.

I shook my head. "Not good for you."

Zainab coughed, then laughed. "I'm not feeling well, just came in here to buy soda." Her face became serious. "And I was going to come to your house to give you this."

I felt like crying. In Zainab's hand were folded up naira bills. After what happened last night, she was still the only friend I could count on.

"What made you change your mind?"

"It's a long story," I said.

"I enjoy long stories."

CHAPTER TWELVE

"Three chances! Three chances to Akarika!"
shouted the bus conductor.

Zainab and I got on the bus and I brought her
up to speed.

"So, Peter had taken the car after all?" asked Zainab.

I nodded.

"Did he bring it back?"

"I think so," I said.

"One chance! One chance to Akarika!" bellowed the
conductor.

There was constant traffic of people coming in and
leaving the bus, but the driver kept on shouting that there
was only one space left.

Everything around me was suspicious. I expected
Auntie Halima or Peter to show up soon and drag me out of
the bus.

I watched the conductor for about thirty minutes and
found out that most of the earlier passengers were touts,
paid to occupy the seats. Once a real customer showed up,
they would leave and get a kickback from the conductor.

We didn't leave Lamija until three hours later. Only then did I heave a sigh of relief. The hustle and bustle of town life gave way to clusters of houses here and there as we drove out of town.

Zainab and I sat next to each other. I couldn't believe I did it. This was the first time I'd done anything like this. The next step would be to convince the teachers not to send me back. I dozed off with that thought on my mind.

The bus stopped by the sign on the main road that read, "Welcome to Akarika Girls Government Secondary School." I got off the bus, yawned, and stretched. I shielded my eyes from the brutal noon sun.

"I still don't believe you're here," said Zainab.

"Better believe it. There's no going back for me."

"Let's go see if we're the first to arrive."

"I doubt it," I said.

We grabbed our bags and started off toward the school gate.

A green agama lizard with some brown on its back scurried toward us, pursued by a big male with a red head and blue body. They froze when they saw us. So did I, ready to flee. I knew they were harmless, but I just don't like lizards, and less so their cousins, the snakes. The lizards looked at us for a second and darted off in different directions. The female disappeared inside a bed of flowers while the male scurried up the school fence. It lay there, watching us and nodding its head.

Zainab bumped me on the shoulder. "You're so faint-hearted."

"As if you're not," I shot back.

We walked in through the wide-open gate. Hausa music blared from a radio in the security post, but no guard was there. I looked at the administrative building and classrooms on our right; the louvers were all closed, no sign of life. To our left were the dormitories; the windows were open, evidence of life. We walked across the soccer field that separated the hostels from the administrative buildings.

By the time we arrived at our dormitory, Mary Slessor House, I was sweating profusely. The rectangular building was built with the same design as the other two dormitories, Victoria House and Ekpo House.

We'd learned about Mary Slessor in history class in our first year. She was a Scottish missionary to Nigeria in the nineteenth century who helped stop the practice of abandoning twins in the forest to die of starvation or be eaten by animals. Back then, twin births were considered demonic in some parts of Nigeria. Now the name "Mary Slessor" always reminded me of twins.

Four windows kept the dormitory aerated and well-lit with natural light during the day, and the mosquito nets and burglary-proof bars kept insects and intruders out. At each end of the building was a door, one permanently blocked with a bunk bed. Only one was available for use.

To the left of the functional door, in the corner, was a spot reserved for the head girl, Aminata. From this vantage point, she was supposed to monitor all traffic coming in and out of Slessor House.

As we walked in, I felt a sudden onset of nausea. Aminata was already there, talking to a group of girls. Our eyes met, and her eyebrows shot up.

"Ngozi Bashiru, what are you doing here?" asked Aminata and headed in our direction.

Aminata was a big girl. No, she was a big woman, and you don't want to get on her wrong side. Rumor had it that she was married and had two kids at home. She'd refused to graduate from secondary school by not showing up for exams. As the oldest, most experienced student, she'd been head girl three years in a row. Her motivation was to supplement her family finances by taking food from the school's store for her family. Fellow students were not spared either.

Aminata waved a piece of paper in front of me. "You're not on the list, why are you here?"

"She's on the list," said Zainab.

"I'm . . . I'm on the list," I stammered.

Aminata eyed Zainab. "Show me."

My mouth went dry. I didn't want to be sent back. I knew I was not on the list, but we went through the list anyway.

"Where's the other list?" asked Zainab, her face very serious.

For a second Aminata looked confused, then she hissed. "Get out of here, there's no other list."

Zainab pointed at a group of girls. "Both the twins are here, but only one of them has her name here. There must be another list."

Aminata wagged a finger at me. "See what's going to happen. Write your name on the list and you can stay for the night. Tomorrow we'll see what the teacher says." Aminata flipped the list over, and there was the name of the other twin written in blue ink, while the names on the front were in black.

"I don't know why people can't stay at their homes during the holidays," murmured Aminata. "As if something is chasing them at home."

I nodded. "Okay, sounds good." I wrote my name and turned to walk away.

"Wait, we're not done. I have an errand for you first," said Aminata. "Go to the snack kiosk and buy me a loaf of bread, two sardines, two bottles of Coke, and three boiled eggs." She handed me a folded naira note.

"Don't forget to bring back my change," said Aminata, her face impassive.

I took the money, she turned and walked away.

"I'll go with you," said Zainab. "This is what I call scratch my back and I'll scratch yours."

Aminata had given me only a fifty-naira note. The items she'd rattled out would cost more than two hundred. I used two hundred of my own money, or what was left of Fatima's money, to buy Aminata's provisions. When I gave her the goods, her face was passive and only contorted into a smile when I gave her back her fifty as change.

"Welcome to Akarika Girls special session," said Aminata.

CHAPTER THIRTEEN

T he analyst rushed through the main door at the offices of Hamza Tarbari for President. His eyes glanced over the empty bank of computers housed in cubicles with black monitors, ready to work, lacking only personnel. Dr. Tarbari would have been here, in the open, going over a website with the other analyst or browsing on one of the computers. *Where was Dr. Tarbari?*

The analyst had seen him come in a few minutes ago with the campaign manager. He checked in the conference room, which housed an overhead projector and white board walls. Nobody was there. Even the other analyst they had hired was gone. Two of them watched over the bank of twenty computers on this floor and another twenty on the floor below, the same layout as this one.

He stopped and listened. He had hoped to hear her black heels striking the corridors. Two people searching would make this faster. All he heard was the pounding of his heart.

Less than a minute ago, the campaign manager had taken a call. Beads of sweat had appeared on his forehead, despite the frigid air inside the reception area delivered by two air conditioners that looked like refrigerators. He nodded a few times, pushed the mute button on his phone, and had whispered, "Inform Doctor that his wife is on the way."

The analyst's mind came back to the present moment. He knew there were a few more rooms to go before he checked the main office. Since he'd been hired from his job as a computer analyst at Diamond Bank, he'd done little in his new position. In fact, he'd done nothing, but his paycheck came like clockwork. During his interview, Dr. Tarbari had told him about his plan to run for the presidency. He'd been in the United States when Barack Obama ran, and he liked their strategy. He would like to run a similar campaign, focusing majorly on social media and mobile penetration.

The analyst had agreed with him that Nigeria's mobile phone penetration was on course to reach eighty-four percent in the next four years. With a good jingle and excellent message, he could get to the masses.

But he wasn't going to mention that it didn't matter, since the incumbent always dictated the outcome of the election. Maybe it was time he looked for another job; once the primaries were over, there wouldn't be any job here. Unless Tarbari had a plan he was keeping close to his chest. He knocked at the next closed door. Dr. Tarbari was not there. *Where was he?*

The analyst heard the faint sound of metal scraping on concrete outside. *The gate is being opened.* He looked out of the corridor window as he passed and his body went rigid. Mrs. Tarbari—the other Dr. Tarbari's car was pulling into their parking lot. In a panic, the analyst thundered down the corridor, passed a bank of printers in one corner and the fully stocked pantry, still full but for the few drinks and pastries he'd removed.

The analyst skidded to a halt in front of Dr. Tarbari's office. He knocked quietly. No answer. He swallowed and knocked louder. "Dr. Tarbari. Mr. President." Still there was no reply. "Mr. President?"

Knowing that Mrs. Tarbari could get to this office within a few more minutes, the analyst turned the handle and pushed open the door.

"*Wallahi!*" the analyst gasped as he looked into the palatial office. Dr. Tarbari sat behind his huge Mahogany desk, his head thrown back, supported by his intertwined fingers, his eyes shut.

The analyst cleared his throat. "Mr. President. Your . . . your wife is on her way—"

Tarbari's eyes flew open. "Stall her five minutes," said Dr. Tarbari, cutting the analyst off. "Now! Go!"

Fearful, the analyst left the room and shut the door quietly. Dr. Tarbari sounded different, as if he was under stress. The analyst's mind raced. How was he going to stall the wife of his employer?

At the same time, he wondered if he was seeing things. Was that the other analyst's shoe he saw under Dr. Tarbari's table? The analyst raced off to intercept the footsteps he was sure he would hear soon. He knew his paycheck would depend on that.

CHAPTER FOURTEEN

Malam sat alone in his home office and looked at the newspaper again for the millionth time. Muzo was dead. It was a mixed feeling that passed through him, elation, sadness, and trepidation. He let out a deep sigh.

It was time again to execute, thought Malam. Nobody wins by accident. *Success is always intentional.* Becoming an achiever can be summed up as one deliberate step after another. You might stumble, but if you remain focused and steadfast, success will find you. The main thing is coming up with a solid plan in the first place.

Malam knew that the next stage of the plan would be tricky and may result in more deaths. A similar incident took place a week ago, and it didn't even make the news. *This should not either*, thought Malam. He was more concerned about the boys recruited by Gambo over the years. Would they keep their mouths shut and remain loyal to Gambo and the course?

Malam was no scholar, and he knew that. But he

believed in common sense and learning from experience. He read a lot, of note, the works of great men.

One quote rushed to his mind. A quote that would help him see reason in what he was about to do: "The tree of liberty must be refreshed from time to time with the blood of patriots and tyrants." That had been Thomas Jefferson.

Malam whispered aloud, "And the blood of the innocent."

Malam reached for his phone, punched a fast-dial button, and waited.

"*As-salāmu ʿalaykum,*" answered the voice on the other side.

"*Wa alaykumu as-salam.* Go ahead as planned. Remember, keep casualties to a minimum."

CHAPTER FIFTEEN

I looked around, amazed by how fast time had flown. It was already late evening, and girls exchanged stories about their vacations so far and what they would do after the two weeks here were over.

Joy Okafor, who was in the same class as me, picked the bed on my right. Her locker had no lock—she had arrived too late. I lay on my back, a novel in hand, and tried to read.

"Ngozi, can I put things in your locker?" asked Joy. "I promise I'll remove them tomorrow once I buy a staple and padlock."

Joy was skinny and tall, about six feet, compared to my five feet ten inches. She was a conscientious student, and we were study partners. She always had a smile on her face, a scarf over her braided hair, and a small Bible with her at all times. A member of the school's CSU, Catholic Scripture Union, she never compromised when she believed she was right.

"Thanks so much!" said Joy.

I watched her put an iron, two packets of cabin biscuits, and a tied-up plastic bag into my locker. She slipped a trav-

eling bag under her bed and changed into a blue embroidered top. She knelt down, said a prayer, and stretched out
on her bed. Within minutes, she snored. I wished I could
fall asleep without effort.

As the night darkened, the heat lingered on. My
stomach rumbled, reminding me I had skipped dinner. I'd
bought a small tin of powdered milk, sardines, a sachet of
margarine, and a loaf of bread when we were at the kiosk. I
popped the lid of the powdered milk open with a spoon
handle. Someone had removed the protective foil cover of
the tin. Instead of white powder, they had filled the tin with
sand. My heart sank. Somebody had pulled a fast one.

I wanted to scream. All these things happening to me in
one day. I showed it to Zainab. She had been dozing off.
"We'll sort it out tomorrow."

It wouldn't be nice pointing fingers at any of the girls.
My anger dissipated just as fast as it had built up. But I was
still hungry. Then I had an idea. I looked at Joy, who was
fast asleep. The time on the wall clock was 8:00 p.m. I was
sure Joy wouldn't mind if I borrowed her iron.

I cut off two slices from my loaf of bread. There was a
power socket on the wall next to me. Good thing we still
had power. I plugged in the iron, and while it heated, I
opened a tin of sardines and applied margarine on both
sides of the sliced bread. Next, I tore out two sheets of paper
from the middle of one of my notebooks and laid the
buttered bread on it.

"What are you doing?" asked Zainab, resting on her
elbows on her bed.

"Making a fish sandwich, the way Efome does it." I put
the fish in between the bread and wrapped it tightly with
paper. I ironed the whole thing, one side after the other. In
no time, the dormitory was filled with the aroma of toast as

the hot iron heated the bread. Girls glanced in my direction. When they looked, they only saw me ironing. Before I started cooking, I'd checked and made sure Amanita wasn't in her corner. She would have made sure that I made a few sandwiches for her from my provisions if she was around. When it was ready, I offered some to Zainab.

"I'm not hungry," said Zainab.

That was fine with me. I devoured the whole thing, and it was one of the best meals I'd ever had.

Junior lights-out during regular school session was at 9:30 p.m. and the senior lights-out was at 10:30 p.m. Because this was an extraordinary school session, Aminata fixed it at 10:30 for everybody. After lights-out, we were all supposed to be asleep, and the hostel quiet. But there were still conversations here and there and the occasional flash-light piercing the darkness.

"Who's still making noise?" thundered Aminata from her corner. "Everybody be quiet before I come over there and break your coconut heads, foolish girls!"

Bed springs squeaked as girls tried to find a comfortable sleeping position. In no time, the hostel became quiet and the chirping of crickets outside got louder.

"Ngozi, are you asleep?" whispered Zainab.

I shut my eyes tight as soon as I heard Zainab's voice. I knew I could whisper, but I didn't want any more trouble, even though Aminata was several beds away from me.

"Shh!" I whispered back. "Sleep, before you get us into trouble." I turned away but didn't fall asleep. Slessor dormitory got quieter, the silence punctuated by rhythmic snoring.

A gentle breeze coming through the windows kept the room cool. Now and then, someone whacked a buzzing mosquito, breaking the silence. Those insects were quick.

Despite mosquito nets on the windows and the insecticide we sprayed in the dormitory, mosquitoes still buzzed around. Zainab and I joked that the mosquitoes in our school put on gas masks to protect themselves.

Moonlight streamed in through the windows as I wished sleep would take me. I lay on my back and gazed at the ceiling and wondered if I'd made a hasty decision running away. Now I was at the mercy of Aminata. Did Auntie Nkechi respond to my text? Slowly, as my eyes drifted shut and sleep stretched out its hands to grab me, my thoughts drifted to Auntie Hamila, Fatima, Maryam, and Peter. Were they looking for me? As I thought about this, I drifted off to sleep.

I didn't know how long I slept, but a continuous thumping sound threatened to wake me up for good. I heard distant voices and the sound of car engines. Were those male voices? Where was I? The shouting got louder and louder. My eyes flew open. I saw one, two, three . . . five men in the dim moonlight. Was I dreaming? I sat up in bed and glared. There were men in our dormitory. Other girls sat up too. This was no dream. My heart galloped like a thousand horses.

CHAPTER SIXTEEN

"**B**eat up anyone who resists!" a male voice yelled.

A bolt of raw adrenalin rushed through my veins. I bolted up. This must be a dream. Torchlight bounced off the walls. I wanted to scream, to hide, to make the images disappear. Metal scraped on the cement floor. My head jerked in the direction of the sound. The bunk bed barricade slid away and the door was shoved from outside. Dark images came through the door. I couldn't move. I couldn't breathe. I couldn't do anything.

A few beds away from me a girl let out a high-pitched piercing scream that snatched me out of the fugue state I was in. This was no dream. Furious men were in our dormitory. They seemed to be everywhere, and more were coming in. I felt an incredible urge to pee.

"Everybody outside. Outside now!" yelled a male voice in Hausa. He carried a huge gun, and a belt of bullets was draped around his neck over his army camouflage. For a moment, I thought he was a soldier. Soldiers should be on our side. But these men were breaking things, yelling, and ordering us out of our beds at this ungodly time of the night.

"THE BLOOD OF JESUS!" a girl screamed. A flash of light and a deafening bang simultaneously followed her shout. Someone had been shot. The sound came from Aminata's side of the room.

My ears rang. My head felt like it was stuffed with cotton balls. I seemed to be out of my body watching. Everything seemed to move in slow motion. I had to get out of there. My eyes darted to both ends of the room; the doors were clogged with girls and men.

"Who did that?" a voice yelled. I could barely hear. "Don't fire your gun again!" He sounded angry. "We are here for food and women! We have no use for dead girls!"

For the second time, words spurred me into action. Behind me was a window. I got off my bed and pulled at the glass louvers. There were so many. Should I take the glass louvers out or smash them? The school would charge me for them. And there was also the mosquito net and burglary-proof bars to deal with. Zainab would know what to do.

"Zainab," I muttered and turned to look at her bed. It was empty. I looked at the door. It was wide open, the clog of people gone.

The sound of screaming girls and angry men shouting filled the air. If I stayed here, I would be caught. I took a deep breath and headed for the open door. The darkness outside invited me. I pushed and shoved my way past hysterical girls and determined men. It seemed like a path had been cleared for me. I got closer and closer to the door, to freedom. One more step and I would be out.

Something grabbed me from behind just as I was about to step through the door. A hand squeezed my neck. The light dimmed and got darker as the pressure on my neck increased. Pain exploded in my throat, but most of all I couldn't breathe. The air was being squeezed out of me.

"Small girl, going somewhere?" asked a deep male voice in Pidgin English.

I grabbed the hand on my throat with both fingers and tugged with all my strength. But I was no match. The man held on like a vice. My neck burned and a feeling of impending doom overtook me. I was going to die. My bladder let go and the hot liquid trailed down my leg.

I clawed and kicked. The man held on tight.

"You want to go outside, eh?" said the man. He dragged me through the door, and we were outside.

CHAPTER SEVENTEEN

This couldn't be happening. Fresh, crisp air caressed my skin all over, but there was no time to appreciate it. My eyes adjusted to the moonlight. This was no dream. It was chaos. Girls screamed, and men barked orders at the girls and at each other. The same was going on in the other two dormitories. An open-top pickup truck idled in front of each building and men ushered girls into them. Some girls climbed on their own onto the vehicles while the men dragged others and tossed them in. By the kitchen, men loaded bags of rice, tubers of yams, and baskets of tomatoes onto a truck. *They are stealing our food. I have to get out of here!*

"Quick! Quick! Quick!" shouted another man. "Have you located the freezer? Don't forget the meat!"

Some of the men wore military camouflage while some wore black. They all had rifles and thick beards—there was no way they could be the army or police. The hand on my neck tightened and yanked me forward just as the words "Boko Haram" formed in my mind. The sound of my heartbeat thrashed in my ears. Gurgling sounds escaped my throat as I struggled to inhale and exhale. I clawed at his hand again.

"Aliyu, she can't breathe!" thundered a voice in Pidgin English. "You'll kill her!"

At once, my tormentor, Aliyu, relaxed his grip on my neck. I coughed and spurted, filling up with air, taking in great lungfuls in rapid succession.

"No more casualties," said the authoritative voice.

"Sorry, my sister," Aliyu muttered. He placed his palm over my face and pushed me with his other hand toward the open truck. I inhaled through his thick, rough fingers. The smell of sweat, tobacco, and shit overwhelmed me. I stopped breathing. Within seconds, my lungs burned, and I gasped for air.

Aliyu had hurled me against the tailgate and pain exploded in my waist as my hip bone connected with the vehicle. I massaged my neck, then my hip.

"*Oya*, up!" said Aliyu.

My legs shook, barely able to support my weight. I raised my right leg to climb and felt the dampness of my sleep T-shirt. Shame washed over me, but it passed, replaced by fear as girls brushed against me, thrown into the truck like sacks of rice. I whimpered and struggled to lift my body off the ground. Strong hands grabbed me from behind, hoisted me up, and I was airborne. I landed on the tangled-up bodies of the other girls. They broke my fall and moaned in agony.

"The dormitories are empty, let's go!" shouted one of the men. He looked at us and pointed his rifle. "We've just killed one of your classmates. If any of you tries to jump out of this truck or escape, I will shoot you."

"Oh God," a girl whimpered.

The man that had been talking reached out and struck her with his fist several times. "If I hear any more sound, I'll use more than my fist!" He pointed his gun at us once more, and every whimpering or moaning mouth went silent. Aliyu and another armed man jumped into the back with us and slammed the tailgate shut.

At first, nobody moved. We all cowered on the floor of the truck. I looked around, recognizing some of the girls from Slessor, Ekpo, and Victoria Houses. A girl crawled to one of the wooden benches placed on each side of the truck and sat down. She hugged her knees, and her body shook with sobs.

I glanced at the guards; they didn't seem to notice. Dazed, I got on my knees, crawled to a bench on the opposite side, and sat down. Some girls sat with me while others remained on the truck floor, a mass of whimpering and quivering flesh.

The truck jerked forward, and I held on to the metallic tarp frame on the side of the vehicle for support. Our driver headed toward the school gate, the other two trucks leading the way.

There was a loud boom and the night sky lit up. Girls screamed, and we ducked our heads. Had it been more than a gunshot?

"*Kai*, it's the gas in the kitchen," said Aliyu. "We should have taken it with us, loaded it into the truck with these girls."

I looked in the sound's direction. They had set the kitchen and the dormitories on fire. The truck drove past the security hut and out of the school gate. Just a few hours ago, Zainab and I had walked through this gate without the slightest idea of what was going to happen. I remembered the lizards that had startled us and wished I was as free as they were. I shuddered as a terrible sick feeling washed over me. A terrorist group had kidnapped us.

CHAPTER EIGHTEEN

In 1906 the British merged the small colony of Lagos and the Southern Nigeria Protectorate into a new colony of Southern Nigeria. Eight years later, in 1914, Lord Lugard amalgamated the Northern Protectorate of Nigeria and the Southern Protectorate into one: the Colony and Protectorate of Nigeria. This joining of different ethnic and religious groups into one federation created internal tension, which persisted in Nigeria and is still going on to the present day.

Hamza was all dressed, sipping coffee and listening to the news in his main living room. Another oil pipeline bombing in the south and some expatriates kidnapped. In the north, churches were being bombed. He wondered what Nigeria would have become today if Lord Lugard had taken the vast differences among the people into consideration before joining them together.

Hamza sighed. Problems always seem to appear from nowhere to harass you. He thought of his narrow escape yesterday when Ali surprised him at the office. By sheer luck, the analyst had stalled her long enough. Had he not, it would have been calamitous.

Hamza knew he was lying to himself. He was the source of his problem. There was no other person to blame. People fight temptation, but he was the one who gave in, not fighting. He also knew what to do about it. Nobody said forming a new habit was easy, but you have to avoid situations and people who encourage you to indulge in whatever bad habit you're trying to get rid of.

Just like the country, he would have to take matters into his own hands to rid himself of his addiction. Nigeria needed a trickle-down change. All hands must be on deck. A change that would start from the top and trickle down to the man or woman at the last rung of the ladder.

As the second son of one of the wealthiest men in the country, growing up, his father had shielded him and his brother from the everyday hardship of living in Nigeria. Decaying infrastructure—roads, water supply, power supply, health, and the education system. Things taken for granted in other countries, where things work, do not function in Nigeria. The sad thing is that Nigeria had the resources to make it happen, but for corruption and mismanagement.

Hamza thought of car lines at petrol stations and laughed.

"What . . . what's so funny, sir?" said a voice.

Startled, Hamza turned to face his campaign manager, Kola, whom he had invited to the house, his first step in trying to break his bad habits. He had forgotten about him.

Kola Abioda was one of the few people who worked for and reported to Hamza's father. In his early forties, Kola worshiped the ground the elderly Tarbari walked on, and was an excellent manager. His job was his family and friends.

"Ah, I forgot you were here," said Hamza. "Nigeria is one of the world's largest producers of crude oil, yet it doesn't have refineries that function at full capacity. It sells crude to other countries and buys it back as a refined product at very exorbitant prices. Why? So that the middleman gets a huge payday."

The campaign manager shifted uncomfortably. "Sir, Tarbari and Sons have a fleet of oil tankers dedicated to that trade. It's a service someone has to provide. In fact, I managed that division before Oga said I should come and . . . assist you with the campaign."

Hamza nodded. His father's company, which he was a part of, had made a lot of money from government contracts. He was part of the problem.

Kola coughed. "Sir, you know if we don't do it, the job will go to someone else, and that money won't come to us."

"That's the problem!" said Hamza. "The refineries should never be allowed to break down. The refineries' maintenance should be the first agenda. There's no account-ability, and the bad habit continues in perpetuity. Every-body wants a share. The result, you have pockets of well-connected individuals here and there making millions of dollars." Hamza stabbed a finger in the air. "Then they park the money like a classic vehicle in some Western bank. Who suffers? The man on the street."

The manager pointed at the sixty-inch flat-screen TV hanging on the wall like a framed picture. "Oga, they are talking about you and the chairman."

Hamza picked up the remote control and turned up the volume. A picture of him and his father was on TV. A female newscaster was speaking.

"The opposition party will have their primaries in a few days. It is speculated that Dr. Hamza Tarbari, son of business magnate and billionaire Tarbari Tarbari, will be nominated by his party as their candidate for the presidential election. Young Tarbari, if nominated, would have to address accusations leveled at the opposition for sponsoring terrorist attacks and kidnappings in southern Nigeria as a voter-suppression strategy."

A male newscaster turned to face his colleague:

"Since the president is from the south and Dr. Tarbari is from the north, it seems like . . . No! It will be a north and south showdown. Hmmm, it might get ugly. The religious and ethnic tensions would take a front-row seat."

Hamza lowered the volume. "By putting our picture there, they are insinuating our involvement. How can we be sponsoring such a terrible thing? We don't even have the nomination yet."

The manager smiled. "But you will, sir. You . . . you have a . . . a solid concrete wall behind you. The accusation from the other party, from Aso Rock, is a preemptive strike. That means they're thinking ahead. To put you in a defensive position from the onset."

The more Hamza stared at the TV, the more he felt himself being drawn in. The problems of Nigeria are many but could be solved. Nigeria needed a leader whose focus was in moving the *country* forward, not his bank account, his village, or his friends. There must be accountability. He knew what must be done.

CHAPTER NINETEEN

The wind roared in my ears as the truck picked up speed. I shivered; my wet T-shirt clung on me like a second skin. What do I do now? Why tonight? The truck swerved, throwing us around. The two guards in the back with us gripped the metal tarpaulin frames for support.

A few girls had fallen off. I couldn't say if they fell off or jumped on their own, but the bus roared on. Either the guards didn't see or they saw and didn't care. What would they do? I had to jump.

It was dark outside, and all I could see were bushes and lights from a few houses. We were still within Akarika town.

The truck made a sharp turn, and I landed on the girls on the floor again. The girl sitting opposite me screamed as she lost her balance and fell off the truck. I gasped. Is she all right? The guards I think saw but didn't seem to care. *Jump off*, I urged myself. But instead of doing that I scampered back to my position on the seat.

"Take it easy!" shouted Aliyu. "We're losing girls!"

I doubt the driver heard him, but I did, and the effect it had on me was to dampen my intention.

The driver did not slow down but continued to move at breakneck speed. I held on to the tarpaulin frame and reconsidered. But some force, fear, kept me frozen in my seat. After what seemed like an eternity, the truck reached a good patch of the road, and the bumping up and down stopped.

"This is better," said one guard and turned in to face us.

We drove for another five to ten minutes, then another girl at the far end of the truck got up and crouched low. She glanced in my direction, at the two guards, who were looking elsewhere, and then jumped off the vehicle.

I jerked forward. Energy surged through my veins. The two guards seemed very interested in their discussion and smoking. Who knew where they were taking us? I might break a leg, but that would be better than wherever we would end up. I let go of the frame and looked outside the truck. All I could see were fast-moving dark shadows. *Ngozi, jump, save yourself.*

I raised myself up, muscles tensed. I glanced at the two men. They would talk, laugh, glance at us, and then look away. They were talking about us. The throbbing sound in my ears and the roar of the wind all became one. I'll jump at the count of three. One, two—

One of the men whirled around, laughing.

I sat down fast. The knot in my stomach tightened.

Aliyu reached into his pocket and held up a pocket flashlight. He pointed the flashlight at his colleague.

"Remove that from my face!" hissed his colleague. His open mouth showed he had lost a few of his front teeth.

"Sorry, I was just testing it," said Aliyu. "What do we have here?" He shined his flashlight on the face of the girl on my right. "This one is not bad!" he muttered. He continued to pass the flashlight from face to face. Then it was my turn. I felt the light beam on my skin. I squinted and raised my hand to my face.

"Come on, remove your hand!" he bellowed.

I put down my hand and continued to squint. After what seemed like an eternity, the beam left my face and landed on the girl next to me. She was sobbing. I didn't dare to look. I was just glad he hadn't said "okay" when he looked at my face. The light lingered on the girl's face.

"Shine the light again on the last girl," said his colleague.

The light landed on my face once more.

"Where do I know you from?" he asked in Pidgin English.

I squinted and held my breath. My whole body shook.

"Do you sell oranges?" he asked me after a few seconds. He grinned. "Ah, she's the orange girl." He nodded. "Where's your friend?" His voice was slow and deliberate. "Is your *toto* as sweet as your oranges?" He chuckled.

"You are always helping yourself to hawkers," said Aliyu. "If it's not a young girl selling bananas, it's ground-nuts. Now it's an orange seller." He shook his head.

I did not understand what he was talking about and had never seen him before. Armed robbers killed people that recognized them to protect their identity. I shivered; goose bumps spread all over my body. Trouble seemed to find me at every turn.

CHAPTER TWENTY

I must get off this truck. There was no other way. I watched the guards, waiting for a time when they were not paying attention. But they looked in at us as they talked. I berated myself for not jumping off when I had the chance. It seemed like an eternity had passed. Then Aliyu turned away, and the other guard joined him.

I looked at the other girls in the truck not knowing for sure who was who. Where was Zainab? I looked around again, hoping that I would see her, but she was not on this truck. Did she escape? Was she in another vehicle? I remembered the last time we spoke earlier in the night before we descended into this nightmare. If anyone could get away from all of this, it was Zainab. I had to wish she got away because any other outcome would break my heart. I knew wherever she was, she had me in mind too.

The guards who had been talking and smoking, content to face the bushes and watch the night, turned inward to us again.

"Do you think we have enough girls," asked Aliyu. "Some of them fell off the truck when the driver was driving like a madman." He counted us. He counted all the way to twenty-three girls.

"They won't be enough," said Aliyu.

"What do you care? You only need one," said his colleague. "Let's hope there are more on the other trucks."

What are their plans for us? I wondered. Did the other girls hear?

Aliyu and his colleague continued their discussion, and I continued the search for an opportune time to make my move. After a few minutes, I decided that there would never be a right time. I had to make my move. I looked around. The men were not paying attention. The truck was traveling at a decent pace. I rubbed my sweaty palms together. *Do it*, I urged myself.

A girl laying in the small pile on the ground moaned and cried.

"I can't take it anymore, I can't," said the girl.

She got up. There was no pretense. Tears streamed down her face. Her nightgown was wet and clung to her skin.

"What is it?" barked Aliyu.

Both men reached for their guns.

"Sit down!" Aliyu's colleague hissed in Hausa.

"No! No!" sobbed the girl. "I can't take it anymore."

As if in a trance, she scrambled to the edge of the truck and jumped off.

"Stop the truck! Stop the truck!" barked Aliyu. Holding the rails, he walked toward the front of the vehicle. Girls whimpered in pain as he stepped on them to get to the driver's cabin.

Aliyu banged on the roof of the truck. "Driver, stop! Stop!"

The truck screeched to a halt.

"Flash your light," said the other guard.

Aliyu jumped down from the truck, brought out his flashlight, and pointed in the direction where the girl was last seen. This was an excellent time to run in the opposite direction. Pulse racing, I stood up. This was the only chance I would get. I leaned forward to haul myself over the back frame of the truck when the driver's-side door opened. I sat down. The door remained open, but the driver didn't come out.

"This light is useless," said Aliyu's colleague. "I can't see anything. Should we chase after her?"

In reply, Aliyu removed his gun from his shoulders and released several shots in the direction where the girl had jumped off. The sound was deafening.

"Do you want to kill her?" asked Aliyu's colleague. "I thought you were complaining we didn't have enough girls."

"I can't see anything," said Aliyu. "If we can't have her then she should not be useful to anyone."

"Let's turn around and use the truck's headlights to look," said Aliyu.

"No," said the driver. "We have wasted a lot of time already. Cover the truck with the tarpaulin and keep your eyes open!"

The man in the truck appeared to have more authority than Aliyu and the other guard.

The two men turned around and came back on the truck.

"Get up, get up," said Aliyu as he kicked and shoved the girls to the side. He bent down and lifted a tarpaulin we had been on. "Come and help me," he called out to the other guard.

None of us girls dared make a run for it. We all wanted to live. The men spread the tarpaulin over the metal frame welded to the top of the open section of the truck. The tarpaulin was in bad shape with holes on the roof. In some parts, large chunks of the waterproof material were missing. It then dawned on me it was made to allow air in and out. The bottom part of the tarpaulin was intact and secure.

With the new arrangement, the guards only worried about the entrance. I ran my hand over the lower part of the tarpaulin; it was tight. So was my luck. The time I was ready to make my escape bid was when they made it more difficult.

CHAPTER TWENTY-ONE

We'd been on the move for hours. I'd tried to keep track of the turns we took, but there were just too many. To complicate things, the driver had made a few wrong turns and had to trace back the same way, confusing my already overburdened mind. For a time, I'd fallen asleep.

Earlier, before they put the tarpaulin over the back of the truck, it would have been easier to trace our path. The occasional headlights of oncoming trailers loaded with goods had showed we were still on a major route, and they left in their wake the smell of exhaust fumes long after they'd groaned past us.

But now there were no lights, just emptiness. The smell of car fumes was gone, replaced by a putrid odor that hung in the air like a dark rain cloud. We had made no bathroom stops, and I believe I wasn't the only one who had lost control of their bodily functions when the men attacked our dormitory.

Inside, I felt numb and empty. I let out a long exhale

and wondered for the millionth time how I ended up in the back of a truck in the middle of nowhere.

Aliyu and his colleague with the missing front teeth continued to talk and smoke, holding on to the tarpaulin frame for support, their guns hanging from their shoulders. They were still awake but the glow from their cigarettes showed tired faces.

Moonlight streamed in through the tears in the tarpaulin's roof. I recognized some girls based on their silhouettes. The rest had their heads bowed in sleep. The girl on my right seemed to be crying in her sleep. *She must be having a nightmare*, I thought, *but who wouldn't after what we were going through*. I heard a sob here and some whispered words there. Everyone tried not to provoke the guards.

I tried to piece together all that had happened so far. It looked like something out of a Nollywood movie. I thought of my only friend and wished for her safety.

A girl in a blue T-shirt got off the floor, stretched, and squeezed in beside me. Then she mumbled something I didn't pick up. She was courageous to have gotten off the floor, but I didn't want her to draw attention. *What was she mumbling about?* I wondered. Maybe stress had gotten to her.

I turned to get a better look, and something around her neck glistened in the moonlight. I recognized the cross fastened by a black thread. Only Joy would have the courage to pray, even if it meant getting into trouble. I reached out and squeezed her hand. She looked at me, nodded, and continued with her mumbling.

Relief washed over me like warm water on a cold morning. I felt relief knowing we had a prayer warrior with us. I'd given up on prayers a long time ago. Where was God when my mother died? Then my uncle. Where was He when Auntie Halima mistreated me, and where was He now?

I hoped a miracle would happen for Joy. Prayers were something we all needed. I remembered the guards and glanced over my shoulder toward the end of the truck where they stood, resting their legs on the tailgate. They paid no attention to us.

"Who do you think they are?" I whispered close to Joy's ear.

Joy did not answer but continued with her prayers, her lips moving nonstop.

The girl sitting next to her leaned forward. "I think they are Boko Haram."

My mind drifted to yesterday morning before my altercation with Maryam. The newscaster had talked about suicide bombings and the killing of Christians by this terrorist group. Akarika Girls wasn't a faith-based school, but a high percentage of Christians to Muslims attended. Some abducted girls were Muslims, and so was my best friend.

My problems just grew wings ready to fly. I pinched myself for not escaping when the opportunity had presented itself. The unvarnished truth stared at me in the face. I couldn't even take the necessary steps to save myself.

I rocked from side to side in rhythm to the truck as it continued on the unpaved road, driving deeper into the lair of the terrorists. *Should I make another attempt to escape?* I asked myself, even as the probability of success faded from my mind.

CHAPTER TWENTY-TWO

Joy beside me continued to pray. At some point, exhaustion must have taken over because her lips stopped moving. I'd been watching the guards, waiting for them to sleep. I was sure it would be daylight soon, or at least we'd get to our destination. I wrapped my arms around me and rubbed my palms up and down against my arms. The air had become crisper. The guards had dozed off too, tired from the long day of standing and enticed by fresh air.

"I'll sleep first," said Aliyu in a groggy voice to his colleague. "Wake me up in fifteen minutes, then you can sleep."

Aliyu wedged himself in the corner between the tailgate and the wall of the truck and snored. His companion sitting on the tailgate watched him. Within seconds Aliyu nodded off. At one point, he lost his balance and almost fell off the truck.

"Aliyu, Aliyu," called the other guard. He stood for a moment, hissed, and sat in the opposite corner as Aliyu. A few minutes later, he too was snoring. I couldn't believe what had just happened. I watched them and waited a few more minutes. Adrenalin pumped through my veins. *Ngozi, this is your chance, take it,* I told myself. I moved my shoulders and shifted Joy. Her head rested on the person next to her. *Should I wake her?* I wondered. What if she didn't want to go? That should be her decision, not mine. Would she wake me if situations were reversed? There was still danger involved. It wasn't like we were walking out the door. I decided to go alone.

My heartbeat sounded so loud that I thought it would wake up the others. It would be tough to move without stepping on someone. As I got up, my knees cracked. It sounded like a gunshot, and I sat back again. I looked around; nothing moved. My best plan would be just to get up and go for it.

I felt a nudge on my right side. Nobody else was awake, to my knowledge. A girl peered at me when I looked. Her face was familiar.

"What's your name again?" I asked.

"Senior Ngozi, it's Mary, Mary Ibe," she said in a low voice.

I remembered a junior girl in class two. I didn't know junior students came for this exam thing.

"Are you jumping off? I'm scared," Mary whispered. Tears glistened on her cheeks. "I had a dream that they shot Aminata!" she blurted.

"Shh!" I whispered and wrapped my arm around her shoulder. I glanced at the guards; they were still sleeping.

"Aminata was a bully, but she didn't deserve that. Nobody deserves death."

"I know," I said in a low voice.

"Where are they taking us?" asked Mary.

"I don't know." Outside the door, I could see a trace of the coming day.

"Please stay, don't go."

The truck was no longer speeding. I rocked from side to side as we traveled over rough terrain. I held Mary tighter and felt her body shake with sobs. My mind was made up, to protect her.

"What will happen to us," whispered Mary.

"We'll be all right. We'll survive this. The police will look for us." In my heart of hearts, I knew it was a lie. Only our parents and families would care. In my case, nobody would.

Growing up, Uncle took us to church every Sunday. He believed strong religious exposure was good for a child. Auntie used to bring us after his death, but when terrorists blew themselves up in churches, we stopped going altogether. I wondered whether being kidnapped was my punishment for not going to church. Then I thought of Joy, who never missed church and prayed all the time, yet she was right here beside me, plus all the other girls. I would leave that to God to sort out.

I would not be the one who doomed the group because I'd stopped praying. I ransacked my brain to find a prayer to say, but nothing came to mind. *This must end well*, I said to myself. Psalm 23 popped into my mind, and I recited it in my mind.

The Lord is my shepherd, I shall not want.

He makes me lie down in green pastures. He restores my soul.

Even though I walk through the valley of the shadow of death, I fear no evil.

CHAPTER TWENTY-THREE

Gambo sat in his hut and waited for the cargo. He hoped their trip had gone well. The early morning atmosphere, the sun displaying brilliant colors as it rose, reminded him of another time many years ago when he witnessed the same bright colors of the sunrise while waiting.

He was young and desperate. He and a group of young men, teenagers from Edo State, were in Libya. They stood on the shores of the Mediterranean, and across the horizon, their handlers had pointed.

"The light you see is Europe, the promised land where money grows on trees, the roads are paved with euros and pounds sterling. Where you get paid truckloads of money for a day's job." He, Gambo, was going there.

But that wasn't where the story started. Gambo was an only child. His father worked as a clerk at the Ministry of Agriculture, and his mother sold groundnut cakes. The little money his father made never reached home. He consumed it at Sabon Gari, the abode for non-Muslims, where alcohol was permitted.

See, the religion forbids drinking, but his father was undeterred. He would drink, and when sober pull out his praying mat and ask for forgiveness. Allah was always merciful. Many times, Gambo and his mother would find him and lift him unconscious from a bar in Sabon Gari and bring him home. When he woke up and found himself at home, he would go into a rage. "You should have left me there." He was only taking a nap to make room for more. Father would dish his anger on Mother in the form of slaps and beatings.

One day in a drunken rage, he pounced on Mother and beat her to a pulp. She lay on the ground where she fell. But she never woke up. Remorseful, Father jumped in front of a speeding train. His body parts were picked up along the track in polythene bags and buried. Gambo's maternal grandmother took him in, but he never forgot who took his parents away from him. The nonbelievers who sold alcohol to his father were to blame.

When Gambo was eight years old, Kaka put him in religious school to get him out of her hair. He roamed the streets with some other youths after school. They would beg for money on the streets and stand at the gates of rich men. Sometimes the rich men threw money at the poor souls as they exited their gates. Or they would send a servant out with a pot of steaming white rice and lamb stew.

One day, when he was eighteen, Gambo met some youths who were embarking on a trip to seek their fortunes. They invited him to come. They told him how much they needed, and he stole half the money from Kaka, her life savings. They set off from Kano.

A man called The Handler met them at a designated stop. There they met other young people, boys and girls from the south, mostly Edo State. The Handler took them to a bus, and they handed over their fee to him. The Handler gave them free condoms and invaluable advice.

"If someone tries to rape you, don't resist," he had said.

Gambo remembered that after a fourteen-hour trip, they arrived at Agadez in Niger Republic. The driver was talkative. He told them that the town was an ancient caravan town where smuggling had been their way of life for hundreds of years.

"Everybody off the bus," said the driver. "Wait here for the smuggler!"

As soon as the bus left, a group of men approached them, and the nightmare started. They asked for their money and started with one newcomer from Edo State. When he refused to part with his money, one man pulled out a pistol and shot him in the torso, point-blank.

Gambo and friends emptied out their pockets. The men took the money. The condoms gave them ideas. Gambo and friends did not resist.

Their contact later showed up and took them to Sabha in southern Libya, from where they would head to the beach.

"Can we bury my dead friend?" Gambo had asked, still shaken from the ordeal.

"We'll drop off the body at the desert. The sand will consume the corpse," said their contact.

Gambo and the rest of the crew crossed the treacherous Sahara and entered Libya. With no money to get to the coast, they had to prostitute themselves. One by one his companions started to disappear, thrown into prison by Libyan authorities during a roundup of foreigners or captured and sold as slaves by a local crime group. Only God knows why he survived as long as he did.

Gambo knew it was only a matter of time before his

luck ran out. He had learned a lot about how the syndicate worked. He approached one of the cartels and offered his services to lure people from his country in. They'd wanted to make an example of him and sell him off, but after he told them how much they could make, they tried him.

Gambo's work was easy. The new fortune seekers from Nigeria were nonbelievers most of the time. Gambo still blamed them for all that had happened to his father, making his job easier. In a short time, deceit became second nature to him. They would kidnap the illegal migrants once they arrived at Sabha. Gambo would introduce himself as a Nigerian who could help. Their trust was absolute. They would give Gambo their relative's phone number in Nigeria with joy. The person would be set free after ransom money was received.

After months of saving, Gambo traveled to the coast. He was skeptical as to whether the leaky boat would make it, but there were scores of people ready to take his place. He said a prayer and boarded the boat. *I will cross the sea to my destiny.*

Gambo, like the rest of the men, women, and children, had climbed onto the boat as it rose and fell with the waves. The sea was calm for most of the journey until it was not. Huge waves poured into the boat, and it took in water and began to sink. *Death has found me,* thought Gambo. Within minutes, the cold water of the sea engulfed him. All around him people were screaming and splashing trying to stay afloat. He went under twice, and after the third time, everything went black.

Gambo felt his body being dragged.

"Is he dead?" a female voice at the point of hysteria asked.

"I can feel a pulse, but it's faint." The voice was male.

Gambo's mouth felt dry. "*Ina kishin ruwa*," he whispered.

"You're thirsty?" asked the male voice, excited. "The man spoke Hausa!"

Gambo lost consciousness again. When he awoke he was on a bed, an intravenous line reviving his system, and at the foot of the bed sat a man with a smiling face.

"Ah, you're awake now," said the smiling face. "You were lucky we found you."

Gambo looked at the man. He was young, good-looking, and tall. He looked like a man whose worries were not about his next meal.

"Are you Nigerian?" the man had asked.

Gambo hesitated, but there was nothing else to lose. He had nothing to hide. The trip had robbed him of his last drop of decency. He nodded.

"On your way to Italy? What happened?"

Gambo thanked the young man for saving his life. He took a deep breath and told the man his life story.

"You're fortunate," said the man. "A braver man than I am. I've rented a villa close by the beach and was taking my daily walk when I found you. Allah spared your life. If you come back with me to Nigeria, I'll find you a job. If you want to."

Tears flowed down Gambo's cheeks. Never had he felt so comforted since he lost his mother. Gambo was never an enthusiastic believer in God. Since coming to Libya, he had given up hope, but today he again believed in Allah. This man was sent by God to intervene.

"Who are you?" asked Gambo.

The man smiled. "Sorry, I forgot my manners. It doesn't

matter who I am. I was in the right place at the right time. But my name is Hassan Tarbari."

The next day Gambo left on a private jet for Lagos, Nigeria.

CHAPTER TWENTY-FOUR

I must have dozed off again because I lunged forward and awoke. The truck had come to an abrupt stop. We were in a forest clearing. The sun peeped through the trees surrounding the area. Only the vehicle we rode in was there. Where were the other two?

This must be their hideout. There were a few rows of bungalows and huts with trees and bushes growing right out of some of them. Some were missing doors, windows, or both, with pieces of cloth or ragged curtains as a replacement. It looked like an abandoned settlement.

Most of the girls had stopped crying during the long trip. Like me, some had dozed off. With the truck stationary and the rhythmic movement gone, we all stirred.

"Wake up! Wake up!" barked Aliyu. He kicked the girls closest to him. The second man jumped down, lowered the tailgate, and motioned us out.

I got up and helped Mary up. The stench of dried urine hung in the air like an old friend who had overstayed her welcome. We huddled together. I held Joy on one side and

Mary on the other. I recognized Blessing, Amara, and Sade; they were from the other two hostels.

A short man dressed in a dirty blue kaftan rushed out from one hut. "The girls are here! The girls are here!" he croaked.

More men came out from the huts and bungalows. Some wore army camouflage, some were in black. Most were groggy from sleep. What struck me was how young they looked, in their late teens, early to late twenties. Some of them rubbed the sleep out of their eyes and yawned. Some gathered around a huge white rusty sign with a faded inscription, "Welcome to Sambisa Game Reserve", and peed in the bush with their backs to us.

"I want my mommy," a girl cried.

"I want my mama," mimicked the short man. "She abandoned me in the market to fend for myself when I was two!" He put his hands into the pocket of his flowing light-blue gown and doubled over in laughter.

The driver's door of the truck opened, and the driver came down. He slammed the door shut, stretched, and walked to the laughing man. "Little Stupid, call Gambo."

"Ah Oga Danladi, you did well!" said the man called Little Stupid. "All these girls in one night, wonderful." He turned, still laughing, and ran toward a bungalow with intact windows and a door.

The man called Danladi looked familiar. I didn't want to stare. I remembered what happens to victims who recognized their captors.

In less than a minute, Little Stupid ran out of the bungalow. "Danladi, line them up! Gambo wants to inspect them."

I looked at all those men and felt a knot tighten in my

stomach. My teeth chattered as cold fear descended my spine.

Danladi reached into his pocket and pulled out a sheet of paper. He looked at it, then handed it over to Little Stupid.

The man I perceived to be in charge, Gambo, emerged from a bungalow. He stood for a second. Once the men noticed him, there was silence. He approached us, dressed in military camouflage and, like some of the men, with a rifle slung over his shoulder. Unlike the rest, his uniform wasn't worn, and he looked alert.

He looked about thirty, bug-eyed, with a dark complexion and a scraggly beard. I trembled as he got closer. In his hands were prayer beads. A religious fanatic? I broke out in a cold sweat. Were they going to separate us based on religion?

He seemed like the no-nonsense type. He came to a stop a few feet away from us. His eyes darted from girl to girl as he stroked his beard.

"Did you burn down the school?" he asked in English, addressing no one in particular.

He spoke in a manner like the male teachers I had at school. Did that mean he was educated and not the riffraff the rest of the men were? In his eyes was a hungry look that reminded me of Peter when he chased after lizards to kill or when he was about to twist off a hen's neck. A hunger only quenched by bloodshed.

"Yes, we did," Danladi said.

"Any casualties?" the man asked.

Danladi hesitated. "Yes. Someone shot one of the girls. Another ran away." He handed the list of paper he had pulled out of his pocket to Gambo.

Gambo took it, looked at it, and nodded. "Call out the names. Let's see what we have."

My throat jumped into my mouth. What was I going to do? My first name, Ngozi, was an Ibo name, and that gave me away as a Christian. I wasn't the only person with an apparent Christian name. I could give a northern-sounding name. Then I realized one of the other girls could give me away just to curry favor.

Little Stupid raised the paper. I recognized it at once. It was the list Aminata had given me to write my name on. He read the names out.

"Amina Shehu!"

Amina Shehu raised a shaky hand. She was wearing a nightdress like most of us, which was now dirty.

"Right," said Gambo and pointed to his right.

Amina Shehu's eyes bulged with fear. Hesitantly, she moved to Gambo's right.

"Mary Ibe!" said the short man.

Mary gasped, and tears rolled down her cheeks. I squeezed her hand and let go. She raised her hand.

"Left," said Gambo.

Mary walked over to the left and stood.

Next, Latifah Usman was called and was told to go to the left. She stood beside Mary.

"Nkechi Okoye," called the short man.

"Right," said Gambo.

I noticed a girl dressed in a black veil standing close to Gambo and watching. Her face was impassive. Who was she? Just then she looked my way, and our eyes met.

"Ifeoma Umeh."

I turned to look at Ifeoma and see which side they would send her to.

"Right," said Gambo. "Efome Bankole. Right. Afra Musa. Left."

Then it was my turn.

Little Stupid's eyes widened, and he grinned. "Ngozi Balogun Bashiru." He laughed. "This is a good representation of the whole of Nigeria. You have an Ibo first name, Yoruba middle name, and a Hausa last name. *Haba*, what type of name is this? Your mother couldn't decide who your father was?"

The rest of the men burst out laughing. I lowered my eyes. What I was trying to avoid had happened. Of all things, my name had drawn attention to me. I wished he'd send me to the same side as Mary.

"*Wazobia!*" said another man.

Gambo laughed. "Left!"

I wasn't happy he hadn't sent me to the same side as Mary and wanted to protest by staying put. I raised my head, and my eyes met the girl's again. It was a subtle shake of her head, but I caught it. What was the signal? Did she want me to move or stand firm? Somehow I trusted her. She moved her head to her right. Filled with trepidation, I scurried to the left.

CHAPTER TWENTY-FIVE

The second girl after me he sent to the right. She went to the left and refused to move. Gambo pointed at two of his men, and they descended on her. They beat her to a pulp and carried her off with them. No other girl thought of disobeying orders. This continued until he had separated all the girls into two groups.

"What about the girls whose names are here but who are not here in person?" asked Gambo.

"We lost some on the way," said Aliyu. "The rest should be on the other trucks."

Gambo nodded. He seemed satisfied with the answer. He paused and looked at the lineup. First to his left and then to his right. "Raise your hand if you're a Christian?"

Nobody moved. I'm sure most people saw the news yesterday morning or had at least heard about it. Was that his intention? I strained my eyes, looking out of the corner to see who else had raised their hands.

"How many of you attend church every Sunday?" asked Gambo. "Churches spring up like mushrooms. How many of you attend Sunday services?"

My hands shook first, but now it spread to my whole body. Would I be called out? We were a mix of Christians and Muslims in school, yet I had seen no hands go up. I knew I shouldn't lie. But I shouldn't be stupid either. Then I heard a gasp to my left. I turned. Only one hand had gone up. It was Joy's.

"How many of you are Muslims?"

All hands except Joy's hand shot up, including mine. I felt ashamed. I'd denied my religion at the first sign of trouble.

The man's eyes bulged. His mouth dropped open. His eyes darted from left to right as if looking for an explanation. Then he laughed. He doubled over laughing. Soon, the other men glanced at each other, then laughed too. They must know.

Gambo stopped laughing just as he had started. He turned to the girl in the black burqa.

"Bello, wake up Kaka and the other women right away," said Gambo. "The girls must be reeducated and prepared as soon as possible."

"Yes, sir," said the girl and walked away.

I watched the girl walk away too. Who was she? Was her name Bello, and why was she wearing a burqa?

"Dismissed," said Gambo. He turned and headed toward his bungalow.

Some men walked away. I looked around at the other girls, all dressed in an array of sleeping attire, nightgowns, or oversized T-shirts, with confused looks on their faces.

Rays of sunlight streamed in through the canopy of trees as if ushering in the end of an era and the start of another. What do they want from us? If they wanted to harm us, they would have executed their plan right away.

What's next? I wondered. I was angry with myself. Just

like hesitating to jump off the truck, I'd failed this one too. I'd wanted to raise my hand and damn the consequences. But that would mean antagonizing the people who kidnapped us. I looked at Joy. She did raise her hand, and she was still standing. I knew the easiest way to have issues with someone was to disagree with them. People had problems with those who opposed them. To survive, I would have to agree with them. I thought of all those men and knew it would only be a matter of time. The sooner I got out of here, the better it would be for me.

As if on cue, birds called out to each other as if to say it was now safe. A man tossed firewood into a fire pit and fanned it with a raffia fan. Thick and heavy smoke rose from the fire. He must have used damp wood. He placed a kettle on some stones over the fire. The smell of wood smoke filled the air. If it weren't for the uncertain situation we found ourselves in, it would have looked like just another beautiful morning in northeastern Nigeria.

CHAPTER TWENTY-SIX

Two women dressed in black burqas emerged from one bungalow and walked toward us. Three tribal marks adorned each of their cheeks. Zainab's scars looked like child's play compared to these. Zainab. I'd forgotten about my friend. Was she all right? I wondered what had become of her.

One woman got to us first and spoke to us. We stared at her. The language, I knew, was Kanuri, a dialect spoken in Borno State, in the Sambisa area. I understood only bits and pieces of it.

The woman cocked her head and spoke again. *"Duk abin zai zama shi ke nana."*

She spoke in rapid Hausa. Everything would be all right? Was she kidding me?

"And this is Danuwa, close friend." The woman pointed at the woman standing beside her.

I felt like a boulder had been lifted off my shoulders. I looked around and noticed other girls nodding their heads. We all understood her; there was an authority in her voice. Since our abduction, I was never sure if we would survive this. I hadn't expected to see a woman at all. But there were three. I wanted to believe her, trust we were now in safe hands.

The furrows on Kaka's forehead and the crow's feet around her eyes deepened as she spoke. Her eyes, cold like a snake's, looked alert as they moved from one face to the next.

Whose grandmother was she? What was she doing out here in the middle of nowhere with terrorists? Was she a captive too? A cry interrupted my thoughts.

Mary, still with her group, began to cry. Kaka walked up to her and hugged her. "Shh! Shh! Everything will be fine. Nobody is going to hurt you. Your mother is here now."

Danuwa did the same. She placed her hands over the shoulders of the girl closest to her and comforted her.

I was confused. The two women sounded so genuine.

"If everything is okay, why are we here in the first place?" asked a voice behind me in fluent Hausa.

I knew that voice. Joy stood, hands folded over her chest. "When do we get to go home?"

Kaka glared at Joy. She looked angry. Then her face softened.

I bit my lip. I didn't want to look at Joy. She would get herself and all of us in trouble. But she was right. Why remove us from our school in the first place? I wished I had half her courage. She was fearless. My eyes were on Kaka, looking for any sign that would betray her true intentions.

"First, we'll clean up and then eat," said Kaka. She turned to Joy. "With a full stomach and some rest, we can then address other concerns. First things first."

She sounded sincere. I wanted to believe the words that came out of her mouth, but that would be dangerous. Even though I knew we were in trouble, I couldn't help but hang on to every shred of hope Kaka offered.

Bello appeared again. She seemed to hang around or just materialize like a ghost.

"Bello!" said Kaka. "Take them to the stream, don't waste time. Come right back and pick up the clothes for them from the hut. No idling."

"Yes, Kaka," said Bello. "Come, follow me. I'll take you to the stream."

Kaka sounded annoyed when she spoke with Bello. Did she upset her? Like sheep to the slaughter, we followed Bello downhill on a bush path. The earthy smell of the stream was unmistakable, even before I saw it. It seemed to materialize from a huge stone, collected in a pool and flowed away as a small channel, then disappeared in a cluster of bushes.

I wanted to talk to Bello and find out more about her. But as soon as we reached the stream, she turned around and went up again. Kaka and one woman came down to watch over us.

"You can take off your clothes and bathe," said Kaka. "Nobody will come."

Some girls did, but I kept mine on. I waded into the water and shivered. Its greatest depth came up to my knees. It was crystal clear, and I could see the occasional fish dart about at the bottom. Despite all that had happened, and having just witnessed a girl beaten and carried away, I picked up a few conversations.

Kaka and Danuwa stood by the stream banks in in-depth discussion. They would now and then glance at us and smile. They were not there as guards. They moved like older people; just one shove would send them to the ground. I glanced at the bushes. If I made a dash for it, there would be no way they could catch up with me. Maybe there was more to it than met the eye. Water splashed behind me, and I turned. Joy waded over.

"I saw you looking at the bushes," said Joy. "Do you have any ideas?" Her nostrils flared with each breath.

My eyes darted to Kaka and the other woman and then back to Joy. She was my friend, but she should have kept her mouth shut. She'd drawn attention to herself. I looked at the women by the bank again. They were still talking. I shrugged. Our eyes met, and I looked away.

"I can't stay here. God won't let it happen," blurted Joy.

"We'll figure something out," I whispered, covering my mouth with my palm as I spoke, my eyes darting around. I saw the third woman return, carrying a large bundle wrapped in multicolored cloth. She laid it down on the grass.

"All right, girls, come out of the water," said Kaka.

The sun was out, and I could feel its warmth on my face. I hadn't taken off my clothes. There were no towels, so I wrung them the best I could.

"Put these on," said Kaka. They had untied the bundle and handed out clothes from the pile.

I got a gray dress and Joy took a black one. I couldn't wait to get out of my wet T-shirt.

All around, excited girls grabbed the clothes. Some used their old nightgowns as towels to dry themselves. I pulled my T-shirt off by the shoulder and slid the dress over my head. It smelled of incense. I rinsed off my T-shirt in the stream, wrung it, and dried the rest of my body with it. It felt so good to be clean, dry, and in clean clothes. I got a glimpse of Joy.

"What's wrong?"

"It's a burqa!" She dropped hers to the ground.

I knew where she was coming from.

"Think of it as temporary," I said in a whisper.

"Do you think Kaka would have done the same if the situation was reversed?" asked Joy. "I don't think so."

I jerked my head from side to side to see if the women heard us. No one paid us any attention. I understood her sentiments, but I wanted to survive.

CHAPTER TWENTY-SEVEN

Hamza and Kola traveled together to the building that housed their campaign offices and they went straight to his desk. Hamza had a simple plan, to do his own part in salvaging his private life and country. The two analysts were there, and there was no sign of what had transpired the day before.

Hamza smiled at the three people in the room. "Emmm, we have to employ more people to fill the computer terminals and start the social media campaign that I employed you for. If you have friends and colleagues who might be interested, you can invite them to apply."

Hamza wondered whether to talk to them about himself now or after they hired more people. He went with addressing them now. He would still speak to a new group, but these two could spread the word talking about his background and education.

After primary school at Kano, he went to Eton College in the UK. His summer vacations in his secondary school days were spent traveling the world. The last two weeks were always spent in Kano with his father. So were all other breaks. After secondary school, he came back to Nigeria for medical school.

"I don't want you to be a stranger in your own country," his father used to say.

"Which medical school did you attend, sir?" asked the male analyst.

"The one in Kano," said Hamza. "While I was there, the late Dr. Muzo was my mentor." Hamza picked up the newspaper with the headline news about the late doctor and handed it to the analyst. "I will get to that later."

The analyst took the newspaper, looked at it, and handed it to the girl.

"I did my house job at the teaching hospital in Kano and the NYSC in Enugu."

The National Youth Service Corps was established in 1973 as one way to heal a country that had come out of a three-and-a-half-year civil war, the Biafran War. Graduates of universities and polytechnics were sent to states other than their state of origin to spend a year, with a stipend from the government as a way to encourage exposure to different cultures and promote national unity. More than forty years later, the jury was still out on whether it was a good idea.

Kola smiled. "You went to the East, sir?"

"I didn't want to," said Hamza with a chuckle. "At the time, I preferred to pursue residency training in the United States right away but changed my mind. It was an eye-opening experience, culture-wise, learning about other parts of Nigeria."

"Since I'm from Lagos State, they posted me to the north," said Kola. "And I never left."

Hamza noticed the unease in the female analyst. Maybe she didn't take part but still got her certificate. He moved on. "After that, I went to the US for postgraduate training. I did a residency in medicine and a fellowship in cardiology. Took a leave of absence and squeezed in an MBA from Harvard. Went back to medicine as an attending in New York until . . . until the accident."

Kola pursed his lips and shook his head. He looked at the other two but said nothing.

Hamza looked at the two analysts. "So, questions?"

"No, sir," they said at the same time.

The male analyst raised his hand. "But, sir, the primaries are in five days. Do you think we will . . . still be here?"

Hamza laughed out loud and turned to the campaign manager.

"You can answer that."

"You've asked an idiotic question," said Kola. "Of course we will still be here. But, you might not—"

"I'm very sorry, sir, please disregard the question," pleaded the analyst. "I misspoke, sir. Sorry for the foolish question, sir!"

Hamza knew what the young man was talking about. He'd done nothing yet to establish an interest in taking part in the primaries, apart from what Kola did, mobilizing people to hold rallies and distribute banners. Until he saw the paper about Muzo's death, he was just going to satisfy his father's insistence that he participate in the primaries.

"It's all right," said Hamza. "Like I said, invite capable people you know and we'll hire them. We hope to clinch the primaries and take it from there."

It would be close to impossible for an incumbent to lose an election in most African countries, thought Hamza. There was something about power that, once you wrapped your lips around that teat, you could never let go.

"All right, back to work," said Kola and watched them leave the room. As soon as the analysts shut the door, he turned to Hamza. "What do you think of this plan: we assume we have already won the primaries and focus on the main election?"

"Why should we make that assumption?" asked Hamza. "I haven't played an active role in the party. And I don't think we should take the votes of the people for granted."

"We have a unique candidate," said Kola, making emphasis with his hands. "Well-read, reasonable, well-traveled, and with new ideas. Look at the politicians in the system today. The same ones who have always been around. They are stuck in their ways. No new ideas and preferring things remain the same. You scratch my back, and I scratch yours as we loot the government coffers."

Hamza nodded. So far he liked what he heard.

"You're young; you're not going there to enrich yourself," said Kola. "If we can bring the youths to your side, and the election is free and fair, you'll stand a good chance."

Hamza smiled. "I like the plan. We'll talk more about details." Hamza laughed. "But free and fair—that would be the day."

"If we can get a repeat of June 12, '93," said Kola. "The candidate that appeals to the masses wins."

Hamza remembered June 12, 1993. He was still in medical school. Then military head of state, Ibrahim Babangida, had been credited with organizing Nigeria's freest and fairest presidential election by national and international observers.

The election was so transparent that the eventual presumed winner, Chief MKO Abiola, a Muslim from the west, beat his opponent, Bashir Tofa, in his home state of Kano.

MKO Abiola with his "Hope" campaign had appealed to a large cross-section of Nigerians. However, IBB—Babangida—in a nationwide broadcast on June 23, 1993, annulled the election. IBB stepped aside in August, leaving behind an interim civilian government. By November of the same year, General Sani Abacha, IBB's second in command, took control in a bloodless military coup.

There was a knock on the door.

"Yes," said Hamza.

The female analyst poked her head into the office, stepped in, and shut the door. "Sir, two men, they said they are CIDs, are here to see you."

Kola frowned. "The Criminal Investigation Department of the police, what for?" Kola walked rapidly toward the door. "I'll see what they want."

Hamza's whole body went tense. *That was quick,* he thought. He drew in air and forced his body to relax as he exhaled through his mouth.

CHAPTER TWENTY-EIGHT

I came up the footpath from the stream into the clearing and stopped in my tracks. Young girls carrying infants in their arms and children three to five years old ran around without a care in the world. Where did they come from?

"Move, move," said Kaka. "You're blocking the way."

Girls behind pressed us forward to get a glimpse for themselves of what the commotion was all about.

"Girls, let's go. Over there to the kitchen." Kaka pointed to the fire pit, Danuwa was keeping busy, while the girl Bello approached the fire pit with a bundle of different sizes of sticks. She dropped them in a pile on the ground and headed toward the bush.

Danuwa picked up one stick, snapped it in two, and added it to the burning sticks under the pot.

Who were the women with the children? My stomach rumbled as soon as the smell of *masa*, fried rice cakes, hit my nose. I pulled my eyes away from the children and looked toward the felled tree used as a table. Plastic plates and spoons lay on the table next to a blue plastic tray piled with white cakes. It looked like a pyramid of odd-shaped tennis balls. A calabash of *fura de nunu,* a yogurt drink made from millet, sat next to the cakes like a bowl of whitewash paint. House flies dove into the creamy mixture one after the other to get their share. Shooed away by the women, they always returned within seconds, like a bad habit.

"Eat, eat," said Kaka. "There's enough today. Not always like this, so eat as much as you can."

We dug in, flies and all. When you're hungry, everything becomes delicious. Food has a way of making you forget your immediate problems. We'd bathed, got clean clothes, and now our stomachs were being filled. Our captors, like a nighttime rat nibbling at your toe ever so gently, were winning over our hearts and minds.

Kaka watched as we ate, nodding her head to music only she could hear. For me, as I satisfied one want, another one arose. The central predicament came to the front burner: Why were we taken and when were we going home?

Kaka cleared her throat.

"You'll go back to your school when the time is right," said Kaka as if she was in my mind. "God willing."

CHAPTER TWENTY-NINE

The mention of school got our attention.

"Left to me, you are free to come and go, but Gambo and his men see things a lot differently. As long as you are here, they see you as under their protection. So, I wouldn't advise you to leave on your own without a guard and guide. The place is full of poisonous snakes, man-eating boa constrictors, hyenas, and . . . even animals we hear only at night. One could eat you." She dropped her voice with the last sentence.

It had the desired effect. A gasp escaped the lips of some of the girls. Heads and eyes darted all over the ground, looking for anything slithering around. The thought of a snake crawling on me sent a cold shiver down my spine. Even if I escaped, which direction would I go? Which way was salvation? All around us was bush.

I looked around our surroundings. The buildings were in rows along patches of tar, remnants of a road that ran between the premises when the place functioned as accommodation for visitors to the game reserve. The camp reminded me of the gutted and sometimes abandoned buildings you would see in bushes far from villages as you traveled on some highways or local roads. The buildings were huge and always came in pairs, but not close together.

Fatima once told me on a trip to her village that those houses were constructed by the Babangida Administration many years ago as local offices for the two political parties then. The government had wasted taxpayers' money yet again.

"Explore your surroundings," said Kaka, breaking my thoughts. "But don't go near the children and their mothers."

Why kidnap us in the first place if we were not here for a purpose? My thoughts drifted to home. Fatima must have raised the alarm. But I left in a hurry. Nobody knew I was leaving. Musa must have delivered the sugar. Fatima would ask questions and tell Auntie Halima what was said. It would be apparent to her I ran. The realization hit me like a brick: nobody would be looking for me.

CHAPTER THIRTY

As the sun went down, black flies and mosquitoes made their presence felt as the end of our first day in captivity approached. I tried not to think of how I got there; there would be a time for that. To survive, I needed to learn, and the only way was to watch.

Later, the men led Mary's group away. Some girls wailed and wanted to stay with us. One girl tried to run back to our group. They caught her and slapped her around. I couldn't say if they were being taken to a better place. Every girl obeyed after that. The rules became obvious—do what you're told.

That night, we were all put in a large room with a rectangular opening. The door had been removed from the hinges. Nobody guarded or restricted our movements. Nobody dared to venture far—the sound of the night kept us indoors.

We had to relieve ourselves right beside the open-door frame. There were raffia mats for us to use as beds, but it became apparent there wouldn't be enough to go around.

There was a scramble, and at the end, those who got none had to share. I'd grabbed one, and so far nobody had asked me to share with them.

As it got darker, it became evident there was no light in the room. Light fixtures on the walls and the sockets were gone, vandalized. The thought of this building deep in the forest having power, while houses in major cities didn't, almost brought a smile to my lips, but nothing was funny.

One girl found an old bucket and placed it in the corner of the room. It became our piss bowl. None of us thought it was a good idea to venture outside again as the night deepened.

Another girl found a stub of candle and matches used by the last occupants. She lit it, and our shadows came to life, dancing on the walls like evil spirits waiting to pounce. When you're scared, everything becomes a threat.

Joy brought her mat close to mine. This time, I didn't move away. There was no reason to. It was just us girls in the room.

"I wish I had my Bible," said Joy. She touched the wooden crucifix on her necklace.

"I wish I wasn't here," I said. "We've been here only twenty-four hours, and it feels like a week."

Joy nodded and continued to run her hands over her crucifix.

An owl hooted in the distance. A snarling sound like dogs fighting pierced the darkness, and the crickets went quiet. The snarling noise subsided, and the crickets resumed chirping until the snarling started again, and the process repeated itself.

A girl cried.

"We'll be okay," said another girl's voice, shaky and on the brink of tears.

All right for now, I thought. I doubted the terrorists brought us all the way here to be pampered. I laid on my back, awake and alert, my eyes fixed on the missing part of the roof, expecting an animal to jump in at any time. Some girls talked amongst themselves, while some murmured to themselves. There were sobs here and there. Some had already fallen asleep, their snores adding to the sounds of the night.

I couldn't sleep. My eyes were alert, kept open by the fear of the uncertainty of the night and what tomorrow might bring. I knew death was an end everybody would meet, but I feared if I closed my eyes this night I would never wake up.

Beside me, Joy was on her knees, her eyes shut, her mouth moving with no sound, her body rocking back and forth.

I watched Joy and wondered again if prayers would save us. Why would God put us through this in the first place? Was it to teach us a lesson, or were Joy's prayers in vain?

I remembered all the children we'd seen earlier with their mothers and wondered if that would become our lot, my lot. How did they get here? Were they abducted too, helpless and forgotten—the story of my life?

I thought of the people who had helped me since Matron died. My late uncle, Fatima, Zainab, and my godmother. I felt sorry for myself. But I had to pick myself up. Nobody would do it for me. I pushed the thought to the back of my mind.

Exhaustion got the better of me, and my eyes flickered. I could still hear Joy beside me mumbling. The night had gotten cold, and I used my nightshirt, which was now dry, as a blanket.

"Joy, get some sleep," I mumbled as I drifted off to sleep.

The image of Aminata and the sound of a single reverberating gunshot played in my mind.

CHAPTER THIRTY-ONE

"Wake up, wake up," said a familiar voice.

I opened my eyes. I felt like I had only just drifted off to sleep and now it was time to wake up. At the entrance to our room was Danuwa. She bent over and shook the two girls sharing a mat closest to her.

One girl stared at her. Her eyes widened and she drew back. She was wide awake in an instant as she realized where she was.

"Everybody, to the stream," said Danuwa.

Joy was already on her knees, praying. I wondered if she'd slept at all. She concluded her prayers, got up, and hurried after me as I ran toward the door.

I'd made up my mind. I would survive, and I would not give the terrorists a reason to target me or see me as a problem.

Outside, the day was breaking, but the camp was still asleep. I stopped in my tracks. The truck that brought us was gone. Why was I surprised and sad? Maybe my subconscious always believed our stay would be temporary. With the vehicle gone, it was looking permanent.

"Take one and pass it down," said Danuwa.

I received the small bundle. Chewing sticks, held together by a black strip of rubber band. I took one and passed it along. I munched down one end, got it soft, and scrubbed my teeth with it. The chewing stick reminded me of Fatima. She sometimes had one dangling from her lips early in the morning as she cooked and cleaned. I don't know why I was thinking so much of a home where I didn't belong.

A girl screamed and ran out of the room we had slept in. Tears poured down her face. She was in Ekpo House.

"She's not moving," sobbed the girl. "I've been calling her to get up. She's not getting up."

Danuwa's eyes narrowed. "Who's not moving?"

"My bunkmate, my bunkmate!"

Danuwa went into the room. I dragged my feet, my hand clutched over my chest. An intense feeling of doom descended on me. Some girls followed Danuwa and soon sobs came from the room.

"Bello, Bello!" yelled Danuwa as soon as she came out of the room.

"Yes, Ma!" said a breathless Bello. She ran forward.

"You're never around when you're needed," scolded Danuwa.

"Sorry, I was helping Kaka."

"Always excuses. A snake bit a girl. She's dead. Tell Kaka and call Danladi!"

Bello ran off. I stood there, my chin trembling. I couldn't tell who it was, but the girls in the other dormitory knew. They gathered together in a group hug, crying.

"One has to be very careful," said Danuwa. She raised

her hand and waved. Kaka, Bello, Dan, and Aliyu rushed toward us.

Danladi approached the entrance to our room, forehead furrowed. His eyes darted from girl to girl, searching. Just before he entered the room, our eyes met. I saw the tension leave his face, then he was gone. For the second time, I felt I'd seen that face before.

Minutes later, Kaka came out. "It is unfortunate. Just like I was saying yesterday, there are dangerous animals here. Bello, take them to the stream now. We have a long day today."

As we walked away, I turned around and saw Aliyu and Danladi carrying the corpse of the dead girl wrapped in a mat. Aliyu winked at me. I looked away. I couldn't understand. He had a dead body in his hands, and all he could think of was a wink at another girl.

We went down to the stream. I felt weak from the shock of witnessing yet another death and from lack of sleep.

Would I survive this? I waded into the stream, and the coldness sent a jolt through me, waking me up. I knew too that I'd just become the focus of unwanted attention.

CHAPTER THIRTY-TWO

"Good willing, you'll become proficient in two things while you're here," said Kaka after we came back from the stream.

We sat in the kitchen area silently. Death and beatings had become a common occurrence in our eyes. Kaka and Danuwa had already moved on from the events this morning.

"The two are religion and preparing good food, the two things that nourish the body as a whole. Danuwa will divide you into two groups." She snapped her fingers and motioned at Danuwa and Bello.

They separated us into two groups again. It seemed like they liked groups a lot here. Lami and Ronke, the twins, were in different groups, and Lami tried to cross over and join the other group. Danuwa stopped her.

"Let . . . let me join my sister," stammered Lami.

Kaka looked from Lami to Ronke. "Ah, *tagwaye*, twins." She shook her head and smiled. "They bring good luck. I wonder who will get them." Her voice was low, as if she was talking to herself. "Girl, be quiet. The time for struggle is yet to come."

There was no humor in Kaka's voice. It seemed like she was a different person. A chill ran down my spine. Struggle for what? I looked at Kaka. She looked harmless, as if she had said nothing. Lami stopped struggling, as if someone had doused her with a bucket full of icy water. She too must have read meaning into what Kaka said.

What was going through Ronke's mind? They were inseparable. When you saw one, the other was always close by. The twins started at Akarika Girls in our second year when their father, a manager in the company he works for, was transferred to Borno State from their native state of Lagos. They looked so much alike. Ronke wore the letter "R" pendant and Lami the letter "L," which helped a lot. The school had invited only one of them to the special session. The other crashed like I did.

Danuwa led Joy, Efome, Lami, Latifah, and the rest of the girls away to sit under a neem tree. Its long branches and leaf cover provided ample shade. I was sure Joy would complain soon.

We remained with Kaka in the kitchen area. Firewood smoldered in the fire pit amongst three huge stones. Bello poked the wood with a long stick. The fire came to life and filled the air with the smell of burning wood, animal fat, and spices.

"Raise your hand if you're a good cook," said Kaka.

I didn't hesitate; my hands shot up. I must make myself useful to survive.

"Only one person can cook amongst all you girls?" Kaka nodded.

I knew most of the other girls could cook too. They

didn't want to volunteer that information until they knew the reason behind it.

Two men approached and dumped something on the ground beside the fire pit. It was the carcass of an antelope. I gasped, and so did many of the girls.

Its huge glassy eyes stared into space. I'd never seen one up close before, dead or alive. Flies flew in and out of a red hole in its neck, staking their claim to the meat. A round metal contraption with jagged edges trapped the antelope's right hind limb. For a second, I looked at it, mesmerized by its simplicity. It looked like a big metal mouth, with iron teeth biting into the antelope's hind leg.

"Gin trap," said Kaka. "It's placed all around the camp to trap animals." She looked around and smiled, mischief written all over her face. "Never leave the camp without a guide. These things can and will snap your leg clean off if you step on them."

Nobody moved. You could hear a pin drop. The realization that we were prisoners in this camp despite Kaka's claim to the contrary hit home. Kaka opened an oil-stained, dirty white sack, with "Akarika Girls Government Secondary School" printed on it in black. She removed spices and other condiments. *They must have stolen them from our school kitchen*, I thought.

"You'll learn how to make *suya*, spicy barbecue meat," said Kaka. "Men find it irresistible. Beef is preferable, but since God has provided us with an antelope, that's what we'll cook with."

She looked at us, again with what I considered a fake smile.

"Once it's all spiced up and roasted on sticks, we'll call it beef."

Kaka's motherly nature and her gentle, non-aggressive

manner disarmed me. As the morning progressed, women and children came out from the huts and bungalows on the side. Their presence, even though not in our immediate vicinity, gave suggested safety and normalcy. Most of the other girls felt the same, I guessed, because nobody complained.

Kaka had Bello skin the antelope's thigh, berating her every move.

"Don't peel the skin too far. Make the slices thinner. You good-for-nothing *karuwa*, prostitute!"

Bello mixed cayenne pepper and salt in a large bowl. She sprinkled oil on the sliced meat and was about to coat the meat with the mixture when I blurted, "Wait!"

Kaka frowned. "What is it, my daughter?" asked Kaka.

My heart pounded so much I thought it would burst. "Sorry . . . sorry," I stammered. I . . . I make *suya* a lot at home. If you add these too, it will enhance the taste." I glanced at the sack. "May I?"

Kaka smiled. "Show us."

I went through the bag and brought out ground ginger, onion powder, paprika powder, and roasted ground peanut paste from the sack and added them to the mixture.

"Good," said Kaka and looked at Bello. "Add them."

Bello rolled the meat in the now brownish mixture. She speared the meat onto thin wooden sticks and stuck the sticks into the earth close to the open flame, setting the cooking in motion.

On and on Kaka went, accusing Bello of being such a terrible person and doing such a shoddy job, although Bello did everything expertly, as if she'd been doing it all her life.

Bello never stopped smiling and was always polite. Even when Kaka called her a prostitute. My blood boiled and I wanted to speak up for her.

"Your turn," said Kaka, looking at me.

My anger dissipated at once, replaced by a fluttery feeling in my stomach. "Me?" I asked in a voice I didn't recognize.

"No, not you," said Kaka. "The girl behind you. You're one twin, right?" She pointed at Ronke.

"Yes," said Ronke in a shaky voice.

"Come and learn."

Ronke stood up and walked to the front.

With Kaka's attention on Ronke, I turned toward Bello and whispered. "Thank you for yesterday. Don't mind her, you're the best."

The side of Bello's mouth twitched, and she nodded. Her eyes glistened with tears.

"This is how it's done," said Kaka to Ronke as she peeled off another part of the antelope's thigh. "Have you made suya before?"

"No," croaked Ronke.

"What can you cook?"

She rattled off many soups: okra, egusi, tomato, nsala, and jollof rice.

"Impressive. You'll make some for us later, yes?"

Ronke nodded.

Kaka looked at Ronke's work. "Excellent. Bello, watch and learn."

Ronke's work was mediocre compared to Bello's. Kaka invited me and some other girls to try our hands at it.

"The most important thing in suya are the spices," said Kaka and nodded in my direction. *Make yourself useful*, I reminded myself as a warmth spread inside me.

In no time, there was a circle of meat on sticks around the flames. As the meat cooked, my stomach rumbled as the familiar aroma of spicy suya hit my nostrils.

CHAPTER THIRTY-THREE

As we waited for the meat to cook, I watched the other group a few yards away. The girls huddled close to each other, a mass of black and gray.

The girls watched Danuwa like a hawk. She stood in front of a chalkboard with a long stick in hand. She would point at something on the board and they would recite it.

"Western education is sacrilege," the girls chorused.

Danuwa pointed. "Again!"

This went on and on until they satisfied Danuwa, then she would shift to another part of Western education she wanted to dismantle and destroy. Where was Joy? Then I saw her standing apart from the group.

The suya sizzled and made popping sounds. I focused on it.

"You seem eager to join the religious group," said Kaka.

I lowered my head and wanted to run and hide. I didn't know what to say. Before I could answer, she continued.

"Don't worry, tomorrow you'll get your chance," said Kaka. She pointed at Bello. "Help this good-for-nothing pick the right spices."

I didn't look at the other group again, but I wanted to. I thought Danuwa would have descended on Joy by now, but for some unknown reason, nobody had bothered her. Maybe it was because of the girl who had died earlier.

Kaka was busy examining the suya, so I shot a look at the other group. I gasped. Joy was on her knees praying. I gasped and turned away. I willed myself not to look again. We all knew what happened to people who disobeyed orders.

I braced myself, waiting to hear a cry of pain, a shout for help, or girls gasping or sobbing. All my senses were alert. Every rustle of fabric, cough, sneeze, or whisper sounded like Joy's voice. When I couldn't hold it anymore, I looked and gasped.

As many men as had come out the morning we arrived were around Joy, but they ignored her. A man, I think it was Danladi, was taking photos or shooting a video of the girls with a camera. Joy was still there unmolested.

Kaka laughed a dry, hoarse laugh that sounded like nails on a chalkboard. I whirled around, sure she would let me have it.

"Look at them," said Kaka pointing at the men. "It was inevitable, the smell has drawn them out."

Kaka fanned the flames more with a fan made of palm fronds. "As long as I'm in charge of the food, they must wait. Look at their faces; they hunger for meat, both the edible and the physical."

That night, I lay on the raffia mat beside Joy, exhausted from cooking and drained from watching Joy. My eyes burned from the fumes, now made worse by the animal fat torch Kaka had provided in the snake's wake.

We searched the room and uncovered a nest of baby rats. We killed them. Snakes preyed on rats. We found a few scorpions hiding in the mats and crushed them with rubber slippers.

Should I say something to Joy? Was it my business? She was my friend. As much as I wanted to be like her, disobeying them would not be helpful—if you wanted to survive. I was surprised nobody had hit her yet, or any of us.

"How are you feeling?" I asked.

"I don't know," said Joy. She sounded like she was about to cry.

I turned and looked at her. She blinked, and a tear rolled down her cheek.

"I'm a born-again Christian. My belief is my life. Even you . . . I know you're a Christian, but yet . . ." Joy's voice trailed off.

"Yet what?" I asked.

Joy's tears came faster. "You embrace their religion!"

My pulse raced. I knew she was right. I was selfish. But I'd seen what they did to people who resisted them. "It might be better not to antagonize them," I said.

"Are you saying I should go against my beliefs?" asked Joy.

I didn't answer. I didn't know what to say.

Joy was quiet. "Give them a hand today, and tomorrow they'll want an arm," she murmured.

"Joy, we didn't ask to be here, but we're here," I said in a shaky voice. "We have to survive this in one piece. They have the upper hand. I don't think it's wise to make them angry."

Joy inhaled and lowered her head. For a few seconds she stared at the floor. Her head jerked up. "Have you read the Book of Daniel, about Shadrach, Meshach, and Abednego?"

I nodded. I knew the story about the boys who refused

to bow to a foreign god and were thrown into the fire. "God protected them from being consumed by the flames," said Joy.

"But we have to help God help us. We have to keep ourselves alive," I said.

"He saved them," said Joy. Her voice wavered then strengthened. "Their faith was strong." She raised her head and looked at me with big wide eyes.

I couldn't argue with that. I'd lost the battle. *God help us*, I thought. I lowered my head onto my arm, exhaled, and waited for sleep to come and take me.

The next thing I heard was the tweeting of birds. It was morning. I felt ashamed. Despite the situation we were in, I'd slept like a dead donkey.

CHAPTER THIRTY-FOUR

arly the next morning, the camp was quiet, just like it was the previous day. We came back from the stream, and I wanted to rush off ahead of the others and report for duties just as Kaka had instructed.

All I wanted to do was keep my head low, do my job, and bide my time. I didn't know what Joy was up to, but I didn't want her to get me in trouble.

Lami, Efome, and Latifah walked ahead with me. The rest of the group followed behind. My group went to the tree with the chalkboard. For a second I wondered if I was doing the right thing going with the wrong group.

"Aren't you going in the wrong direction?" asked Lami, eyebrows raised.

"You'll get yourself in trouble," said Latifah.

"Kaka told me to report here this morning and help with the meat."

"Ah, Ronke told me you were the star of cooking yesterday," said Lami.

"The suya tasted good," Efome added. "Where did you learn to make it?"

It was ironic. I'd resented Auntie Halima for pushing me into the kitchen over the years. "At home."

Ronke glanced around, then moved closer. "What do you think they have planned for us?" She looked scared.

Latifah glanced around and whispered. "Anybody thought of running away from here?"

"We should talk to that girl, Bello," said Ronke. "She seems like she's been here for a while."

Latifah shook her head. "She looks comfortable. She might give us away. I wonder how long she's been here."

"I worked with her yesterday, and I'm supposed to help her today," I said. "Let me ask her." I didn't tell them about the subtle nods she gave me after we arrived. "I don't think Kaka likes her."

When we arrived at the kitchen section, Bello was already there. She waved me over. This time they had a smaller antelope. It too had a gin trap wrapped around its leg.

"Good morning," said Bello.

"Good morning." Everybody called her Bello, but she didn't look like a Bello. "Do you have another name besides Bello?"

"Faith."

My eyebrows shot up. "Faith Bello?"

Faith nodded and smiled. "My mother is a Christian. What's the story behind your name?"

"I don't know, but once I find out, I'll let you know. Can I call you Faith?"

"Yes, but make sure Kaka doesn't hear," said Faith.

Where do you come from?"

"About a two-hour drive from here, close to the border," said Faith in a soft voice.

"Which border?"

"Cameroon," said Faith. "It's close to where the group with the smaller girls went to."

She must mean Mary Ibe's group. "The group you told me not to join?"

Faith nodded.

"Why the separation?"

"The girls are younger, easier to handle," said Faith. "They took them to be sold into slavery and they'll end up in North Africa."

I couldn't believe my ears. "Slavery . . . slavery? Like buying and selling . . . people?"

"Yes, they become house girls or domestic servants. Some will earn money for their new masters as prostitutes. The lucky ones would become wives."

I shook my head, refusing to believe slavery still existed. I thought of Mary and wished it was a lie. I saw Mary's crying face in my mind's eye and felt an emptiness inside. I changed the topic. "Do you ever think of home? Like, will you ever go back home?"

Faith lowered her eyes. She focused on the antelope and tugged on the trap. I asked the next question, eager to get to the one I wanted to ask, the one that was burning a hole in my head.

Faith raised her head. "Are you going to go home?"

I wondered how best to answer the question. "As soon as the terrorists say we can . . . or I'll run away."

"Where's your home?" asked Faith.

"Lamija, but they took us from our school in Akarika." I looked around. Nobody paid us any attention. "Why does Kaka maltreat you?"

Faith's eyebrows narrowed. "Maltreat me? No. She doesn't like my faults."

"If she addressed me all the time the way she talks to

you, I might find it difficult to control myself. I . . . I might roll my eyes or pretend I didn't hear her when she wants me to do something?"

Faith laughed. "You won't do anything like that. Even if you did, she'd probably hand you over to the men to teach you how to respect your elders. You'll gain nothing. They'll beat you and maim you, and you'll do whatever she wants you to do. And by then you'll have made yourself an enemy."

I stared at Faith in disbelief.

Faith didn't flinch. "It's better to endure than lash out because the consequences would extend to all connected to you."

I paused. That was what I'd told Joy last night. Maybe it only makes sense when it's somebody else's decision to make and not mine. I let that go for now too.

"You said Kaka doesn't like your faults, but all I see is goodness. Even the first day I was here you helped me, and you didn't even know me."

"But I have flaws," said Faith. "Kaka is right. I drop things, I forget messages, I don't hear when I'm called, and sometimes I forget to say my prayers. These things, even though minor, annoy both Kaka and Danuwa."

"But you're human. Don't they forget things too sometimes?" I said.

"Not like me," replied Faith.

Faith refused to say anything wrong about Kaka and Danuwa. I couldn't understand why she was so passive. When people maltreated her for no reason, I thought it would be adequate to treat them the same way. Otherwise, the wicked people would always prevail. They would never feel challenged and would never see a reason to change their ways.

"What are you thinking?" asked Faith.

"When someone does something bad to me, I always strike back."

Faith looked at me with sad eyes. "Don't do that here. Violence rarely overcomes hate, nor can revenge fix wrongs—"

"What then?" I asked, cutting her off, eager to hear.

"You should do what Christ said in the New Testament," Faith said. "Love your enemies, love those who despise and use you, and turn the other cheek."

"Turn the other cheek? Even Joy, my friend, a born-again Christian, has refused the burqa given to us to wear. I have a cousin that lies about me for no reason, an auntie who hates me, and another cousin Peter who beats me up to deflect his own shortcomings. I resent them all. And you say turn the other cheek. If I did that, they'd slap me on that check too."

"Maybe, but life is too short to bear a grudge. All that hatred occupies space in your head," said Faith. "Think about it, if I bore hatred for Kaka for everything she did, it would cloud my judgment to enjoy other good things of life. And I would need a bigger head too." Faith smiled.

I couldn't laugh. "Kaka called you a prostitute!" I said in a loud whisper.

Faith didn't reply. She busied herself mixing spices as I'd done yesterday.

"You! You're not in my group."

I turned and saw Danuwa's menacing face glaring at me.

I jerked back. "Ka . . . Kaka told me to help out," I stammered. My posturing with Faith evaporated in an instant.

"Help Bello? Come on, get out of here. Your group is over there. Goat! You cannot follow simple instructions."

CHAPTER THIRTY-FIVE

Heat rushed to my cheeks. I looked down as I walked over to the other side as fast as my legs could carry me. Instead of getting on Faith's good side, we ended up arguing. I looked behind me as Kaka approached the kitchen area. I walked faster.

"Danuwa, I'm ready," said Kaka. "You can go over to your side now."

I took a seat on the ground with the others and waited for Danuwa to come over. I glanced over at Faith. Kaka was already harassing her. Would I have another chance to talk to her?

"Western education is forbidden," said Danuwa and pointed at the board with her stick.

We repeated after her.

Danuwa's eyes blazed. "God willing, with time we will succeed and wipe out all the nonsense they've taught you in school. We must live the way our forefathers lived. We must live by Sharia."

On and on Danuwa went. Reciting religious text as if we were in kindergarten wasn't challenging. A few girls dozed off, and Danuwa descended on them and knocked them on the back of their hands with her stick. She made an example with one girl.

"Pick a pin!" Danuwa barked.

The girl assumed a posture as if she was about to pick an object from the floor, bent at the waist, palm on the floor, and one leg in the air.

"Stay in that position," said Danuwa. "If you fall, I want you to remain where you've fallen until this class is over."

The girl assumed the position. I counted in my mind. She fell at the count of ten and remained on the ground. Tears and sweat flowed freely down her dust-covered face. I pinched myself to keep awake, reciting whatever Danuwa wanted us to repeat. It had no effect. I might as well have tickled myself. I'd almost dozed off when Danladi and Aliyu approached.

"Good morning, Danuwa," said Danladi.

"My son, how are you?"

"I'm fine," said Danladi.

Aliyu was busy ogling the girls.

Danuwa looked at Aliyu. "You, you are not fine? Looking for something to snatch?"

"Forgive me, Ma, good morning," said Aliyu. "The beautiful girls you have here are confusing me. I'm looking for the right one before Gambo comes."

"We are making videos and taking pictures," said Danladi. "To post on YouTube and give to newspapers."

Danuwa shrugged. "Okay." She laced her fingers together on her lap and pursed her lips.

Danladi continued. "We want to shoot videos of you teaching the girls. Gambo wants it fast."

Kaka's face changed like a flash flood. "You and Gambo are trying to kill me," said Danuwa. "Don't you know each time you take a picture you steal a year from my life? Take ten pictures, and I've lost ten years."

She unloaded on him in rapid Kanuri first, then switched to Hausa. I gave Danladi full credit; he stood his ground.

Danladi laughed. "No, Danuwa, it's not true."

Danuwa shook her head. "Take as many pictures as you want of the girls. Call me when you're done. I'll be in my hut." Danuwa walked away.

Danladi raised his camera and took pictures. Girls tried to move away. He lowered the camera. "Don't move away. I don't want to do this again. Now smile, we want you to look happy."

They want us to look happy. I turned the words over in my head. Is someone looking for us? I did not hesitate. I did as they told me. Some girls still had not gotten the memo. I didn't think it was a bad idea to be in a picture if it would be featured somewhere. It was evidence we were alive.

"I will not say it again," said Danladi. "Please do not move away from the camera."

The same girl that Kaka had punished earlier stepped away. Maybe she had a death wish or was just a magnet for trouble. Danladi nodded at Aliyu. He rushed the girl and within seconds rained blows on her. Tears, snot, and blood rolled down her face onto her top.

"Now you have a reason to stay out of the picture," said Aliyu.

Danladi shook his head and continued clicking on the camera.

What type of people are these? Animals. Pulse racing, I looked around for Joy, then remembered she was in the other group. I found her crouched on the ground wearing black with the others. She had somehow turned her burqa to a hijab. I heaved a sigh of relief. At least she was taking part in cooking.

I heard repeated clicks of the camera and turned to look. Danladi had the camera on me. He took a lot of pictures.

"You have a beautiful smile," said Danladi.

My body tensed. I covered my face with the scarf.

"Relax, I've been watching you through the camera lens. I took video and stills. I'm sure you'll like them. I'll show you later when I sort through them."

A few steps behind Danladi stood Aliyu watching us. Our eyes met, and he smiled.

CHAPTER THIRTY-SIX

Hamza walked into his office and marveled at the level of activity and amount of personnel in the building. It was just five days ago that he met with his people. Kola had put things in motion right away.

It was also the same day he had learned that Dr. Muzo was strangled in his office. Murdered. Who would do such a thing?

The detectives saw Hamza for one reason, and one reason only. Dr. Muzo wrote in his journal of an appointment with him the day he was killed. They'd wanted to know what the meeting was for. The older detective with gray hair had asked the question.

"Do you know who would have killed Dr. Muzo?"

Hamza told them the truth. "I don't know."

"Who requested the meeting?"

"He did." Hamza raised his hand. "Hold on, am I a suspect?"

"No, sir. These are just routine questions, sir."

"All right, carry on," said Hamza.

"Were you surprised with the request?" asked the detective.

"Not really. Dr. Muzo was my mentor and teacher back when I was in medical school in Kano. Over the years, occasionally we would meet for lunch. And remember, he's my personal physician."

The detective nodded.

"You know how it is," said Hamza. "No matter how big or successful you become, your teacher can always pull your ear—you always have that respect for them." Hamza held his breath. He hoped the detective would buy that and shift their investigation in another direction.

"You're right!" exclaimed the detective and gave a knowing smile. "Mine is fear. I once saw my fifth-grade elementary school teacher, Mrs. Biodun, at the market. She was now old and shriveled, and my first instinct was to run and hide. She terrorized me when I was in her class."

Hamza exhaled. They talked about teachers, schools, and the economy. They both agreed the government was to blame but left alone who the government was.

Before they left, Hamza had asked them to keep him up to date and let him know if they would require his help in any way.

"Is there any information you would like to share with us about Dr. Muzo?" asked the older detective as Hamza walked them to the door.

There was an incident when Hamza was doing his internship. It was something Hamza would rather forget. He did not believe in volunteering information.

"No, but if I think of anything I'll let you know."

If it ever came to light, he would address it. He pulled out a drawer on his desk. It contained a brown envelops stuffed with cash. It was something he had seen his father do countless times—make people who come to visit you an unexpected gift. That way they are indebted to you, and if for any reason you need a favor from them, they can't say no.

Hamza shut the drawer. If given a chance, he would rebuild Nigeria one step at a time. He shook hands with them, and they left, the disappointment on their faces evident.

Hamza was surprised at himself. He had gone from noncommittal to wanting to give this his best shot. He had tried to kill the idea when his father suggested it, asking for a state-of-the-art, modern campaign office, which he thought would faze his father, who believed money should always be put to good use.

"You shouldn't waste it just because you have it!" Father would say.

But Hamza got the office with all the bells and whistles, and he was still nonchalant about running for office. You just don't wake up one day and decide to run for office. But since he saw his name in the newspapers linking him to terrorist attacks in the south, he got angry and decided to at least try. Now doubt had crept into his mind.

Was all this just another of his father's pet projects he would start and later abandon? Hamza knew his father had his own agenda, which he knew nothing of. Would he support him all the way or run out of steam when he tired of the whole thing? Could he lead? Running a country was not the same as running a hospital.

Hamza also knew he would inherit a huge chunk of his father's estate when he passed on. Father had given him a copy of his will to read, and minutes later asked about his marriage. The reason was obvious. Hamza would one day have to pass this on to someone.

He sat in his office and sighed. The old man was still alive, and without his financial support and connections, his efforts would come to naught. He could not continue to ignore his father anymore.

CHAPTER THIRTY-SEVEN

By the fifth day, I was still helping Faith early in the mornings before our teaching for the day started. Sometimes we would go to the stream to do laundry for Kaka, Danuwa, or Gambo. Gambo was the head of the group. In second place was a tie between Danladi and Aliyu, depending on Gambo's mood. Kaka and Danuwa were like watchdogs.

The food the terrorists had stolen from our school kitchen had dwindled, so we spent more time on religion. Kaka joined the two groups together. Cooking was no longer as elaborate as the first few days. The amount we had to eat had also gone down.

The visits by the men to watch us cook and recite the Koran went up. They were becoming restless. You could see the hunger and fire in their eyes. It was around this time that Kaka talked about our conversion to Islam and marriage.

"The men are looking for wives!" said Kaka. "How many of you would like to marry?" A giggle broke out. *Teenage girls will be teenage girls*, I thought. Suddenly, they all sounded like my cousin Maryam. I searched the group and soon found who I was looking for. Joy had resolved to stay away once the emphasis shifted to religion. She stood apart, praying.

"We know you all said you were Muslims, but we want you to convert before witnesses. We do things the right way. These men will take you as wives when you are of the same faith." She pointed in the general direction where the men were.

It sounded like a joke, but it wasn't. There was no other reason we were here. The evidence had been there right from the start—the women and children. I wondered when it would escalate from asking to demanding.

"Think about it," said Kaka. "You are young and beautiful. Your whole life with four or five babies is ahead of you."

More giggles broke out at the mention of babies, but nobody agreed to convert and take a husband. Even the girls that were Muslims did not volunteer to get married.

Bello was single. I don't know how she did it. What I wanted to do was get away. The other girls were bugging me to find out from Faith. I resolved to speak to her next time we were alone.

Later, on our way to the stream to wash, I asked her if she knew how to get away from here.

"You just got here, and you want to leave?" asked Faith. "This is the middle of nowhere. Unless you have a truck, you cannot get very far. I've been here for one and a half years, and the only girls who have gotten out of here were in the belly of an animal."

My pulse raced. So, there was a way out. The belly of an animal. "How?"

Faith rolled her eyes. "Animals ate them when they tried to escape." There was anger in her voice. Faith made a sweeping hand gesture. "There are more groups like Gambo's scattered out here in Sambisa. They make a living organizing raids into villages and towns stealing whatever they need, and most do not have a Kaka to protect the girls. Believe me, there are worse groups out there." The veins in Faith's neck jutted out. She shook all over, nostrils flaring.

My mouth went dry. I stood there numb. I didn't know what to say. It was out of character for Faith. Moments later, Faith's breathing came back to normal.

"Sorry," said Faith.

I felt the tears in my eyes. "You've been here for one and a half years?" A lump formed in my throat. "I didn't know," I croaked.

Faith nodded and smiled. "Life is strange. We find ourselves in situations that are no fault of ours, and we have to make the best of it."

"Like you've made for yourself? But you never thought of escaping?" I wanted to hear her story.

Faith nodded. "Like I've made for myself." She paused. "You heard Kaka earlier."

I nodded.

"It's no joke. For you, it would be Danladi or Aliyu. And Gambo decides, not you. Prepare your mind. Come on, let's go."

CHAPTER THIRTY-EIGHT

Danladi sat in his hut and scrolled through the pictures in the camera. He stopped at every photo Ngozi appeared in. He'd liked Ngozi from the first time he saw her at that business center. It was like seeing something you couldn't have. You acknowledge it and move on. He hadn't realized she was the same girl until they arrived at Sambisa. What are the odds? From Lamija to Akarika. Danladi wanted her, and he would do what was needed.

Danladi knew Aliyu was sniffing around too, but only because he didn't have a mind of his own. He wanted whatever Danladi wanted. But this time Gambo would not let him come close. But what was going on with Gambo? *Nowadays, he was a little secretive about things*, thought Danladi.

Danladi knew Gambo was in touch with some big men, movers and shakers who had given them weapons, cars, and food, whatever they needed. He also had a strong feeling that there was more to the kidnapping of the schoolgirls.

Danladi remembered a few years ago when Gambo had

resurfaced. He had shown up at the computer workshop where Danladi worked. He told him he never made it to Europe and had been in Libya. They had talked about their past foray into a religious school. Gambo then told him about the connection he made while away. Contacts with like-minded holy men that are not happy with the direction Nigeria was going and would like to do something about it. He convinced him to join him in forming a group that would bring the people back to the true religion.

Danladi left his job, and they recruited youths with money and ideology. Soon they moved into Sambisa and started harassing fellow Muslims. They added Christians to their enemies, and now he didn't know what they were fighting for. Maybe he should have stayed back in his old job.

Danladi looked out of his window and saw Kaka hunched over a fire pit cooking. His mind drifted to another time many years ago when he watched a woman hunched over a flame cooking. The woman was his mother.

He lived with his mother and two sisters in a slum in the outskirts of Kano with a hundred other families. Just by thinking about it he could smell the filth as if he were there. Decaying garbage, urine, feces. The odor came from the vast drainage gutter that divided the slum into two.

His father was never there. Danladi's mother had sent him to buy bean cakes from Kaka and he'd met Gambo for the first time. Kaka had brought Gambo back with her to the slum where she lived after his parents died. Kaka was not happy having to look after a six-year-old boy, but once Gambo began to run errands for her and helped with her fried food business, she'd stopped complaining too much.

Danladi and Gambo had become fast friends. They were sent to religious school in the slum. Memorizing the

Koran was no easy work. Neither of them had the patience. They looked forward to after classes when they would go out to the main road and watch cars and taunt students who went to the regular schools as they passed.

One day Gambo was detained by the teacher.

"Go ahead," Gambo had said. "I'll meet you once I'm set free."

Danladi rushed off as usual and walked along the gutter following it to where it met the road. Halfway he saw a crumpled paper. He picked it up. It was a hundred-naira note. Danladi gave a small yelp, then clasped his hand over his mouth. He looked around, but no one seemed to be looking for it. He wanted to take the money to his mother, but he was also sure that would be the last time he would ever see it.

Danladi looked for the man that sold homemade candy shaped in the form of sugar canes. He wasn't there. He only saw another man selling real sugar canes.

"Give me a whole cane," Danladi had said.

"Do you have money?" asked the man with a skeptical look on his face.

"Yes!" Danladi showed him the hundred-naira note.

The man hesitated. He thought Danladi had stolen the money. But he picked out the tallest cane, cut off the ends, and smoothed out the roughness with a sharp knife. He cut it into five pieces and handed them to Danladi.

Danladi's mouth flooded with saliva as he waited for his change before taking a bite. He looked around for Gambo. "Gambo! Over here."

"Take your change," said the man and stuffed a handle full of notes into Danladi's small hand.

"What happened?" asked Gambo. His eyes darted from the money to the sugar cane in amazement.

"Help me," said Danladi and handed some canes to Gambo.

As they walked toward the culvert in the road, Danladi told him how he found the money.

"Put the rest in your pocket out of sight," said Gambo. "Before someone steals it from us."

They sat on the culvert and watched cars and people pass.

Danladi removed the hard outer part of the sugar cane and bit into the soft part. He felt he had died and gone to heaven as the sugary water flooded his mouth. He sucked it dry and spat the chaff out. Beside him, Gambo was doing the same.

Without warning, something grabbed Danladi by the neck and pulled him to his feet.

"Where's the money?" spat a hoarse voice.

Overwhelmed by the smell of decaying teeth. Danladi spat out the chaff in his mouth, gasping for air, and noticed his assailant was the local bully.

Danladi's voice came out strangled. "It's my money, I found it by the gutter."

The bully fumed. "Anything found on the ground belongs to me."

Danladi noticed other boys with the bully. A hand dug into his pockets, and soon it was empty, his money gone. People and cars continued on. Nobody paid attention to them.

"Let him go," said Gambo. He jumped to his feet and walked toward the bully.

The bully was taller and bigger than Gambo, but he let Danladi go.

"Okay, I'll punch you instead. You are dead!" said the bully.

Gambo rushed the bully. They struggled, and the bully connected a few punches to Gambo's face. Gambo's nose and lips were bleeding. They separated and stood opposite each other, breathing hard.

"Do you give up?" asked the bully.

Danladi wanted to run. The bully would come after him when he dealt with Gambo.

"No!" screamed Gambo and rushed the bully. He shoved him hard on the chest and pushed him into the road, just as an eighteen-wheeler drove by. There was a pop sound as the wheel rolled over the bully's head.

"Run!" said Gambo.

Gambo had saved my life. I was sure the bully would have killed me or maimed me for life. Nothing came out of the bully's death, he was just another slum rat. Good riddance, the police had said. But I owed Gambo. Things were peaceful for many years until Gambo traveled to Italy. He never made it to Italy but came back years later a changed man with money in his pocket and an ideology.

A knock on the door brought Danladi out of his reminiscing. "Yes, come in."

Aliyu walked in grinning from ear to ear. "Oga has agreed. It's going to happen sooner than later."

"Agreed to what?"

"Here," said Aliyu and handed a folded piece of paper to Danladi.

Danladi unfolded it. His eyes traveled down to the signature. It was Gambo's writing. He read and felt like he had been kicked in the stomach. Someone would be executed.

CHAPTER THIRTY-NINE

On the morning of the seventh day, we woke up at 5:30 a.m. and headed for the stream. Ronke, Joy, Lami, Latifah, and I walked together. I didn't want to convert, but after my discussion with Faith, my resolve was still firm but conflicted.

The girls had been pestering me to tell them what I got from Faith. I didn't want to. It would destabilize them too. My zeal to make it out of here was gone. Faith's predicament was real. If I told them, it would rob them of hope.

"She said we are in the middle of nowhere and the only way out is on a truck." I didn't mention she had already been here for one and a half years.

"Like the way we arrived?" asked Ronke.

I nodded. The girls left me alone as they pondered how to get on a truck.

We returned to our usual spot under the neem tree, and to my surprise, Faith was not there. Neither were Kaka and Danuwa. *Very unusual*, I thought. I looked around. Even the hungry men hadn't shown up. But I knew they would come. They had gotten bolder, like wild dogs. They circled their prey with lust in their eyes. I knew it was only a matter of time before they pounced.

"What's going on?" asked Latifah. "Something is not right."

The door to Kaka's hut opened, Faith stepped out and walked away. She was in a hurry and didn't look at us.

"I wish I'd jumped off the truck," lamented Ronke. "Even if I'd broken a leg, it would be better than being here."

I glanced at Ronke. Her eyes brimmed with tears.

"I wonder what they're planning for us inside there," continued Ronke in a shaky voice. Tears rolled down her cheeks in a torrent.

"Maybe they are just delayed," said Lami, crouched next to her.

"Delayed? Delayed how?" sniffed Ronke. "I spoke with one girl with the babies . . ." She turned and pointed in the direction where the women and kids played. "Do you know what she told me?"

Ronke didn't wait for an answer.

"She said when she was thirteen, she had gone to the market. On her way back, two men had stopped her and told her to come with them. She refused. They grabbed her and took her, despite onlookers. Nobody lifted a finger."

"They took her and her baby?" I asked. Once the words came out of my mouth, I knew it was a foolish question.

"Don't be stupid," said Lami. "She had the baby here. They—"

"*Yarinya!* Girls, why are you crying?" Kaka stepped out of her hut accompanied by Danuwa.

Ronke froze. For a few seconds, she stared at them, as if

in a trance. Then she wiped the tears from her face. "No, nothing," said Ronke. "I wasn't crying. Sand got in my eyes."

Embarrassed by my question, my abaya and hajib felt incredibly hot. Thank God for Kaka's timely intervention.

Kaka was all smiles. She didn't challenge Ronke's answer. "We have good news."

CHAPTER FORTY

"You girls did well. We're proud of you!" said Kaka. She paused for a moment. "Anybody ready to convert and accept a husband now?"

Just like yesterday, the question elicited more giggles, but nobody stepped up.

"No?" asked Kaka. "No problem. Today, we move to the next stage—"

A voice interrupted Kaka.

"The blood of Jesus . . . the blood of Jesus." It was a man's voice, weak and strained.

We turned to look.

"Jesus! Jesus!" someone cried.

A girl screamed. "Oh God!"

Someone cried. The sight that met my eyes chilled my blood. A dirty, shirtless man, one eye swollen, covered in bleeding cuts, was being dragged by Danladi and Aliyu toward us, prodded with sticks by other members of the group.

Gambo and his men wore black. One of them carried a black cloth attached to a stick with a badly drawn white-washed image of a gun and some Arabic characters on it. He waved it in the air, shouting in Arabic, "God is great!" at the top of his lungs.

"Yes, yes, yes," said Kaka. "God willing, tomorrow, each one of you will get a husband!"

The word "husband" turned my stomach. I shivered. At last, they had unmasked themselves, and their intentions were out in the open.

"God willing, to make you good wives, you must declare your faith before witnesses! This unbeliever is here to provide encouragement, listen to him."

What was he going to say? The prisoner was under extreme duress. It was whatever Gambo wants him to say. Danladi and Aliyu forced the man to his knees.

Gambo took a step forward. "Declare your faith!" He hit the man across the face and grabbed him by the neck.

The man grimaced and yelped in pain. He could not defend himself. His hands were tied behind his back.

I saw Danladi video recording Gambo and the prisoner with his cell phone.

Gambo asked the prisoner three more times to declare his faith. The prisoner remained silent. He only whimpered in pain when Gambo applied pressure on his wounds. Despite his injuries, the prisoner seemed at peace.

I clutched my stomach and bit inside my cheeks until I tasted blood.

Gambo was ready to kill. He pulled out his knife and in one swift movement slit the man's throat. A red mist of blood sprayed from the prisoner's neck. Then he fell to the ground and Gambo held the body down with his boots until it stopped jerking.

My body went rigid. I could not believe my eyes. Girls whimpered, afraid to cry out.

Kaka flinched, lips curled. She tried to speak but clasped her hand over her mouth and averted her eyes from Gambo and the corpse. Even Kaka was disgusted by this.

I shook my head. Danladi had captured the whole thing on video.

Kaka cleared her throat. "Raise your hand if you're ready to declare your faith."

The hand of every girl shot up.

CHAPTER FORTY-ONE

"**D**o not say no to your husbands," Danuwa said.

It was her final statement before she walked away with Kaka. We had declared our faith and were now on a conveyor belt to marriage.

Two men grabbed each of the dead prisoner's legs and dragged him away. Who was he? Where did he come from? Did our refusal cost the man his life? If I knew Gambo would kill him, would I have raised my hand earlier to save his life? Too many questions, few answers.

The rest of the girls and I dragged ourselves back to our room in silence. All I wanted to do was mourn in peace for a man who refused to give in to the end.

Tears streamed down Latifah's face. "I was listening. He didn't say anything, he didn't say anything." Her body wracked with sobs.

I hugged her. I was numb. We had held on to our grief until we got back to our room and then we let it go. In the past few days, I'd seen so many deaths close up. How could people be so cruel? But it was not over.

They wouldn't let us grieve in peace. Soon Faith led

some wives of those terrorists into the room to talk to us. Most were the same age as us, or younger. None of the wives wore black or gray like us, but they instead wore colorful wax-print materials, which they had wrapped around their heads as a hijab and then let flow down their shoulders, covering their blouses. Some of them had it all the way to their skirts.

Faith stood in a corner and stared into space. I looked at her, but she refused to acknowledge me. I didn't blame her; there was nothing to say. I was the one who had refused to accept reality. She knew all along what would happen.

One wife walked up to where I was on my mat and spoke. "My husband takes care of his family." She spoke in Pidgin English mixed with Hausa. "He only wants to follow the correct religious teachings."

I didn't say anything, still in shock. How would this terrorist wife feel if I hit her and slit her throat in the name of religion?

"I love my husband, and I followed him here. This is our beautiful baby, Ahmed. He is two years now. I had him when I was fourteen." She raised her child up. She laughed and cooed at her son.

I made no move to touch the baby, carry the baby, or lie to her that her son was the prettiest I'd ever seen. I wanted nothing to do with a terrorist's wife or child.

Seeing I made no move to hold the child, the woman placed the child on her shoulder. "Maybe soon you'll have one too."

My stomach churned. Saliva rushed into my mouth, and I felt like throwing up. "How can they be good when they kill?" I mumbled.

She didn't answer. The smile faded from her lips. I had no more questions. After some time, she left with the other wives. The rest of the day was a blur. I lay curled up on my mat. Beside me, Joy was on her knees in lamentation. Minutes later she got up and walked over.

"Ngozi," said Joy in a shaky voice.

I looked up. Joy's whole body trembled. Eyes red, face swollen, cheeks stained with dried tears.

"I . . . I can't do this," Joy blurted. "Can't stay here. Today, I've already committed one sin . . . failed."

I reached for her hand. Though I didn't see her do it, I knew Joy had declared her faith too. No sane person who watched that man murdered in cold blood would refuse any request with the threat of a similar fate.

I squeezed Joy's hand. I didn't know what to say to her. Staying or leaving meant death. For a second, I thought it would be better to flee and face certain death in the forest than uncertain death in the hands of these monsters.

Kaka called them husbands, but I call them monsters! That's what they are. Deep down, I felt I would die here. But if I gave them what they wanted, maybe they'd spare me. Perhaps a chance would come to escape.

I thought of Faith and how she had survived so far. She did what she was told, and on only one occasion I'd seen her invited into the huts by men. She would go in of her own free will, spend a few minutes to half an hour, and come out still alive. I remembered Faith's words: sometimes it was better to be safe than right.

Suddenly, Joy stopped crying and wiped her eyes. "It'll be all right," she sniffed. Her lips twitched in a smile. "I'll be fine," she said again. "Don't worry about me."

"What is it?" I asked. She had a peaceful look on her face, like the prisoner's before his death.

Joy ignored me. She went to a corner, removed her hijab, and the black dress. Underneath it she had on her blue shirt from the night we were kidnapped. She adjusted the black thread of her wooden crucifix, knelt down, and continued to pray.

Something had clicked for her. Exhausted and terrified of what was to come, I pushed it to the back of my mind. In the morning I would ask her what she'd figured out. The nightmares found me once I drifted into sleep. A younger version of me was about to go through a door. I screamed at her not to go in. But she did. I woke up covered in sweat.

"You screamed," said Joy in a whisper. She was still on her knees.

"Just a bad dream," I said and drifted off to sleep. In the morning, the mat beside me was empty.

CHAPTER FORTY-TWO

I looked around the room. Joy was not there. Maybe she'd gone ahead to the stream. Unlike her, but I hoped. Deep down I felt it. She had left. When we got to the creek, there was no Joy.

It seemed like none of the girls noticed Joy's absence. They were deep in their own thoughts about the murder and the news we'd received yesterday. Now and then, I looked around hoping I'd see Joy's sulking face hanging about.

"What do you think will happen to us?" said Lami in a low voice.

We were on our haunches in the kitchen area. It was a whisper, but I glanced at Kaka. She didn't seem to have heard. She rummaged through a basket Faith had just put down.

Ronke's lips trembled. "I . . . I don't know."

She sounded subdued, not her usual boisterous self. My mind shifted to the present danger we faced. Maybe I should have disappeared like Joy. It was a sweet, sad feeling. Sad that I was still here, but happy for her. She had escaped. I wished I had her courage. I said a silent prayer that God be with her and lead her to safety. She could go to the police or someone who would act fast, without inducement to do their job.

All the other girls wore long faces. I remembered the man with the slit throat. If he had just cooperated, he would still be alive.

"Bello! Bello!" yelled Kaka. "Useless girl, where's the smaller basket?"

"Sorry, Ma, here it is," said Bello.

"Don't just stand there like a fool, bring each one out and raise it up for them to see."

Kaka didn't ask for an assistant this time. Even if she did, I didn't know how to make the yogurt drink.

Each time Faith brought out corn, dry millet, pepper, garlic, and ginger. Kaka named them out in that order.

"We'll make *fura de nunu* today," said Kaka. She placed the ingredients into a mortar. "Fool, come and crush them."

Faith crushed the ingredients in the pestle. She went over to the fire and tended to it.

Danuwa walked up to Kaka and whispered in her ear. Kaka nodded and then gave her instructions. Danuwa stepped back and counted, pointing with her fingers, her lips moving. "*Daya biyu uku* . . . one, two, three . . ."

They must know Joy left. My eyes followed Danuwa like a hawk. What was I going to do? Suspicion would fall on me. What did you know? Nothing, I would answer. I hoped she'd believe me.

Faith handed Kaka the ground-up powder.

"One of you left last night," said Kaka.

All at once everything stopped. I kept my gaze straight, but I could feel all eyes burning a hole in my head.

"Girls, you know you can leave. But for your sake and

our peace of mind, we prefer that you let us know before you go. The Sambisa forest is dangerous and full of many wild animals." She paused, her eyes still fixed on what she was doing. She scooped up the fine powder and let it slip through her fingers back into the mortar.

"Does anybody know who is missing?" asked Kaka.

I focused on Kaka. I didn't want to turn around and meet somebody's gaze. Girls around me murmured.

Kaka leaned over on her stool and picked up a blue plastic kettle. She added water to the fine powder and kneaded the mixture with her fingers until it was malleable. She scooped up some paste and rolled it into a ball.

There was silence except for the crackling of wood in the fire and the laughter and cries of children as the camp came to life. I felt uneasy. The worse was still to come.

"Girls! Look around you. Who is not here?" Kaka yelled in a shrill voice, her eyes wide.

I jumped, startled. What had gotten into her?

Girls whirled around, fear written on their faces.

"Who is not here?" some murmured.

A few seconds later, I heard "Joy, Joy." Then, as if I was wearing a sign that said, "Over here!" all eyes turned.

Kaka's eyes narrowed. "Joy? The one who refused to take part."

"Yes, yes," murmured girls.

"Where did she go?" asked Kaka.

My lips trembled. *I don't know*, I wanted to say, but the words wouldn't come out. I felt a sharp itch in my armpit, then on my head and along my back.

"Tell her," a girl to my left said.

"Ngozi, if you know where Joy went, tell her," another voice echoed.

"I . . . I don't know," I stammered. "When I woke up,

she was not on her mat. I thought she probably went to the stream." My hands were shaking, and I pressed them together. "I . . . I thought I'd see her at the stream."

"Hmm, she didn't tell you she was leaving or where she was going?" asked Kaka.

I shook my head.

"We count you girls every day, and today it was off by one." Kaka bowed her head and put on a grim expression. "There's nowhere to go. She'll die in the bush. An animal will eat her."

Some girls gasped. I exhaled. I didn't realize I'd been holding my breath. Relief washed over me. I felt more confident, as if I'd just passed a rite of passage.

Kaka put the balls into a pot of boiling water. "Later tonight, I will assign you husbands." Her eyes were on the pot.

Again, there was dead silence, as if we were in a vacuum. This was happening too fast. Was it because Joy left?

Kaka pointed at a large calabash covered with a plastic tray. "That's *madara*, milk. A passing Fulani herdsman shared with us. It's already boiled, cooled, and the curd skimmed off."

She retrieved the spicy balls from the hot water and mashed them down again. "We're a family here and should remain as one." Kaka went on and on about women sticking together, testing the mixture with a finger as she spoke, until it had cooled. She put two balls on a plate and added milk to it.

The sound of girls whimpering and the flow of tears from silent cries lasted throughout the rest of the *fura de nunu* preparation. I knew what I would do.

CHAPTER FORTY-THREE

That evening, more wives of the terrorists came to our room once more. I didn't want to interact with them, know their names, or play with the children they brought with them. The more they talked, the more they sounded like a typical family. I saw the possibilities. *Maybe this could work.*

One of the women called Rakiya claimed to be Gambo's wife and showed off a gold ring she said he had given her as *mahr*, dowry.

"It's mine to keep!" she boasted. She brought out a bundle of foreign currency and waved it in the air. "Gambo gave them to me when he came back from his travels to Abuja and Lagos. Sometimes he goes to the Middle East and brings back jewelry."

With the mention of jewelry and cash, Rakiya had our attention.

Rakiya smiled. "If you're good wives, your husbands will take care of you too. So when you visit your families, you can help them." She waved money around again.

"You visit your family?" asked Efome, her voice high-pitched at the end of the question.

I turned my head closer to Rakiya and massaged my neck. *Tell us more.*

"Of course! I give them money whenever I go. They're happy for me and shower me with blessings."

The next question was *how*. If I asked, I would draw attention to myself. I stared at Rakiya to conjure her. Such things only worked in stories and movies.

"Come over here," said Rakiya. "I'll draw henna on anyone who wants it. Ideal for your bridal night." She brought out from a plastic bag ink and brushes. Next was a bottle of cough syrup and a small bottle of soda. She opened both and emptied the cough syrup into the drink. *Another syrup-drinking machine like Zainab.*

To my surprise, Amina and Efome agreed to the henna. Soon they were getting painted and sipping cough syrup with Rakiya and the other wives. Why not?

"Ngozi, come on, it's fun," said Amina.

As the women drew the black tattoos on their hands, more girls joined them. I moved away and went outside.

I stood outside, sad and confused. Giggles from the girls didn't make me feel any better. I watched the tall elephant grass around the camp sway in the gentle evening breeze, beckoning to me.

It seemed like the only hope was to wait for Joy to come with help. By then it would be too late. The image of me a year from now looking like Rakiya flashed through my mind. The life of a terrorist's wife and mother to his child.

That would become my reality if I did not escape. It was tempting; a few steps and I would be free from here. Free of marriage or maybe die trying. Death too is freedom from the misery my life had been so far.

Laughter drifted out from the room. The wives seemed happy. They had families that cared for them and appreciated them. My classmates from Akarika had families they could visit. I closed my eyes, and a single tear trickled down my cheek. I had nobody.

CHAPTER FORTY-FOUR

D usk crept in like a thief and stole the last hopes for escape I had. We stood, waiting for our rendezvous with Kaka. Occasionally a girl would turn her head to the spot where the man had died yesterday. The fear and disgust registered on their faces put us all on the same page.

Danuwa cleared her throat. "By going into the hut, you consent to the marriage. Kaka and I are witnesses."

"You! Go over there!" barked Kaka. "You, there!"

I was in the middle. Just like the first day we arrived, I decided to survive. I would obey all instructions. The trembling started from my lips to my chin and down my whole body. I shook like I had malaria. One after the other the girls before me got husbands, then it was my turn.

"You, over there!" Kaka pointed toward a hut on the far right of the camp.

I was in a daze. I don't remember walking to the hut, but there I was, inside a poorly lit room, greeted by the smell of burning candles and stale sweat.

There seemed to be no one inside.

"What's your name?" asked a melodious male voice in Hausa.

I gasped and followed the sound of the voice. A man sat on the floor. He had nothing on but a pair of shorts.

My mind focused on the advice I'd given myself. My legs trembled, and I squeezed them together to keep my balance. I clenched my fists tight and found relief in pain as my nails dug into my palms.

"Ngozi, have no fear."

My heart jumped. "Danladi?"

I didn't know what to feel—relief, fear.

He had something in his hands that he pushed toward me.

I hesitated.

"Come and look at this. I don't bite."

I walked closer to him. It was a picture of me. The one he took under the tree.

"I've been staring at that picture all day," said Danladi. "I was already in love before I printed it." He raised a bottle of soda to his lips and drank. He lowered the bottle and placed it next to several containers of cough medicine. I shot him a look.

"Don't judge me. You know our religion forbids alcohol." He raised the bottle and took a sip. "But not cough medicine."

My pulse raced. I wasn't safe.

Danladi smiled. "Who's Nkechi Amadi?"

I felt like someone had punched me in the stomach. "Who . . . who? How do you know her?"

"You stole my computer and tried to e-mail her, remember? Lamija?"

What is he talking about? "Computer . . . e-mail. The business center!" It all came back in a flash. The young men trying to upload a video. No wonder his face had looked familiar that first day.

"After I printed the picture, I knew I'd seen you somewhere before. Then it clicked. It was at Lamija."

I didn't know what to say or do.

"I fell for you that first day, and thanks be to God, now we have to consummate," said Danladi.

"Consummate? I'm not married to you!" I shrieked. "All Kaka did was point me toward a door!"

"But you came in of your own free will. You are now my wife," said Danladi. He got up from the mat and walked toward me.

I dashed to a corner of the room. My knees knocked together as I stood there. I did not speak, could not speak. My lips trembled.

"*Kai*, what's the problem? Why are you running?"

A muffled scream somewhere outside pierced the silence of the night. I whipped my head from side to side. More screams, sobs, pleading, and silence followed.

"Somebody is having a good time," said Danladi. He grinned and took a step toward me. "Is this how we will live as husband and wife?" He raised his right hand. "I will protect you until we leave this place."

I covered my head with my hands. The blows I'd expected didn't land. I opened one eye and looked at him.

He placed a rolled-up paper to his lips and lit it. His face became more visible from the glow of the match. His eyes were glazed over and distant. He blew smoke in my face.

It smelled like a sweaty armpit. It must be *wee-wee*, marijuana. Zainab had warned me about it. "Trouble you can smell a mile away," Zainab had said.

I walked backward, but there was no more room. My

back was against the wall. I pushed into it, hoping it would yield and absorb me. The smoke made me dizzy, and my head throbbed.

"*Wee-wee*, do you want some?" He offered me the joint.

I shook my head in a nervous twitch and watched him like a hawk. He thought for a moment and smiled. He walked back to his mat, to a pile of clothes that lay by the side, and rummaged through them.

What is he going to do now, pull out a knife?

Danladi pulled out a bottle of soda, drank a little, and then emptied a syrup container inside it. "Good for you. Calm you down," he said in Pidgin English and winked.

Maybe the wink was to reassure me. It was okay to have things done to me against my will. Danladi was a different person. I shook my head. I saw frustration and impatience on his face.

Danladi took another drag of the joint and blew smoke my way. He drank from his bottle as he contemplated what to do next.

The cloud of marijuana hung in the room like an early morning mist. My eyelids felt heavy, and when I blinked, it was so dark I thought the candle had burned out. I felt like I would faint at any moment.

"Come on," said Danladi and reached for me.

I jerked back. To survive was to give in, and that was my plan coming in. But my mind was yet to accept that plan. All the muscles in my body seemed to agree with my mind. I don't know how or why I felt energized. Before I could stop myself, I worked up a mouthful of saliva and spat in his face. "I thought you were different!"

Danladi's face changed. In a flash, he struck me across the face with his palm. He grabbed my shoulder and threw me down on the mat and straddled me.

The violence surprised me. *Give in. Don't fight.* But my fingers were out of earshot. I clawed at Danladi's face and tried to gouge out his eyes or rip out his nose.

Danladi was strong. He grabbed my wrists and locked them together with his right hand. I was no match for him until my knee connected with his soft middle.

He groaned in pain and rolled away, both hands on his privates.

I wanted to scream with joy. I'd won the battle but the war was just beginning.

Danladi was on his knees, his face a mask of rage. With a perfect move that could only have come from practice, he grabbed my right thigh and pounded his fist into it, grunting like an animal.

I jerked my head back as pain shot through my thigh, up my spine, and exploded in my head like a bolt of lightning. He grabbed my left leg and pounded. I shut my eyes in pain.

His knees parted my thighs.

I tried to move them back together, but they felt as heavy as bags of rice. My legs were useless. With terrifying clarity, I realized I had sabotaged my best-laid plans.

"Why did you hit me?" shouted Danladi.

I struck him on the face and his fist connected with mine. My vision exploded into hundreds of lights, like fireflies twinkling in the night.

Tension left my body. Hands were upon me, touching me, squeezing me, and reaching into places I considered private. I couldn't move. Then I felt nothing.

CHAPTER FORTY-FIVE

A cold draft crept up from the floor, reaching places that should be covered. Shivering, I opened my eyes; I sat with my back against the wall, naked. My chin on my knees. Where was Danladi? I raised my head and looked at the mat. I wished I hadn't. Throbbing pain shot through my head. I shut my eyes until the agony subsided. The monster was not in the room. The events of last night came to mind. The more I pushed it away, the more it crept back in.

I remembered coming to after he struck me, my whole body in pain. He was on top of me, grunting like the pig he is. Tears ran down my temples into my ears. I didn't cry or sob, just let the tears fall. When he was . . . done, he'd rolled away. I'd tried to get up, but my body wouldn't respond. I crawled to the corner of the room and sat with my back against the wall. "Don't leave this room," he had warned. "We're not done yet. One more, before an early meeting with Gambo." I'd drawn my knees up and wrapped my arms around my body to stop the trembling. The feeling of being dirty and damaged surrounded me like a damp cold blanket. If prayers were answered, I would've been dead a long time ago. He could then do whatever he wanted with my dead body.

He had snored, a loud rumbling and rattling sound. He sprawled naked across the mat with most of my clothes under him. That was my opportunity to run, escape. I was ready to leave without clothes but scared to move. I'd stared into the night, rocking back and forth. Danladi's snores, and the flickering candlelight, until it died down, were my companions.

Daylight streaming in through the window brought me back to the present. My clothes lay in a careless heap next to the raffia mat. I moved to retrieve them and awakened pain in my thighs and inside me. The pain, I knew, would fade, but my mind would never be the same. The image of him sprawled on the mat would come alive in my nightmares to torment me. I resolved to lock last night's experience away in the atrocious experience compartment in my mind. With great effort, I pulled my dress on. My body felt like a pillow beaten into shape by an insomniac.

I shuffled out of the hut and raised one hand to block out the sun that threatened my vision. I was in a different part of the camp than I was used to. Farther away, I saw other girls gathered in the kitchen area. Some turned to look at me, and our eyes met. Shame washed over me as if I'd done something wrong, brought this attack upon myself. I walked toward them. Where else could I go? They were my schoolmates, familiar faces. The pain in my thighs got better with each step. Each girl I looked at looked away. Nobody made eye contact. There were no happy faces.

Some girls seemed to have had it worse, sporting swollen eyes, cut lips, and scratched faces. As we stood there in silence, a few more girls emerged from other huts.

Efome sobbed as she approached. I got up, went to her, and hugged her, but she was inconsolable. I didn't know what to say. What was the right thing to say in such a situation? I settled for silence. We sat down on the ground and, like those who had come before, came to terms with our situation.

A girl I didn't recognize walked toward us supported by Kaka. Kaka had a guilty look on her face and looked away when our eyes met. When they got closer, I noticed that the girl she was leading had swollen eyes.

Kaka gave us food, applied shea butter to our superficial wounds, and admonished us to be submissive to our husbands next time.

"Next time!" Efome sobbed.

My body stiffened, not believing that this would be our new reality, my new reality. My regrets mounted, I should have disappeared into the bush. How would I survive this ordeal again? Either I escaped or would just fight every time until they beat me to death. I resolved to walk away that night.

Later in the afternoon, Kaka told us to go back to our rooms, the scene of the crimes last night.

"It's your new home. For you and your husband," said Kaka.

The thought of Danladi and his hut brought a bitter taste to my mouth. Instead of going there, I went back to the communal room I shared with other girls.

Efome was in the room and talked about what had happened to her. I listened but blocked off her words. I didn't want more load to burden me.

Conversations died down, and I looked up. Kaka stood by the door.

"Ngozi Bashiru?"

I felt like someone had yanked a rug from underneath me. As much as I wanted to, I couldn't deny my name. "Yes."

"Come," said Kaka.

I stared at her, too surprised to move.

"Come!"

I scrambled to my feet after her.

"You're hiding information!" said Kaka in rapid Hausa once we were outside.

My nostrils flared. "What—" She cut me off.

"Gambo wants to see you!"

My legs felt like jelly. The image of the man on the ground, his body twitching under Gambo's foot, flashed through my mind. Had they discovered that I was a fraud? That I was a Christian? But almost all of us lied. What does he want from me?

CHAPTER FORTY-SIX

Kaka led the way. She walked toward the bungalow Gambo had emerged from when we had first arrived. More than once, I thought of dashing into the bushes, but raw fear stopped me. Why does he want to see me? Then I thought of Joy. Maybe she came back and asked them to set me free. *Don't be silly*, I told myself. Before I knew it, we were in front of the door. Parked under the shade of a tree close to the bungalow was a Toyota truck with four men sitting in the back, talking and smoking. Danladi was there. I looked away.

Kaka knocked three times and pushed the door in. "Gambo, I've brought her."

My legs trembled. Yesterday, they beat and violated me. What would it be today?

They were comfortable with each other. Were they related? With reluctance, I dragged myself through the door into the dark interior.

Kaka stood behind me and blocked the only exit to the outside world. Was there something worse than what they'd already done? My whole body shuddered. I inhaled; the air rattled as it went in. *She who is down fears no fall*. I exhaled. I felt energized. Whatever else they did, I would turn it into an advantage.

My eyes adjusted to the darkness, and I made out a thin mattress in one corner with two people on it. A laptop computer, a cell phone with a huge antenna, and a printer sat on a table. Next to the table was a prayer rug. A gun with a curved thing next to the handle, like the one I'd seen with Taliban terrorists on CNN, rested against the wall. Gambo sat on a swivel chair in front of the laptop and pounded away at the keys.

"Gambo," said Kaka.

The man stopped typing and whirled around. "*Uwarka!*"

The bravado I'd gained a few seconds ago from my pep talk vanished as I stared into the cold eyes of the murderer. Mother? I gulped, not believing my ears. Kaka had said she was our mother when we arrived here. Was she his real mother?

"You two, go to Rakiya's hut," said Gambo. "She might need help." He jerked his head in the mattress's direction.

The two people on the mat got up.

"Hurry! I don't have all day," barked Gambo.

The two scrambled. One moved faster. They hobbled toward the door supporting each other. I saw who they were and clasped my hands over my mouth, stifling a cry.

Gambo must have beaten her. Swollen left eye. Cracked lower lip, twice its normal size. The twins didn't look at me. It was apparent Lami hadn't resisted after Gambo assaulted Ronke.

"Don't forget, she has seniority!" yelled Gambo as they left. "Or she will remind you."

Anger boiled inside me. I wanted to yell at Gambo.

Punch him in the face to give him a taste of his own medicine. My breathing got faster and faster. I felt like crying, but tears solved nothing.

Gambo sprung from his chair and took a step in my direction. My anger dissipated like steam leaving a boiling kettle. My stomach was tied up in knots.

"Are you someone important?" asked Gambo. Then he laughed. "Rich men don't send their daughters to school in the middle of nowhere."

"But there must be something," said Kaka. She walked to my side. "Look at you. You're not pretty. You're skinny and dry, like a bonga fish. Just ordinary, and yet . . ."

"Who is your father?" asked Gambo.

I wanted to lie. "I don't have one."

"You have one, stupid girl," said Kaka. "You don't know who. Who do you live with?"

"My auntie."

"So I should smell my finger and figure out her name," asked Gambo.

"Halima . . . Halima Bashiru," I said.

"For how long?" asked Kaka. "Are you her house girl?"

"Since my mother died when I was six."

Gambo's eyes narrowed. "Even if you're just her house girl, who gets a six-year-old house girl?"

"My uncle took me in after my mother died," I stammered. "My mother was my uncle's senior sister."

"Where's your uncle?" asked Gambo.

"He died in a car accident."

Gambo thought for a second. "Hmm, everybody around you is just dying."

Gambo read from a note. "Who is . . . Nkechi Amadi, MD?"

"Nkechi Amadi?" I glanced from Gambo to Kaka.

"Yes! Nkechi Amadi!" Gambo bellowed. "Do I speak like I have water in my mouth?"

Was that it? I felt the tension leave my body. I exhaled. "She's my godmother." I glanced from Kaka to Gambo. "My late mother's friend."

"Your godmother," said Gambo, shaking his head and muttering to himself.

Kaka laughed. "Danladi has played you. He dropped the name so you'd allocate the *yarinya* to him."

Gambo shrugged. "Well, since he thinks he can write the woman and make money from her, he should do it. I'll send him and Aliyu. They're already going into town to get supplies." Gambo folded the paper and tossed it.

Kaka looked at Gambo and hissed, "You kids, you travel abroad, come back with ideas, and all you think about is money, money, money. What about the message? What about all these boys running around with you, doing your bidding? How would they feel if they found out you're more interested in the things of the world than the word?"

"Bah, the boys are fine," said Gambo with the wave of a hand. "We gave them wives and some money. Most of them had nothing. They were destitute and had no jobs. I gave them hope, a direction, something to live for. Our main problem now is those Chibok girls. There's too much talk about them in the news, and we were not even part of that kidnapping."

I kept my head down. Had they forgotten I could hear what they were saying? There was silence. I glanced up. Gambo was looking at his laptop.

"Even CNN knows about Sambisa," blurted Gambo. "The government could send the police or soldiers here."

"Police? Soldiers?" Kaka cackled and slapped her thighs. "They are useless. They're too busy visiting prostitutes, setting up illegal checkpoints, and collecting bribes from motorists."

"True, true," said Gambo. "But international pressure might force the president to act after years of not looking at the northeast, and this is an election year."

"I'll take the girl back," said Kaka.

Gambo looked up from the laptop. "Yes, we'll decide on what to do once Danladi and Aliyu get back. I'll send them off at once."

CHAPTER FORTY-SEVEN

Hamza felt like a hamster on a treadmill as the party primaries loomed, running fast, getting nowhere. He had not spoken with his father yet but knew he had his full support. Hamza walked a tightrope and had to be careful whom he got assistance from, financial support in particular. Nothing in life was free.

"Don't worry too much, sir," said Kola in Hamza's office as they sat killing time waiting for the clock to count down so they could go to the party's convention office in Abuja.

Hamza forced a nervous laugh. "Just a little worry, right?"

Kola nodded and gave the victory sign. "I think we're in good shape. Your contribution to the party's welfare committee will come last. I have sent out feelers to find out what the serious contenders plan to donate. We'll triple whatever the highest donation is."

It had been a whirlwind campaign the past few days. Hamza had called high-profile delegates himself. It surprised most when they figured out who was on the other end of the line. They happily pledged their support.

The rest of the delegates each got at least two calls from the army of telephone operatives the campaign had hired. Each of them introduced Hamza as a new face, new blood, an outsider with new ideas. They would then explain to the delegate the problems faced by the country, the incumbent's shortcomings, and how Hamza would bring a turnaround.

"Outline the problem and tell them about our detailed solution to tackle each problem," Hamza had told the operatives the first day. He wished he had started this earlier; focusing on the grass roots was also good politics.

Hamza arrived at the convention and did the rounds. He spoke to the other eleven contestants. Clasping cold and clammy hands like his own made him relax. Knowing the others had their doubts despite how confident they appeared on the outside was comforting.

Hamza felt somewhat confident. They had talked to at least ninety percent of the two thousand delegates at least once, then with follow-up text messages after the phone call. Only his campaign took that approach with the delegates, Kola had told him.

Soon after, the elections started, and the delegates cast their votes. In the early hours of the next day, the sleepy-eyed but excited party secretary called a press conference.

"After the votes were collected and counted," said the secretary with a big smile, "it gives me pleasure to inform you that we have a nominee! Dr. Hamza Tarbari will face the president in the general election."

Excitement and fear of the unknown sent shock waves through Hamza's body when the announcement came. Congratulatory messages came in from all the other participants and party members. The presidency was within reach.

There was an after party, which Hamza attended but

left after doing the rounds, keeping to his mantra to avoid putting himself in compromising situations.

"Congratulations, Mr. President!" said Ali once Hamza got home. "I can see it, you will be our next president."

Hamza smiled. "Thanks for all your support." He scooped her up in his arms as she let out a surprised shriek. They headed to the bedroom for more celebration.

The next morning Kola was already in the living room when Hamza came down.

"Good morning, sir! We had to double the security detail," said Kola. "Your father insisted."

Hamza raised an eyebrow. "My father. How is he?"

"He's doing well, sir. He sends his congratulations," said Kola.

Hamza wondered if Kola had become more official when he addressed him. "Relax. Drop the 'sir.' It's still me."

"Yes, sir," said Kola and smiled. "Congratulations." He extended his hand and Hamza shook it, then they did a bro hug.

Hamza stepped back and looked Kola in the eye. "Thank you."

Kola's smile widened. "Anytime, sir. Anytime."

Hamza took the newspaper that Kola handed to him and wondered if it was time he buried the hatchet with his father. It was more of a one-sided quarrel, childish. He quarreled with the man and yet took his money. His eye fell on the circled headlines. "Hamza Tarbari Wins Party's Nomination."

Hamza smiled, and his eyes drifted down. His stomach tightened as he read the second circled headline: "Is Tarbari Involved in Voter Turnout Suppression in the South?"

Hamza took a deep breath. "They won't even let me enjoy my moment of victory." He knew rumors not addressed stuck faster than ones with an immediate response. He continued to read. They also talked about his lack of experience; there wasn't much he could do about that.

"What do we do?" asked Kola.

Hamza looked at his watch. "The battle is on. We'll drive down to the office and continue." Hamza and Kola exited the house to the carport, and Hamza stopped in his tracks.

"Oh," said Kola. "He wanted you to use something with extra security."

He, meaning his father. One of Tarbari senior's magnificent sedans sat in the carport. It was a luxury car that would attract attention, but Hamza was sure it was bulletproof with RCIED, remote controlled improvised explosive device, jammers.

Hamza whispered. "Please make sure Madam's security is improved too."

"Already done," said Kola. "She left for the hospital earlier in a Toyota equipped with RCIED jammers."

Kola and Hamza got in the car. The convoy was more extensive than it was yesterday. Hamza tried to come up with a counter-strategy after he denied the current allegations.

Things were already changing. The driver to the office took a different route from their usual one. *The leaders of tomorrow,* thought Hamza as they drove past a girl's secondary school on their new path.

Kola leaned closer. "We want to alter the road you take each time."

"I noticed," said Hamza as he sat up and turned his head to get a better look at a uniformed school girl that had just gotten off a bike taxi.

Kola coughed and shifted in his seat. "Sir, this . . . this is the . . . secondary school. Emmm . . . The University of Abuja is on the other side of town."

"Yes!" Hamza blurted.

Kola's eyebrows shot up. "What happened?"

Hamza spoke fast. "Some days ago, some girls were kidnapped from a secondary school in the northeast. There was no response from Aso Rock."

"Chibok girls, yes?"

Hamza nodded.

"What are you planning, sir?" asked Kola, narrowing his eyes.

Hamza's pulse raced. "There was no response from the government, even after Boko Haram claimed responsibility."

"That's true," said Kola.

Hamza rubbed his hands. "We'll call a press conference, deny the allegations leveled against me, and then give Aso Rock something to think about. Something to keep them busy. What are they doing about the kidnapped girls?"

"Brilliant," said Kola.

Hamza leaned back in his seat, his mind already coming up with a speech. "Is Aso Rock so focused on reelecting the incumbent they have let Boko Haram run amok?" Hamza feigned disbelief. "They have kidnapped three hundred of our young girls, leaders of tomorrow. Instead of rescuing them, Mr. President hits the campaign trail. He doesn't care about us and yet he's asking us for our votes?"

CHAPTER FORTY-EIGHT

I kept what had transpired with Gambo and Kaka to myself.

As luck would have it, Gambo sent Danladi and Aliyu with some others on the errand right away. I didn't go back to Danladi's hut, but back to our common room. What were they planning? To e-mail my godmother and ask for money? I hoped I wouldn't be here when they returned.

Some girls stopped coming out to the area where we had the religious studies and cooking sessions. Ronke and Lami looked like they were in mourning. They rarely participated in anything. Some girls embraced the marriage thing and had hardly left their husbands' huts. Some were being forced. I considered myself lucky so far.

Faith was always there, and I helped her with whatever needed to be done. She didn't ask me what happened, and neither did I volunteer information. This morning we came out as usual.

"Faith, please hear me out," I said. "I know you don't mind staying here, but if one were to leave, how could it be done?"

"Like I told you and as you already know, this is the middle of nowhere—"

"But Rakiya said she visits her family often—"

"She would love to visit often," interrupted Faith. "When you met her, she had just come back and was still high on having made the trip. The truth is, she and anybody that wanted to go anywhere can only do that when the truck gets supplies or Gambo sends them."

I listened as she explained why it was close to impossible to get a ride on the truck. From what she'd seen so far, you gained trust after you had been here for about a year and had a child. Your child stays back while you go, as security.

"Some of the men planned to defect," said Faith." They wanted to go to groups that allowed them to plunder goods and women as they pleased. They see Kaka as an obstacle to their conquests. So the marriage ceremony was to satisfy them. Some will still leave. I've seen it happen before."

"Where does Gambo get these boys from?" A fly buzzed close to my ears, I waved my hand around my ears to ward it off.

"Sometimes after they raid a village or set up a roadblock, the men and women of the village, or people they find in the buses, are given two options," said Faith. "Join them or die."

I waved my hands around my ears again, pesky insects.

"Like the man who died for the conversion. They captured him on the road minding his business."

I stopped waving my hands, my mind going back to that day that convinced Joy to make her move.

Faith exhaled. "The young boys are orphans who have lost their families in previous attacks. They are looking for something to latch onto and will do anything as long as they get food."

"What's with this buzzing mosquito?" I waved my palm around my ears. "How come they don't bother you? Are they your friends?"

Faith threw her head back and laughed. It was one of the few times I'd seen her come to life. In fact, it was the only time she'd laughed a full-hearted laugh.

"Oh God," said Faith as she wiped tears from her eyes. "Stop waving."

I stopped.

"Do you see any insects?" asked Faith.

I didn't move my head but checked my peripheries. "There's nothing there." I narrowed my eyes. "But . . . but I can still hear them."

Faith nodded. "Sometimes there are insects, but right now, there are not," said Faith. She pointed up in the sky. "I think it's a toy plane. It's been coming around."

I looked up in the sky. "I see only birds."

"Keep on looking," said Faith.

After a moment I noticed the plane not too far up in the sky. If you were not looking out for it, you would have thought it was just a kite gliding above. I remember seeing the little planes on TV during the Gulf War. Drones, they called them. My pulse raced. I recalled what Gambo said about Sambisa being in the news. "I think they're looking for us," I said.

"If they haven't found us, then they must be blind," said Faith. "It's not like we're hiding. For the past week, they've been buzzing around here like mosquitoes."

I shielded my eyes with my hand and looked up in the sky again.

"Don't do that too much," said Faith. "Somebody might

wonder what you are looking at. If only they can send information down. Kaka wants to make *fura de nunu* again. Maybe they can tell me where the Fulani herdsmen are."

I dropped my hand and looked at Faith. "Did you say Fulani herdsmen?"

CHAPTER FORTY-NINE

I woke up and found out I was not pregnant. This was new for me, expecting good news and getting it. I wanted to scream out the excitement, but I couldn't share. Not everyone was as lucky as I was.

Danladi and Aliyu were still away. I promised myself that the day Danladi got back would be my last day in that camp.

I'd been asking Faith the same question for the past four weeks, and she would stop at "the *fura de nunu* came from milk from the Fulani herdsmen," and that was all I expected when I asked this morning.

"They drive their cattle into Sambisa, grazing on lush grass," said Faith. "I go out to them when I see their cattle or smell the cow dung."

"So, why are you telling me this now?"

Faith sniffed the air. "Try it."

I didn't trust her. She was messing with me. I sniffed. "I smell nothing."

"It needs a practiced nose," said Faith with a laugh.

She sniffed the air again. "They're here."

"The cows?" I blurted.

Faith nodded.

I shrieked and hugged her.

"Careful." Faith pushed me away, her eyes darting around. "We don't want Kaka or Danuwa wondering what was getting you excited."

"If the herdsmen can come and go at will, there must be a safe way in and out of this place," I said.

Faith stopped what she was doing. "But remember, it is their way of life. They've been doing this forever and know how to deal with wild animals and people they come across."

I agreed with her. I'd seen similar herdsmen in Lamija too, driving their cattle down major roads, across people's farms and compounds, and sometimes downtown, leaving a mound of cow manure and a trampled surface in their wake. Yet they came out unscathed.

"Kaka always sends me to find the herdsmen, or they come to the camp, not me volunteering," said Faith. "I must find another excuse. Tomorrow, you can come with me to find them. Sometimes it takes the whole day. It's better when they show up at the camp."

The next morning, I went down to the stream. Ronke and Lami would join at some point, I knew. Rakiya made sure she expressed her seniority many times a day. She would send the second and third wives of Gambo to the stream to fetch water, wash Gambo's clothes, and do whatever chore she could think up several times a day.

I saw them coming, carrying buckets. "Why the long faces?"

Ronke took Lami's bucket from her and walked past me to the stream, while Lami walked into the bushes, looking at the ground, minding where she placed her feet.

"Did the first wife annoy somebody this morning?" I teased.

"This is ridiculous!" said Lami. "People should spread out while doing their business. I can't even find a spot to place my foot."

"Lead by example," I said.

"Yes, I will," retorted Lami and moved deeper into the foliage.

I shouldn't make fun of them. Lami stooped down and vanished, covered by tall grass.

"Something is happening," said Ronke. She glanced around to make sure we were among friends. "Gambo is worried. This morning, he talked about splitting us into two groups."

"What do you mean?" I asked.

"Sending us to different places," said Ronke. "One of us would go with Rakiya to help her with her son, while Ronke or I would stay with Gambo."

"Kaka must be aware of what's going on, but Faith has said nothing about it. Or maybe she knows but doesn't think it's important. I would have to—."

"Oh my God!" said Lami from behind some bushes, slow and deliberate.

Ronke sprang to her feet, eyes wide. "Lami! Lami! What is it?"

Lami's face looked like she'd bitten into lime or stone. "I've stepped on something."

I stifled a laugh. "Are you blind, can't you see where you're putting your feet?"

"The nonsense even smells like you," said Lami.

I couldn't hold it anymore and roared with laughter. It was a pleasant diversion from all that had been happening.

Lami came out of the bush dragging her left foot.

"Please stay away. Go far downstream and wash it off first," I said.

"Not yet," said Lami. "I want you to confirm it's yours."

As Lami got closer, I got a whiff and my smile faded. Lami noticed it too.

"What is it?" asked Lami.

"Ngozi?" called Ronke.

Adrenalin surged through me. I rushed toward Lami. She stopped and took a step back, puzzled by my behavior. "They . . . they are back!"

"Who's back?" Ronke and Lami asked.

I looked at two other girls putting on their clothes by the banks of the stream. They paid us no attention. "Come, I'll help you wash it off." I walked farther away from the two girls and the twins followed. I admonished myself for talking too soon. Should I lie to them or tell them the true story? I wasn't sure of my own passage. How could I invite them to uncertainty?

"Where are you taking us?" asked Ronke. "Who is back?"

"All right, put your leg in the water here," I said. "That's not human shit you stepped in, it's antelope."

Lami shrugged. "So?"

I had to think fast. "Emmm . . . Kaka wanted me to make suya again, but the traps caught nothing. One of the men said they must have moved on. But the poop means they are back."

"Stupid," said Ronke.

Lami stepped into the stream and scrubbed her right foot over the left with a vigorous repetitive motion. "You're thinking about suya when others are suffering. Wait till your husband comes back." She glared at me and forced a laugh. "I'll ask you about suya after that." Lami stomped out of the stream.

"Let's go back before that stupid Rakiya looks for us," said Ronke.

I heaved a sigh of relief. They bought it. But I felt bad. My reaction came out wrong. At least they had each other. It's always been me, myself, and I. I walked back to the camp a few paces behind Lami and Ronke, my mind planning on how to leave this place and what it would be like to be free.

I found Faith by the fire pit and told her I found fresh cow dung. "That means they are close by, right?"

"Are you sure?" asked Faith.

"Yes, by the stream! Lami stepped in it."

"No. I meant are you sure you want to do this?" Faith wasn't smiling.

I was sure, but the way Faith asked made me scared. "Why?"

"Once I ask them, it is the point of no return. The herdsmen could help. Or come back to the camp and tell Gambo."

"It will be a risk," I said. "But staying here would be worse. Will you come with me?"

Faith pursed her lips and shook her head slowly. "I know Kaka, Danuwa, and Gambo. I don't know the Fulani herdsmen. Come, let's go pick firewood."

We set off after Faith told Kaka she was going to replenish the firewood pile.

We walked down to the stream and entered the bushes. I showed Faith the dung.

"You're right," said Faith. "They can't be far. Watch out for traps and snakes. Everything would end if you stepped on one."

We gathered sticks as we went. Sweat poured down our bodies as we navigated around boulders, shrubs, and rough terrain. I picked a few sticks, my eyes searching for the herdsmen or their livestock. All we found was dung, but they were getting fresher and fresher.

"We have to go back," said Faith.

"But, they're close," I protested. "The dung is fresher."

"This is the farthest I've ever gone. We don't want to get lost or allow darkness to overtake us." Faith turned around. "Tomorrow we'll try again. They might even come to us. Kaka would worry and get suspicious if we stayed longer."

I had no choice but to agree.

"We'll take this path and gather more sticks. "Carry these."

Faith's hands were full of wood, and I felt ashamed at my singular focus. I had picked little. I took the load from Faith; it was heavy and uncomfortable to carry, but it was the least I could do. *Close, but yet so far*, I thought. We passed a cluster of bushes, and Faith stopped. "What?"

She nodded toward her left. I turned, looked, and dropped the load in my hand. In the valley below were about one hundred white dots, grazing. "It's them!" I'd never felt so happy to see cows. "Let's go down!"

"No. It looks close, but it's a fifteen-minute walk. We don't have time. Tomorrow we'll do it."

"But what will be our excuse for tomorrow?" I asked, my hands in the air pleading.

"*Fura de nunu*. We'll take our chances."

CHAPTER FIFTY

With freedom in mind, I noticed the landscape. Sambisa was beautiful. A mix of dense vegetation of thorny bushes and short trees. Open woodland with a combination of tall grasses of the savanna.

As we trekked along a ridge, I admired the scenery, dark, tall trees and shrubs against a backdrop of a sinking red sun and golden rays behind it.

I peppered Faith with questions about the herdsmen. Did she foresee any problem that might prevent them from taking me? No, she didn't think so. Did she know where they came from and where they were going? No, maybe to the nearest town to sell their cattle. I asked her if she would change her mind and come with me.

"Ngozi, this place is my home. There's no other place for me to go."

"This is nobody's home," I said. Has Kaka brainwashed her mind so much? I tried another approach. "Out there in the bush, you are a natural. Together we'll be able to get out of here in one piece."

Faith shrugged and kept on, walking in silence.

I was soaked with sweat by the time we got back to the camp just before sundown. Time had flown by. Faith dropped her load, and I put mine beside hers. She took sticks from the pile and positioned them in the fire pit. "I'll go tell Kaka we're back."

The more I thought about escaping and how possible it had become, the deeper my fear became. *What if things don't go as planned?* I saw the sense in Faith's reasoning.

Faith came out of the hut. "Only Danuwa is in there. Kaka is with Gambo. We'll sort the firewood and wait for her."

A few minutes later, we sat down taking a break. Kaka was not back. We both looked up at the same time. We heard a noise above.

"Those little planes?" asked Faith.

I nodded and cupped my ears. The sound blended in, like a wind that hummed as it traveled through trees. Like birds, the drones in the sky looked like they belonged there to the unobservant eye. Did they see at night too? Had others noticed them? It also begged the question, if the government knew where we were, why hadn't they come to our rescue?

Faith tapped my shoulders and pointed as I heard the unmistakable sound of a truck engine and looked in that direction. Close to the faded sign that said, "Welcome to Sambisa Game Reserve," a truck, similar to the one we rode on from Akarika, screeched to a halt. The passenger-side door flew open, and Aliyu got out dressed in military khakis. Danladi got out from the driver's side. He too wore camouflage.

"No!" I gasped and shook my head from side to side. Danladi headed for Gambo's door, glancing around as he moved. Then he saw me and stopped. He switched directions and came toward us.

I stumbled back. My whole body went rigid and a whimper escaped my lips. I hadn't seen him since the morning after.

"Be strong," whispered Faith. She took my hand and squeezed.

I wanted to run. I wanted to hurt him, the way he had hurt me and worse. As he got closer, he broke out in a smile.

Faith leaned in. "Be strong," she said again and stepped away.

My nostrils flared. I felt naked and abandoned to face the monster alone.

"*Iyawo*! Wife!" yelled Danladi and crushed his body into mine in a hug. I fought an incredible urge to throw up on him and knee him in the groin.

"Sorry I've been away for such a long time," said Danladi.

He was excited to see me, oblivious of the effect he had on me.

"I promise, we'll always be together." Danladi released me from the hug and glanced over at Faith. "How are you, Bello?"

Before Faith could answer, Danladi turned away and once again headed toward Gambo's hut.

I shook my head. "Of all the days, he comes back today," I said through clenched teeth. My voice cracked. "Faith, I have to go right now." I grabbed her shoulders, my whole body trembling.

"Something is afoot," said Faith. "Let's find out what's going on first. It's not just about getting up and leaving. The herdsmen will have to agree to take you with them."

I knew she was right, but I couldn't be in another room

with him. I would take my chances in the forest even if I had to introduce myself to the herdsmen alone.

Faith was trying to talk me down when the door to Gambo's hut opened, and Gambo, Danladi, Aliyu, and Kaka strolled out. We froze.

"Bello!" Gambo barked and waved Faith over. "Call my wives and all the other new wives."

I could feel Danladi's eyes on me. I couldn't stay in the same place with Danladi. Heart pounding, I turned to follow Faith.

"Ngozi, stop!" said Gambo. "We wait for the others."

Rakiya was the first to arrive. She stormed in looking annoyed. A few steps behind her were Lami and Ronke. Rakiya looked at Kaka, hissed, and turned away. Gambo took her aside and whispered in her ear. That seemed to make her madder.

"Without you?" said Rakiya in a loud whisper. "Nonsense!"

I couldn't believe my ears as I listened to Rakiya. I covered my mouth with my hand as my pulse raced. Gambo would kill her.

Rakiya barked, "Those toy wives you and your . . . Kaka married are the ones going."

"Okay," muttered Gambo and walked away with Danladi.

My mouth dropped open. I thought Gambo would have killed her on the spot.

Efome, Amina, Latifah, and a bunch of other girls arrived, the apprehension on their faces unmistakable.

Kaka cleared her throat and looked at Gambo who nodded. "Tonight, those of you who want to go, *inshallah*, God willing, are free to go."

CHAPTER FIFTY-ONE

Nothing moved. My stomach quivered.

"What?" shrieked Efome.

"We can go home?" asked another girl.

I looked around to make sure I'd heard right. Wide eyes and open mouths looked back at me. I clenched and unclenched my fists. When something is too good to be true, it always is. Why are they setting us free? They must have known about the drones. Maybe Danladi brought back information, and they must move us? Whatever the reason, I would leave this place.

A murmur broke out amongst the girls.

Kaka raised her hands. "Those who have husbands have two options. Stay with your husbands or leave, then work out a time and place to meet later."

With the mention of husbands, the murmurs faded, as if the air had been sucked out. Then it started again. This was a sham marriage. Was I going to ask Danladi to come to Lamija? I swallowed hard; the thought made me nauseous.

"Those who want to go, raise your hands," said Kaka.

My hand shot up. I glanced around; most of the girls

had their hands up. The confused girls who didn't want to go had their hands up halfway. I looked at Faith. Her hands were down, shoulders slumped and eyes on the ground. I grabbed her arm with my free hand and raised it up. I looked at Kaka, waiting for her to say something, but she didn't.

"God willing, you'll leave tonight. You will trek with some guards through the bush to meet up with another group, and you all will travel together to town."

Warmth radiated through my body. I felt like whooping loudly. No matter the plan, I was leaving tonight. If we're trekking, that will work for me, for us. I nudged Faith. She raised her head and looked at me with the saddest eyes. *Why the sad face?* I wondered. I brushed that aside. *When we get into the forest, we should run for it and meet up with the herdsmen,* I thought.

"Trek in the bush at night?" one girl asked.

"What about snakes? What about traps?" asked another.

Kaka spread out her hands and shrugged. "They are there. You don't have to go if you fear those." She glanced around. "Who wants to stay?"

This I must see. I looked around to watch Kaka humiliated.

"The camp is safe," said Kaka. "There's food, we have treated you well. Raise your hand if you want to stay."

At first, no hands went up, then Amina's hand went up. Then Efome's, then another and another.

I stared at them, mouth wide open.

The girls with their hands up stared at their feet, refusing to look up and confront our stares.

Kaka smiled and nodded.

Aliyu walked up to Kaka. "We have to go!"

"Won't you rest? You just came back," said Kaka.

"We don't want to be late meeting up with the others."

Aliyu and another man lined us up in a single file. It had been on a night like this weeks ago that they kidnapped us.

"Be careful where you place your feet," said Aliyu. "If you twist your ankle or get yourself bitten by a snake, we'll leave you behind."

Get yourself bitten by a snake? I thought. *Who would step on a snake?* I looked at his feet; he had boots on. *Take them off, Aliyu, and a snake would sink its fangs into you too. Then we will leave you behind.* Despite my bravado, I glued my eyes to the ground, searching. I hoped Aliyu's flaming torch would keep the animals away from us.

There were no good-byes, no time to pack either. There was nothing to pack. We left with Aliyu in the lead. Like the man bringing up the rear, Aliyu was equipped for the occasion, burning torch in hand, a powerful handheld flood-light strapped to his chest, his rifle slung over his shoulder, and a machete in a scabbard on his belt. He also carried a backpack.

Aliyu seemed to know where he was going. Within minutes we were on a footpath.

About ten to twenty minutes later, I smelled it, cow dung. I got excited. If we saw any of the herdsmen, Faith and I would go to them. They were close by; the smell of manure was strong.

"Watch your steps," said Aliyu. "There's cow shit all over the place."

The sound of crickets and the occasional shriek, maybe a monkey ahead, silenced as we approached. Trees and shrubs, bathed by moonlight, faded in and out of view as clouds drifted past the moon. With each animal cry or rustle in the bushes, I wanted to run away. *What is out there waiting?*

You must make a move, I told myself. But each time I considered dashing into the forest, the darkness and the sounds unnerved me. It was one thing to come up with a plan, and another to execute it in the face of reality. Some actions are borne of desperation. For the first time, I feared for Joy. I hoped she'd found this footpath to follow.

"*Sannu!* Greetings!" said a voice from the darkness.

Aliyu stopped, and then everybody stopped. Faith behind me squeezed my hand.

I turned to the voice. At first, I saw nothing, then the clouds shifted, and I saw them. All around us were the silent white beasts, some standing, some on the ground chewing their cud. I touched Faith on the shoulder as my pulse ticked up a notch. The Fulani herdsmen—it was now or never.

"Greetings! Aliyu here. Who am I greeting?"

"Usman here! Gambo?"

"Gambo couldn't make it," said Aliyu.

"Did . . . did you bring the item?" asked Usman.

Realization hit me like a punch to the stomach. They knew each other. "No," I murmured and shook my head. Are we supposed to go with them? But Aliyu talked about meeting a truck. What is this?

Aliyu gave the burning torch to the girl closest to him. He removed his backpack and brought out the wrapped-up bundle sticking out of it and gave it to Usman.

Usman put down the bow and sheath of arrows he had with him, took the package, and unwrapped it. The metal gleamed in the moonlight. Usman was all smile and teeth. "Beautiful!" cried Usman. "What type of gun is this?"

"AK-47," said Aliyu. "It's the same type we use. Drop it

in cow shit, rain, piss on it, just press the trigger, it will answer. We just came back from a long trip to pick them up."

"*Aboki*, friend!" said Usman and tossed the gun to another man who seemed to materialize out of the darkness.

The man caught the gun, ran his hand along the surface, and smiled. He put it across his shoulders and hung his hands over it as he would do with a stick.

"We have to go," said Aliyu. "Remember our agreement. Let us know when soldiers are coming and keep an eye on our people leaving the camp."

"Don't you trust me again?" said Usman. "I know my job. Today we only saw two girls collecting firewood."

My mouth went dry. Faith and I would have handed ourselves over to them as sheep led to slaughter. Like a long-distance runner, slowly and steadily, doubt crept further into my mind.

CHAPTER FIFTY-TWO

All that walking awakened the dull pain in my knees, legs, and thighs where . . . Danladi had punched me. It had been four weeks, but the pain was still there, and now it was getting sharp. I'd bumped my toes a few times against stones and roots, and the combined impact was taking its toll.

My feet caught on something, and I stumbled forward knocking into Faith, who had switched position with me after the encounter with the herdsmen.

"Who is stumbling like a drunk?" asked Aliyu. He shined his flashlight my way.

Faith crouched down beside me. "Are you all right?"

I nodded.

"Ah, Madam Danladi, it's you," said Aliyu. "No fractures, I hope, because we'll leave you behind."

I scrambled to my feet and rotated my ankle; no pain.

"I'm all right."

Aliyu waved his flashlight in the air. "Keep it moving. We're almost there."

We walked a few more minutes, and the pain in my thighs was becoming unbearable. Once I realized the pain was there, that was all I could think of. The girl behind me stumbled into me a few times. I wasn't the only one getting tired.

"Stop," said Aliyu, his voice a whisper.

He must have read my mind. There was silence. The insects shut up too. Something must have disturbed them. I heard the crackle of a radio close to Aliyu.

The radio crackled, and a voice came on. "We are here. Where are you?"

"We're close," said Aliyu.

It was only a few minutes of rest, but my thighs were overjoyed. We'd walked for about five minutes when I smelled cigarettes.

"Who goes there?" a voice said.

"Bida! Fear not. It's us," said Aliyu. "Were you expecting something else?"

We entered a clearing. Parked close to a tree was an open-backed pickup truck. A beam of light hit Aliyu's face.

"Come on, remove that thing from my face, Bida!" Aliyu raised his hand to block the powerful beam.

"Sorry, you can never be so sure," said Bida.

"Bida, I still have my gun," said Aliyu. "I might have an accidental discharge if you don't stop fooling around. Trekking through the forest at night with all these girls is no fun."

Bida let out a low whistle as his flashlight bounced off our faces, one after the other. "You guys kept all the pretty ones! When you get on the truck, you'll see ours, they look like monkeys!"

"Nonsense, you were there," said Aliyu. "You could have loaded your truck with any of the girls."

The beam hit my face, and I shut my eyes tight. When I opened them, I saw only halos and closed them again. I had a bad feeling about this Bida character. I hoped he was not coming with us.

Bida chuckled. "Which ones have you tried? No, what am I saying, which ones haven't you tried?" He broke out in a fit of laughter.

"That one is Danladi's wife," said Aliyu. "He said he's in love."

Bida chuckled. "Love? What is that? *Abeg*, please, does she have special skills?"

Aliyu hissed and then laughed. "I hope your mother knows she has a worthless human being for a son."

"She tells me that all the time," said Bida. He pointed the flashlight at my chest. "Maybe somewhere along the journey, I'll get to know them better."

For a moment I felt fear, then it passed. I would not be a victim again.

"These two are Gambo's wives," said Aliyu and shrugged. "Just for your information."

"Okay, I've heard," said Bida. "Girls, climb on." Bida lifted his head and spoke louder. "Make room inside that truck. More passengers are coming."

Some girls climbed in; the vehicle shifted each time someone got on. Then Lami, Ronke, Faith, and then it was my turn. My knees trembled as I heaved myself up. There were other girls already in the truck, dressed like us in black and gray, with hijabs on their heads. I couldn't make out their faces.

The seating arrangements were just like on the last truck, with benches on either side of the truck bed. I sat down close to the tailgate.

Aliyu and Bida stood by the driver's side. "Where to now?" asked Aliyu.

I cocked my head to hear better.

"Let's get back on the road first," said the driver.

CHAPTER FIFTY-THREE

Hamza drew international attention to the kidnapped girls and the plight of their parents. Most did not believe it at first, based on the brazenness of the crime and the lackadaisical response from the government, but Hamza stoked the flames by mentioning the offense at every opportunity while campaigning.

Hamza was in his office. He looked at the TV, toggling between Aljazeera and CNN. He listened to the newscaster.

"Our sources tell us that the United States and the United Kingdom have offered to help rescue the girls. Their surveillance planes have located the terrorists' whereabouts, and they are ready with a military team for an extraction.

Hamza felt like the run for the highest office in the country was looking like a cakewalk. Things were going well. There was a knock on the door, and Kola walked in.

Kola handed him a newspaper. "Here, sir. They've pulled out all the stops."

Hamza read the article fast. He sighed and shook his

head. He could not believe how low the opposition would go to smear. "Father was always right."

Kola's head shot up. "How, sir?"

Hamza stroked his chin. "He always said men who long for power and get it live in terror of losing it. That's exactly what we see here. This incumbent would move mountains to win the election."

Kola nodded. "But this is an accusation no matter how they frame it. Everybody reads between the lines."

Hamza knew the opposition had nothing. There was nothing. They were just blowing hot air. He shook his head as he took in the image again.

Kola leafed through the newspapers. "All the papers have the same image."

"That's the only thing they have," said Hamza. "How's the grassroots outreach going?" he asked, changing the subject.

"Expensive. We're now operating on a national level. We cover every part of the country. The response to our outreach is mixed, depends on the part of the country. In the north, it is positive, lukewarm in the south. In the west . . . a wait and see. Most people are keeping it at a tribal and religious level for now."

"The ugly head of Lord Lugard's 1914 amalgamation," said Hamza.

Kola tapped his lips with his finger. "It doesn't help either that you, a northerner, want to replace a southerner."

Hamza had been pondering the situation too. To be acceptable in other parts of the country, he must have a southerner as his running mate. Or maybe someone from the west.

So far, he had kept his father out of his campaigning. But he also knew the time would come when the focus would be against him for being his father's son. The billion-aire who built his wealth any which way he could.

"I have a suggestion," said Kola.

"Go ahead."

"In considering who to pick as a running mate, you should involve the party at one level and your own personal pick at the other level. We don't want to alienate the party. Then you can do your own assessment of who you think would make a worthwhile running mate. If we're lucky, we'll come up with the same person."

Hamza drummed his fingers on the table, his mind far away from a running mate. He felt there was something he did not know. His mind went back to seventeen years earlier. It was still vivid. He went through all that had happened step by step; there was nothing out of the ordi-nary. The relationship between him and his father had changed, and he had blamed his father. He should have fought for what he wanted and not given in to temptation. As he had seen in the past few weeks, he could never stop being his father's son.

"Sir? Mr. President. Hamza?"

"Hmm?" Hamza turned to look at his campaign manager.

"Your mind must be very far away."

Hamza got up. His knees creaked. The newspaper in hand, he walked over to the window and looked at the traffic outside. It was the middle of the afternoon. Cars and people moved up and down the road, the sun blazed as if angry. That was how his head felt. "It's not fun being on the receiving side of an accusation."

"I agree, especially when there's no truth to it," said Kola.

Hamza spun around. "That's the problem. The more

it's being said, the more you doubt yourself. People start to doubt you too."

"Your right, sir," said Kola. "But it doesn't end there. You now divert resources to tackling a non-issue instead of focusing on your campaign. It's like a lawyer in court saying something he's not supposed to. The opposing attorney objects and the judge sustains, agreeing with him."

Hamza nodded. "But the damage was done. The jury has heard. They can't unhear." Hamza wondered if the information he had on the opposition was correct. Was there something other than than selfishness that prevented Aso Rock from looking for those girls? He looked at the damning headlines in today's papers again. He felt the police should have informed him of the progress they'd made so far. His mind drifted to the detectives that had presented themselves at his office.

He and the detective had developed a good rapport. Why hadn't he given him a heads-up that it had progressed to suspected murder? Hamza felt hot under his suit. He was getting worked up.

He took a deep breath, exhaled, and reminded himself he had refused to provide any form of incentives to them. They didn't owe him anything. What was an excellent rapport to them, anyway? Cold cash would have bought them a bag of rice, some meat at the market, or a good night at the beer parlor. Hamza chuckled and shook his head. The country is in a mess.

"What's funny, sir?" asked Kola with a smile on his face, eager to share in his boss's joke.

"I didn't 'thank' the detectives when they came to visit," said Hamza, making air quotes. "I feel they might have informed us of their progress if they had been incentivized.

But you don't get something for nothing." He smiled again. "It's going to be tough to straighten this country out."

Kola bunched his lips and nodded. "The opposition has more than a few media outlets in their pocket."

"We'll double our efforts," said Hamza. "Address the press as the issues arise and keep our focus on the campaign." He looked at the headline again. "Was Dr. Lambert Muzo Murdered to Keep Him Quiet?"

Quiet about what? The newspaper showed the image of a daily planner with "Hamza Tarbari" written in the 4:00 p.m. slot. Hamza's body went tense. He wanted to punch someone. So that was what it felt like to be on the receiving side of bad press. What should he do? Volunteer information or wait for someone to blast it on headlines.

CHAPTER FIFTY-FOUR

We set off once more along the bush path. After about five minutes of slow, bumpy riding, we turned onto a tarred road; the ride became smoother, and the truck picked up speed. Shoulders slumped, I tried to rest. Then, I picked up Aliyu's conversation and sleep vanished from my eyes.

The guards had their rifles slung over their shoulders, relaxed.

"Do you know why we're moving all these girls?" asked Bida.

"We're in the papers," said Aliyu.

The wind roared in my ears. I leaned forward and turned my head to hear better.

"What?" shouted Bida.

"We're famous. Everybody is talking about us!"

"Famous?" asked Bida. "Why now? We've been operating around here with no attention for a long time!"

"Ha!" said Aliyu. "We just came back from town. Those Chibok girls have drawn attention from everyone. Britain, France, Sweden, even America got involved. Everywhere, TV, radio, newspaper, all you hear is, 'Bring back our girls, bring back our girls.' They call us the Nigerian Taliban."

Someone nudged me. It would have to wait. I cocked my head to hear more.

Aliyu continued. "That's why we're moving at night. Those Americans have these little toy planes that look like mosquitoes flying around and taking pictures. They know where we are. We got information that soldiers are coming to Sambisa soon."

Soldiers are coming? I couldn't help but believe Joy made it out alive.

"That makes sense," said Bida. "My oga only told me we're going across the border."

A chill traveled down my spine. Border? Did I hear right? I thought they were taking us home. It all made sense now. People are looking for us, and they're taking us across the border? Which country is across the border, Cameroon, Chad?

I struggled for air. It felt like a heavy mass had settled on me. Every word out of Aliyu's mouth felt like an additional weight.

If I went over that border, that would be the end of me, the end of us all. We would never see our families again. I squeezed my hands together as I tried to collect my thoughts. Here I was, on the back of a truck leaving Nigeria as a captive. If I crossed that border, that side of the fence would never be green, no matter how much I watered it.

I would have to jump off this truck. I felt an awakening inside me, a new resolve to get away. I felt like doing something right away. I inhaled and held it until my lungs burned, then let it out. That calmed me. What do I do next?

I felt a hot breath against my ear.

"They're taking us to Cameroon," whispered Faith.

Just then, the truck hit a bump that sent us out of our seats. For a moment, I thought Aliyu or Bida had hit me. We scrambled back to our positions.

"Find another spot," said Aliyu to the girl sitting opposite me. She scuttled back and he placed his foot on the bench.

"Everybody okay?" asked Aliyu.

Bida produced a flashlight and turned it on.

"Relax, the girls are not going anywhere," said Aliyu. "Fear is powerful."

Bida placed his foot next to Aliyu, their backs turned to us. "I know, my brother. But I'm so tired that even if any of the girls should run, I wouldn't have the strength to give chase. The girl . . . my wife wore me out last night. How was yours?"

I stopped listening, disgusted that that was all they thought about. I thought of pushing them out of the truck. A hard push would do the job. *How do I take care of the driver?* I wondered.

All around us was inky darkness. The truck slowed down as we got to a bad patch on the tarred road, full of potholes and small craters. This was my chance; bad roads don't stretch forever.

I leaned close to Faith and whispered. "I will jump." I squeezed her hand. "Jump after me. I'll wait for you."

I nodded. I knew this was the best time to get off the truck, but I sat there. Maybe I was waiting for instructions. Time was ticking, but my legs refused to move. Faith tapped my leg and gave it a squeeze. She got up and jumped into the darkness. I gasped, looked around, and looked at the guards. They still had their backs to us. Adrenaline surged through my veins. I had to jump.

I gathered my dress and raised it to my thighs, freeing my legs. I looked at Ronke, her eyes were as big as tennis balls.

A chill ran down my back, and I knew I would do it. My pulse raced and I felt like I was observing myself from above. The rumble of the truck seemed like it was right inside my head. As if in a trance, I got up, stepped onto the bench, and jumped.

I landed on my feet, slipped, and slammed my butt on the ground. The impact forced the air out of me. I sucked in air, choking on dust and exhaust fumes. I got on one knee. I'd done it. I had to get off the road. To my surprise, two more figures jumped out of the truck and ran toward me.

"Ngozi, over here," whispered Faith.

"Where?" I jerked my head from side to side. All around me was tall grass and the sounds of the night.

"Over here," whispered Faith again.

The two shadows were almost upon me.

"Ngozi, wait for us," someone gasped.

"Ronke?" I couldn't believe it. They met up with me, and together we scrambled toward Faith by the roadside. At that moment, the clanking sound from the truck stopped. The silence was immediate. Even the insects went quiet. Flashlights pierced the darkness in our direction just as we ducked. But not fast enough.

The bright rear lights came on, and the truck backed up. My mouth went dry. Now my body was ready to move, but Faith held me.

"They don't know where we are," whispered Faith, panting. "If we run, they'll hear us and come after us."

Aliyu jumped down from the truck. "Bida, stay! Watch the other girls. We can't have more escaping."

The closer they came, the more I felt like fleeing. We

hadn't even enjoyed a full minute of freedom, and we were about to be caught. I could hear the cries from the girls on the truck. I wished they could all jump down. That would create confusion for Aliyu and company. They couldn't get us all.

The truck stopped and the driver got out. "I'll watch the girls," said the driver. "Bida, follow him. I'll keep watch. If there's any problem, I'll lean on the horn." The driver turned to the girls on the truck and pulled out a pistol. "If any of you dares move, I'll shoot her like this." He released two shots in the air.

"Why did you do that?" snapped Aliyu. "There's a police checkpoint close by. You've just drawn unnecessary attention to us. Don't shoot unless you have to."

As soon as those words were out of Aliyu's mouth, Lami bolted.

CHAPTER FIFTY-FIVE

"Run! Run!" I shouted.

The three of us ran after Lami. The last thing I remember was seeing the men stop when Lami ran, then give pursuit. I ran as I'd never run in my life. Whoever was in front of me became my guardian angel. I was right behind her.

The closeness of the voices and the sheer terror of what would happen to us if caught pushed more adrenalin into my system, and I ran faster. I caught up with Faith, and for a split second, we crashed through the bushes, side by side, then I overtook her. Grass blades cut my skin, scratched my face, but I didn't slow down.

I couldn't tell if we had lost them, but I kept on going. Faith, or whoever, was as close as could be. Every breath I took felt like inhaled fire. Sweat poured down my face, stung my eyes, and blinded me. My legs got heavier and heavier, but I refused to stop. It was dark in front of us, with the occasional beam of light from the guard's flashlight cutting through.

How far away he was, I couldn't tell. *Please don't trip,* I said to myself. Please don't fall. As soon as that thought passed through my mind, my right foot caught on something, and I fell. Everybody stumbled over me and fell. It happened so fast.

"I hear them! I hear them!" shouted Bida. "Shine your light over there."

One person sprang up. I seconded and took off just as the other two got up. I thought of running off in another direction to split the chase, but I didn't have time to do anything but run.

"Ahh!" someone screamed and fell to the ground.

"Over there!" shouted Bida.

The same obstacle that tripped the person in front got me too. I hit the ground and rolled down and down and stopped going when I hit a barrier. I tried to get back on my feet, but my muscles were too fatigued. Roots, twigs, and someone's legs and arms were in the way.

"My ankle!"

It was Faith. She howled in pain. I reached over and felt for her face, found her mouth, and clasped my palms over it.

"Do you see them?" a voice asked. It sounded like Aliyu.

"Shhh," I whispered, panting. Faith's breath was hot on my hands. I held her close, our heartbeats sounding like war drums. "Lami, Ronke! Who's there?" I whispered.

"It's . . . it's me," said Lami, gasping. "Ronke is still up there."

Lami's voice sounded like she was crying, close to hysteria. I hoped she would do nothing crazy again.

Faith shook my hand off her face. "Are you trying to suffocate me?"

I took my hand away and exhaled, just then realizing that I had been holding my breath.

Light beams flashed close to us. The sound of feet crunching leaves got closer and closer. Running for it was hopeless.

"Check in that hole," said Aliyu.

I knew they were coming to our hole. I gripped Faith. This was all just for nothing. Only a few minutes of freedom was all we got. The footsteps got louder and louder. They would catch us. Beside us, Lami was sobbing like a baby. I wished I could cry too. Crying was good for the soul, but not good when you're facing danger.

"Over here!" yelled Ronke at the top of her lungs.

"Get her!" yelled Aliyu.

The sound of running feet shattered the silence. It had been so close. The footsteps moved away from us. If she didn't fall, she might outrun them. Why did she expose herself? Then it hit me—she'd bought us time. "Come, get up, let's go!"

"Oh God, Ronke, my sister," sobbed Lami.

I helped Faith up. She howled in pain once she set her foot on the ground.

"I think I twisted my ankle," said Faith.

"Lami, come and help me," I said. Faith's nails dug into my shoulder as she tried to stand on her own. Lami came over and supported Faith on the other side.

"Which way do we go?" asked Lami, her cheeks streaked with tears.

We had fallen into some ravine. We climbed up with Faith between us. It was a gentle slope, but supporting Faith to get out of it would take time. We were halfway up when I thought I heard something, like the footsteps. "Stop," I whispered.

"Where are the other girls?" asked Aliyu. "You tried to lead us away. Would your sister do the same for you?"

"Please, please let me go," cried Ronke.

"They caught her," gasped Lami.

"Shh," I whispered. Faith and I shook with her sobs.

"Put me down and run," said Faith.

We stood halfway out of the ravine, easy targets. I didn't know what to do. What would they do to us this time? I would try and fight them, get them to shoot me. Better to die here than go to Cameroon. Just then, the sound of the truck horn shattered the silence, urgent and loud.

"Come back! We have to go!" yelled the driver.

The horn sounded again for a longer time.

"Leave the girls! Just come back!"

"This driver is an idiot," said Bida. "Let me enter that hole and get them."

The sound of the horn blasted again.

"I'll leave you guys behind!" yelled the driver.

"All right, all right, we're coming!" said Aliyu. "Maybe the girls on the truck have overwhelmed him. Let's go before things get out of hand."

Their footsteps got fainter and fainter, and Ronke's cries got weaker.

I didn't move. I couldn't believe our pursuers retreated. We could still hear the men in the distance. Aliyu was chewing out the driver.

"Keep your eyes on the girls in the truck!" yelled Aliyu. "For our sakes, I hope it wasn't the girl Oga was interested in!"

Several doors slammed, and the truck drove off. The sound of the truck's engine faded, and I let out a big sigh of relief.

CHAPTER FIFTY-SIX

I felt giddy as crickets resumed their orchestra. "Thank God, they left." A burst of laughter escaped my lips, then sadness. My body shook with sobs. I didn't know why I was crying, but I couldn't stop. Faith wrapped her arms around me and whispered things in my ear which I didn't hear but which were comforting. All I could think of was Ronke's face the last time I saw her in the truck as I was about to jump. There was no doubt she saved us. If the tables had been reversed, I doubt if I would have done the same for her. I stopped sobbing.

I ran my hands over my face to wipe the tears. Lami sat on the ground, sobbing and shaking her head. I went over, sat down beside her, and hugged her, triggering another round of sobs from her. I didn't know what to say. We were trapped in the middle of nowhere because of me. If I hadn't been so keen on escaping, Faith wouldn't have jumped. Ronke and Lami would have stayed on. I blamed myself.

"What do you think they'll do to Ronke?" asked Lami.

They'll take her across the border, and you will no longer be a twin. But I didn't say that. "It will be all right," I said.

"How do you know?" Lami blurted. "You can say whatever you like to make me feel good, it's not your sister who was taken."

Lami's words hit me like a blow to the stomach. I knew she was hurting and I bit my tongue. "We will hope for good things," I said in a shaky voice. "I don't know how we will get out of here. We have to believe we can."

"We'll get out of this bush in one piece," said Faith.

Something rustled in the bushes. I whirled in that direction, my body tense. All I saw were dark shadows, each one more suspicious than the last. Every sound and shadow a menace. It would be stupid of us to still be here if they came back.

"What should we do?" asked Faith. "We can't go far in the dark."

"Let's get out of this hole," I said.

"But you saw what happened the last time," said Lami with bitterness in her voice. "We couldn't even move while trying to support . . ." Lami's voice trailed off.

"Give me a hand." We took a while, but we made it out with Faith.

"Which direction should we go?" asked Lami.

"As far away from the road as possible," said Faith.

I looked around, not sure which direction was away from the road. Faith placed one arm over my shoulder and the other over Lami's and we started in the direction we were facing. Each step was laborious, and after a few minutes, we collapsed in a heap, out of breath.

"Let's rest and get our strength back," said Faith, who grimaced as she dragged herself to the trunk of a nearby tree.

Lami and I joined her.

"They lied to us to get us out of the camp," said Lami.

"They were never going to set us free." Lami paused. "I'm so happy to be away from Rakiya. Gambo frustrated her and she took it out on Ronke and me," she hissed. "I hope she dies and rots in hell."

I wanted to say we were closer to death than Rakiya but kept my mouth shut.

Lami sighed. "Where do you think they were taking us?"

"Cameroon," said Faith and adjusted her position against the tree. "Aliyu and the new man were talking on the truck."

"I slept off once we got on the truck. Rakiya made us fan her throughout the night while she slept. Ronke and I took turns sleeping, but it wasn't enough. The walk through the forest drained my last ounce of energy. I'd hoped the experience was a dream until Ronke woke me up and whispered in my ear we were going to jump." Lami cried again.

This time I left her alone. In the distance, the first signs of sunrise showed their colors in the sky. We would need water, food, and a lot of patience. Exhaustion tugged at me.

"What do you think tomorrow will bring?" asked Lami. She sounded groggy.

"Maybe a hunter or a farmer will find us," I said.

"Let's hope it's a friendly hunter," said Faith.

Each time I closed my eyes, it would jerk open a few seconds later. Our first morning in captivity would come to my mind. The girl that didn't wake up. I pushed the image away, but it always came back. I didn't want to think about it because thoughts become things.

On my left side, Lami snored softly. I was the only person awake. Faith mumbled something.

"Yes?" I looked at her. She was talking in her sleep. I would not get a reply.

With a sprained ankle, Faith was a liability and could extinguish any chances we had of making it out of here alive. Without her, we stood a chance, at least to travel fast. To be able to get to a village. After all, a drowning person doesn't save another drowning person.

This was my chance to walk away and abandon her with Lami, save myself. At this moment, the sun slipped out from behind a cloud and bathed us with light. Faith scratched her face in sleep. She looked so peaceful. She was only here because of me.

I decided and felt at peace. I shut my eyes for one more shot at sleep.

CHAPTER FIFTY-SEVEN

My cheeks felt warm. I opened my eyes and shut them. The sun was up and doing its job well. I opened my eyes again and got used to the glare, but all around me was grass and shrubs. Where was I? Something nudged my leg. I scrambled away, crouched, ready to run. My body moved in rhythm to my inhales and exhales. The sleep fog cleared, and I recognized Faith, and the events of last night came back.

"You're awake," said a voice.

I jerked my head to my left. Lami was up, brushing grass and leaves off her outfit. Her activity must have woken me. "Did you sleep at all?"

"Yes, woke up a few minutes ago."

Faith lay propped up against a tree, pieces of dried grass and leaves stuck in her hair; her long thin fingers interlaced lay on her lap. Dirt and dried leaves attached to her clothes, her hijab lay discarded on the ground together with one of her slippers. I looked at my clothes; they didn't look any better.

"They have my sister," said Lami. "We have to get out of here. Get help and find her."

I nodded and examined myself—small cuts, bruises, and caked blood dotted my hands and legs. I looked at the culprit, tall elephant grass. The blades swayed and rustled in the morning breeze, looking harmless until they cut you like a sheet of paper. My feet were bare, covered in dust, my flip-flops gone. I noticed a ruptured blister and a cut along my right toe, and right away, the pain came alive. My mouth was dry.

"We have to wake Faith," said Lami. "Who knows where we are."

Every noise sounded suspicious. I expected something or someone to materialize from the bushes and whipped my head from side to side.

"You're so jumpy, relax," said Lami. "It would have been easier for someone to attack us while we slept."

The foolishness of my thoughts was apparent. I relaxed. "I'd hoped to wake earlier so we could travel some distance before the sun came out, but I overslept."

"Faith," I said and shook her shoulder with one hand and tapped her cheek with the other.

Faith woke with a start. "Where are we?" She raised her palm to shield her eyes. She moved her leg and winced.

Her right ankle was swollen and shiny like a balloon. There were no cuts or bruises. She'd twisted it. I felt her pain. I'd experienced it a few times as a kid playing hopscotch. "Do you think you can walk?"

"I hope so," said Faith. "Help me up."

Time to make a move, we faced the dilemma of which direction to go. I couldn't see above the grass. I spotted a small termite hill in the shape of a mushroom. Crumbs of dirt broke off once I stepped on it, but it held my weight. I tiptoed and could see over the tall grass.

"Do you see anything good?" asked Lami.

"Yes, a footpath. We'll have to travel down to it."

"Get down, let me see," said Faith and stepped on the brown puckered earth. "I see it! It must lead somewhere. Let's follow it."

"We might meet a hunter or farmer along the way who can give us water." As soon as I mentioned water, my thirst intensified.

Like we did when we got out of the ravine, we supported Faith as she hopped on her left leg.

"This won't be easy," said Lami after a few steps.

With each step we took, I would feel Faith's body go tense. She was in pain, but not complaining. Last night her pain had been masked by adrenalin.

We kept going, but after about twenty minutes, we were out of breath, exhausted, and soaked in sweat. We had made little progress. I could still see the termite hill.

We collapsed on the ground sucking in air. The sun was merciless, sweat flowed from every pore in our bodies. My clothes felt like a second skin pasted onto my body.

The soles of my feet were on fire. Pain from the cuts I'd received last night, stepping on sharp sticks and rocks, and the heat from the ground didn't help matters. I never knew the soil could get so hot from the sun.

"At this rate," said Faith, panting, "we won't accomplish much. I'm thirsty."

"Please don't mention thirst again," I said breathing hard. I glanced at Lami. She stared ahead. Her nose was flared. Her jaw muscles clenched and unclenched. What was going on inside that head of hers?

"Faith is right," said Lami. "We won't accomplish much at this rate. Let's—"

"Let's travel to that shrub," I said, cutting Lami off. I knew where she was going with that. "When we get there, we'll decide on which direction to follow."

Lami got on her feet and pointed. "The shrub shaped like the letter Y?"

I nodded.

"It's far, let's go," said Lami.

With a definite goal in mind, it was easier. No, not easier, bearable. It took a while. A few stops every now and then, but we got there.

We lowered Faith to the ground and joined her, panting.

"I wonder what time it is?" said Lami.

Faith pointed at a small tree. "You see the shadow on that small plant?"

"Yes," said Lami.

"You can't see much of it because it's short," said Faith. "So, it's probably midday. Shadows are shortest at midday."

Lami exhaled. "We took the whole morning to walk that distance. We have another five hours of daylight. This footpath must lead somewhere that we can get to in five hours."

I looked at the footpath and nodded. We seemed to have the same thoughts.

Lami cleared her throat. "If . . . if we . . . leave Faith here . . . we'll travel faster and bring help."

Nobody spoke. The twenty-foot python in the room sat in full view. I knew where I stood.

"I think you're right," said Faith, fingers laced together, resting on her lap. She didn't look up. "I'll be all right, you two can go."

Faith herself had sanctioned it. I could go without feeling guilty. But it wasn't right. She was helpless.

"Ngozi," said Lami. "What do you think?"

"I think we shouldn't split up. Yes, it is tough, but—"

"I will not stay here and die," said Lami. "You can do whatever you like. I'm going." Lami got to her feet and stormed off down the path."

CHAPTER FIFTY-EIGHT

I watched Lami walk away into the horizon and out of sight. I exhaled and felt good, an unexpected release of all tension. All my decisions at home with Auntie Halima, Maryam, or anybody that wasn't on my side would be dealt with on a "what's good for me" basis. This wasn't about me.

Faith looked at me. Our eyes met. "You should have gone with her." Her voice was a whisper.

I sat down beside her. "You should have stayed on the truck," I countered. "No more talk about staying or leaving, we are in this together." I'd known Faith since we arrived at the camp and I knew nothing about her. I changed the subject. "Are you looking forward to reuniting with your family?"

Faith nodded.

"Do you have siblings? Your parents will be excited when they see you. What do they do?"

Tears brimmed Faith's eyes. "Two brothers and two sisters. My father is a hunter and butcher."

I moved away from that topic, imagining it could be

very emotional thinking about loved ones you hadn't seen in one and a half years. I'd rather be home than with the terrorists. Like how Zainab said to make the best use of it. *Zainab*, I thought. *I hope she escaped that night.* The thought of Zainab and Faith's reaction about her family instilled an urgency in me.

"We have to get going," I said. "At least cover a reasonable distance before it gets dark."

I glanced around to see if I could find a stick we could use for support, but nothing. Just like we had done before, Faith placed her hand over my shoulder, and we hopped and walked. We found a rhythm, but thirst was burning a hole in my mind. The heat from the ground on my bare foot was unbearable.

"The sand is hot, right?" asked Faith. Sweat poured down her face like rain.

"Very," I said and grimaced. "Let's walk on the grass." We got off the path, but hopping on the grass wasn't easier. Hidden rocks and sticks were a hazard for my bare foot.

"Watch out!" said Faith.

Adrenalin surged through me. I jumped. "What? Where?" I could only think of snakes.

Faith pointed at a heap of dried grass.

I looked, and froze. That would have been the end. A rusty circular piece of metal with serrated edges lay concealed in the grass.

"Gin trap," said Faith.

I nodded. Just like the one on the antelope Kaka had shown us. *Now we have to look out for snakes and traps that cause damage*, I thought.

"The good news is a hunter will come by at some time to check his traps," said Faith.

"How often do they check?" I asked.

"Maybe daily, or at the most, every two days. The animals might die in the trap or get eaten by another animal if the hunter doesn't come to retrieve them early enough."

"Maybe we should just stay here and wait," I said. Seeing the gin trap also answered the question of why people stuck to the footpath rather than walking across the brush. The place could be laden with gin traps.

"Let's find shade, at least keep the sun away," said Faith. "Watch where you place your feet. It would be the end of the road for anybody who got their foot in that contraption."

I didn't feel like moving, and my whole body ached, but I forced myself. We hobbled along, stepping away from two other traps we came across. Instead of crossing the bush, it might have been a better idea to get back onto the footpath and avoid all these traps.

"Do you see that?" I pointed ahead, my heart racing.

Faith shielded her eyes and looked. "It looks like somebody in a brown kaftan!"

They were doing something repetitive, like hoeing or pulling weeds from their farm. The sight was a new lease on life. "Let's go."

Faith moved faster too, half-dragged by me in my excitement. As we got closer, what I had seen was not human.

"Is that a scarecrow?" asked Faith.

"If it's not a person, at least they have crops worth protecting." It looked like corn. I could smell and taste it from here. I'd never eaten raw corn, but my stomach rumbled.

We were now close enough to see it was just a piece of cloth caught in the branches of a shrub. There was no corn, just elephant grass that played with our minds. Dejected, we continued toward the piece of cloth. At least we could rest under the shrub.

"If I don't get anything to drink in the next hour, I'm just going to stay here and die," said Faith.

Exhausted, we collapsed under the shrub with a piece of brownish cloth attached to one of its branches. For a while, we sat there, wallowing in disappointment.

"Ngozi?"

"Yes."

"Do you think we should have stayed on the truck?" asked Faith.

I didn't answer right away. I'd been thinking too. "At least we're free," I said.

Faith sighed. "Free to perish in the bush."

"It's not over yet. We're still alive."

"For how long?" Faith blurted.

I jerked my head, startled by her outburst. I'd always looked up to her strength. "We'll get out of here alive, I promise you." I had no idea how. I looked around; nothing had changed. Grass, small trees, the sun, and the heat, all were still with us. Up in the sky, some birds circled; our new companions. I nudged Faith. "Is that a bird or one of those drones?"

Faith raised her head. "Let's see."

"I wish I could stretch out my hand and snatch one from the sky," I said. "Then we'd have a feast." I chuckled and nudged her.

Faith giggled. "Those are vultures. They're getting ready to feast on us."

I sat up. "What? No, that will not happen. We're still very much alive. They only feed on dead things."

"Yes, but they sense when something is about to die, and they wait. I watched them from my father's butcher shop. Once a cow is brought in for the day, the vultures circle and just hang around. They know entrails will come their way."

I stared at Faith, confused about what to do next. My eyes fell on the stupid piece of cloth that had drawn us here. It swayed in the stifling air. I yanked it free from the shrub, intending to use it as a handkerchief. I looked at it; the brown color we'd seen from a distance was reddish brown. It had dark particles of various sizes stuck onto it. I picked up a flat piece of wood with a pointed end to scrape them off. The stick looked like a short wooden cross, the long part broken off.

A thin black thread connected to the wood floated in the air. There was something familiar about it. I went to work and scraped off the dark particles.

"What the . . ." I shrieked. I looked at the piece of cloth again. The area I'd just scraped clean was blue. All the dots connected and a scream ripped through my throat.

CHAPTER FIFTY-NINE

Hamza lay on his back wide awake. Beside him, Ali lay asleep. Listening to her rhythmic breathing would usually calm him, but not tonight. He generally only needed a few hours of deep sleep to recharge, but tonight he couldn't even get a minute. The news that Muzo was murdered just before their meeting bothered him. Politics wasn't an easy business. Before you throw your cap into any race, steel yourself for scrutiny. No wonder people with excellent management skills who can make a difference prefer not to get into politics.

Hamza thought about the press. Were they paid to come up with such headlines? Or were they only doing their jobs. He got off the bed and walked to the window. Sleep was out of the question. Was it possible that Aso Rock put the reelection of the president above finding those girls?

Did they have any idea that a child was a blessing? And three hundred girls went missing, and nobody knew? He couldn't imagine how those parents felt. He looked at Ali and counted himself lucky. She was such a strong woman.

She had endured all he had thrown her way. He turned to face the window.

"Sweetie, you can't sleep?" It was Ali's voice.

Hamza spun around. "I'm so sorry. Did I wake you?" He walked toward the bed.

"No, not really." Ali sat up. "I was thirsty." She reached for the glass on her bed stand and drank deep. "What's on your mind?"

Hamza sat on the bed and took her hand in his. "The headlines, those kidnapped girls . . ." Hamza's words drifted away.

"I hope the girls are rescued," said Ali. "I saw the first lady of the United States on TV holding a sign that read #Bringbackourgirls. People are becoming aware. They kidnapped another group of girls from Akarika Girls Secondary School—"

"Did you say another kidnapping? Of girls again?"

Ali pursed her lips and nodded.

"Oh my God. I hope it's not becoming a trend," said Hamza. He shook his head. "How did you hear?"

"One of my patient's dad mentioned it. Heard it through the grapevine. It happened weeks ago, and it wasn't even in the news. They hoped all the attention on the Chibok girls would rub off on their plight too. Many people all over the world have heard the message and are getting involved. You've done your best." Ali rubbed Hamza's back. "Now get some sleep, okay? Tomorrow is another day." She laid back, closed her eyes and covered herself with the blanket.

Hamza leaned down and kissed her cheek. Her lips crinkled in a smile. He watched the rhythmic rise and fall of her chest for a while. Politicking was becoming too much for

Hamza. Maybe it was time he bailed out. There were a lot of demands on him. He looked at Ali. He would try his best to deliver what she wanted.

CHAPTER SIXTY

"Ngozi, what is it?" asked Faith, her eyes wide.

I swallowed to clear a painful lump in my throat, but it wouldn't go away. I bunched my hands into a fist around the piece of wood. My hands shook as I raised it to get a second look at the wood. The black thread floated in the air.

The marks on the wood looked like what I would make when I started off with a new chewing stick. Tears rolled down my cheeks. Something terrible must have happened. There was no doubt the dark color was blood.

"Joy had this cross around her neck, and she was wearing her blue dress the last time I saw her." My voice broke.

"The girl that left camp?" asked Faith.

"Yes, we called her Scripture Union Joy. She had refused the hijab and black outfit." I stared ahead, not focusing on anything.

"You can't be so sure." said Faith. She sounded hopeful and wrapped her hands around my shoulders.

But I knew. Those were Joy's things. Tears rolled down

my cheeks. "Why do bad things happen to good people?" I said through sobs. "Why must good people always have to prove themselves against evil? It's not fair, not fair. Joy would never hurt a fly." I told Faith about the night Joy left. That I'd always hoped that she would return with someone, the police or the army to rescue us. "When I heard the army was coming, I thought Joy had made it. But now . . ." My voice trailed off.

When the words stopped coming, and the tears stopped flowing, I felt empty.

Faith took the cross from me. "I know you're convinced it's her stuff, but it doesn't prove . . . something . . . bad happened to her." She ran her finger over the surface.

The look on Faith's face changed. "What is it?" I asked.

Faith's eyebrows narrowed. She flipped the wood over and ran her finger over the marks again. "We must get far away from here. They look like an animal's teeth marks. Whatever attacked Joy might come back." Faith looked around. "But how did Joy get here?" Faith's voice was low like she was posing the question to herself.

Faith was right. We had driven an hour or more to get here, then a few more hours on foot. Joy walked all the way. Or did she?

I took the broken cross, wiped the dust off it, cleaned the thread, and tied it to the little shrub. I shut my eyes to pray, but there was just silence. Joy was now in a better place where all the terrible things she had fought against would never get to her. I wished I could go back and take out my anger at Kaka, Aliyu, Danladi, Gambo, and all his men. This was all their fault. It's not fair people have to experience such violence to get to a better place.

I looked at Faith and wondered if it was the right decision to stay with her. Then I posed the question to myself:

How would I feel if the tables were reversed and I was abandoned by people I called my friends or family? If I was treated differently? My auntie and cousins came to my mind. I was becoming them. I was disgusted with myself for thinking that.

My mind was still numb from what we had discovered. Had an animal attacked Joy after she had come this far? We got back on the footpath. It was slow and steady. The sun faded and the heat on the ground dissipated.

I'd hoped we would run into people on the footpath, but we didn't see a soul. Exhausted, we found another small tree and stayed under its branches. The trees here were not as tall as the ones in Sambisa where the terrorists had their camps. Something must have attacked Joy. I intended to climb a taller tree for the night, but Faith wouldn't be able to do that.

We could not move any farther; we must rest. I doubt if we had progressed far enough from where we found Joy's belongings to be out of range of whatever attacked her. Maybe we should just stay in place and take whatever fate handed us. After all, we were trespassing on their habitat. We had invaded their privacy. My stomach rumbled, and it reminded me that we hadn't eaten or had any liquid for a full day. I looked at the long grass and considered eating it.

"Ngozi, I never thanked you for staying," said Faith in a whisper.

"It's nothing. I know you would have done the same for me."

My stomach felt empty and hollow.

We both drifted off to sleep. We must have slept for some time because when I opened my eyes, darkness had crept in. Faith snored beside me. Around us, the foliage looked like grotesque shadows in the moonlight. I woke up Faith.

"Oh, God, it's night already," said Faith.

I yawned and stretched. My stomach rumbled and growled. I felt well rested. I would have given anything for something to drink.

"Should we go on?" I asked.

"I don't think it matters anymore," said Faith. "We are vulnerable whether we move or stay. Since we're tired, we might as well rest and hope for the best."

I agreed with Faith. Most predators had an excellent sense of smell and hearing. Once again, we found ourselves resting outside at night, our condition not any better than the night before.

CHAPTER SIXTY-ONE

"I'm sure someone somewhere is looking up at the sky admiring the moon in the safety of their home," said Faith.

I looked up too, still awake. It was better than looking around. Every bush, tree, or shrub took the shape of something sinister. For the thousandth time, I wondered if it would've been better if we'd remained on the truck. What else could those kidnappers do after what they'd already done?

"How's your ankle?"

Faith sighed. "It needs rest to get better. Hopefully, we'll run into some people tomorrow and get something to drink. I have a good feeling about—"

Faith stopped talking mid-sentence.

I heard it too, a rustle in the dark shadows followed by a loud shrill from above. The hair on the back of my neck stood up. I jerked my head upward just in time to see a black silhouette zigzag its way in the dark sky. A bat. At Lamija I would watch them as they exited from the roof of the house next door, darkening the evening sky. I thought of

Auntie Halima. I doubt if she was looking for me. *Good riddance,* she would say.

I shrank closer to Faith, my body shaking violently in anticipation of what horror lay in wait for us in the dark. I expected an animal to pounce on us at any moment. Then, the night became still. Slowly, very slowly, the crickets started where they'd left off.

It seemed the worst was over. We remained huddled together. There was nothing else to do. A minute later, I heard a snore. I wished I could fall asleep at the flick of a switch. My eyelids got heavier, but my overwrought nerves would only permit fitful snatches of sleep. I must have been startled to wakefulness more than ninety-nine times by animal sounds and rustles in the bushes.

Scarcely had I closed my eyes for the hundredth time when hysterical laughter rang out from somewhere in the darkness close by.

"What was that?" Faith woke up and dug her fingers into my skin. Pain swept through my arm as her nails dug in. I dared not make a sound. There was something out there. Everything was quiet for a few seconds, then the stench hit us, a horrible mix of rotten meat and unwashed bodies. There was howling on our left and on our right.

For a moment, I couldn't move, frozen in place. The smell hit me again and urged me to my feet. "Let's go!" I knew the end was close, as close as the sound and stench that had come upon us. I hurled Faith to her feet.

"Ahhh!" Faith cried out in pain.

With her arm over my shoulders, we hobbled away from our tree, not knowing if we were headed toward danger or away from it. Every step must have been painful for Faith because I dragged her along.

"Ngozi, what are they? Are they coming? Are they coming?" Hysteria crept into her voice.

I didn't reply, but neither did I look back. We would not sit and watch the animals approach. Around us, they snarled and growled. I'd always feared death by drowning and was scared of death by fire; never had I considered being eaten by wild animals.

CHAPTER SIXTY-TWO

The animals were everywhere. To our right, two sinister shadows emerged from the darkness, their bodies silhouetted against the lowering sky, tapered figures from the head toward the tail—*kura*, hyenas. I shook uncontrollably. I wanted to flee, to hide. With menacing dogs, any sudden movement might initiate an attack, and these animals were not dogs. They were far worse.

They would feast on us while we were still alive.

I remembered the words of the man in the market just a few weeks ago. It was all I could think of. I expected them to pounce at any moment.

I'd heard your whole life flashes before your eyes right before you meet your creator, but my mind was devoid of thought, frozen in fear by pairs of yellow eyes glowering at us, waiting, watching.

"We will die!" screamed Faith. "We're going to die . . ." Her voice trailed off. Her fingers gripped my arm like steel vices.

I held Faith tight, and we shuffled off to the right, to the left, forward, backward. Then, my foot caught on something, and the inconceivable happened—we tumbled to the ground. That was the last place you wanted to be when an animal was about to attack.

I'd expected them to charge at us while we were down, but it seemed they preferred to play with their food first.

I jumped to my feet and dragged Faith up.

"Oh God . . . we're dead!" said Faith.

Closer and closer they came and seemed to be everywhere. In the dim moonlight, I counted four.

They snarled, growled, and dashed at us, then pulled back at the last minute.

Faith and I jostled back and forth like ping-pong balls, not knowing which way to turn, which one of them would be first, spurring the others to rip us to pieces. Like bullies in a school playground with a cornered student, the hyenas laughed and jeered.

Despite my tight grip on Faith, my fingers trembled, then my arms. Within seconds, my whole body was shaking.

I sobbed without a sound. In tough times, prayers were the answer. Would our prayers be answered? Why did God deliver us from the terrorists only to abandon us in the wilderness, to be eaten by animals? This was no way to die. I wanted to scream at the top of my voice.

When I was around age five, my mother would lift me in her hands and toss me into the air. I would shriek with fear and then delight. "Again! Again!" I would shout at the top of my lungs. This time, all I felt was real fear; the safety net my mother provided was not here. The animals came closer and closer—and with them came the smell of death.

My lungs opened. "Again! Again!" I screamed at the top of my lungs.

Startled by my outburst, the big hyena closest to us

jumped back. Something snapped like a twig, then there was the rattle of chains, followed by a loud cry like a wounded puppy. The large hyena whimpered and moaned.

It snarled and thrashed around. It had caught its hind limb in a gin trap secured by chains to a tree. A familiar metallic smell filled the air. I stood there, mesmerized by the sudden change of events.

A smaller hyena strolled over to the large hyena to investigate. In the blink of an eye, the trapped hyena wrapped its jaws around the neck of the smaller one. There was a sickening sound, and the small hyena ceased to move.

Smelling blood and a kill, the other two hyenas turned their attention to their dead and trapped comrades. They restarted the death dance, but this time focused on a new target, a target they knew was helpless; there was no hesitation, no question as to whether either would put up a fight. Back and forth they darted toward the trapped comrade. One leaped onto the back of the big hyena and ripped a chunk of flesh out of its back. The animal screamed in pain, and the air became thick with the smell of blood. Another raised its head, sniffed the air, and joined the slaughterous fray.

Faith, cold and clammy, tugged on my arm with so much force I felt it had been torn off. "Let's go!"

My knees buckled and I backed away. The animals were now ignoring us, engrossed in their quarry of fresh meat. The hunter had become the prey.

We turned and hobbled away quickly. The sound of chewing and crushing bones felt like it was inside my head and increased my sense of urgency.

We kept on, alternately running and walking. The sound from the injured hyena suddenly stopped. Silenced for good. The sound of feeding diminished as we put more distance between us and the carnage. A few times, I turned around to make sure we had nothing on our tail. By now we had distanced ourselves from the feeding, but I was sure we were within range if they decided they needed more food.

"I can't go any farther," said Faith. Her voice belied the pain she was enduring. "Let's stop here. The animals won't attack during the day."

We collapsed with exhaustion, weakened by the lack of food and water. Along the horizon, the fingers of daylight stretched out across the sky. At last, dawn was breaking.

CHAPTER SIXTY-THREE

Ahead of us was what appeared to be a hut. With the last of our strength, we crawled toward it. The walls were made from sticks, plywood, and cardboard boxes, with an opening in front. Any determined hyena could get in. For now, it was better than standing in the open. A large piece of plywood placed over the opening served as the door. I moved it aside and we stepped in, then I put it back.

It looked more like a shelter from the sun and rain. The inside smelled of charcoal smoke and the roof was made of dried grass. Streams of light came in through a square hole cut in the cardboard, which was covered with clear plastic. Next to it, a dirty T-shirt hung on a nail.

An old raffia mat lay on the dirt floor next to a pit with the remnants of a charcoal fire.

"It must be a hunter's or farmer's hut," said Faith. "For when he's working late." I looked around to see if there was anything to eat or drink. I found a black plastic bag on the floor and picked it up. My pulse raced. *Please contain something to eat.*

I fumbled with the knot—too tight. I ripped the bag open.

"Groundnuts! Faith, look." I cracked one shell and threw it into my mouth and chewed, it was dry and raw, but it was the best groundnut I'd ever had.

"This is so good," said Faith as she cracked her own shells.

I emptied the bag on the floor, and we ate hungrily. Groundnuts make you thirsty, but we'd cross that river when we got to it. Within minutes the nuts were all gone.

"I think we're close to a village," said Faith. "Whoever has this hut could be the same person who set all those traps. I'm sure he'll be coming around."

"Should we continue?" I asked.

"Even if I wanted to, I don't think I could move. God was on our side last night. Those hyenas, they must have eaten . . ." Faith stopped herself.

"They must have eaten Joy," I said, finishing Faith's words. After last night's close shave, my mind was blown.

Faith and I lay side by side on the mat. I knew I wouldn't be able to sleep. Each time I closed my eyes all I saw was the snarling hyenas and the smell of death they'd brought with them.

"Are you awake?" asked Faith.

"I can't sleep. At least we're resting." We lay there quietly, the light coming in from the window getting brighter and brighter as day broke. In the morning we'd find help.

CHAPTER SIXTY-FOUR

I felt we were close to finding help. Since Faith had been a captive for such a long time, it would be nice to get her home first.

Faith sighed. "I can't sleep."

"Neither can I. Is your home close to this place? Maybe we can take you home first before I head home." I laughed. "I'm sure they won't be too excited to see me."

Faith whimpered and I felt her body go stiff.

"Are you all right? I got on my elbows.

Faith's voice broke. "I can't go home," she sobbed.

"Of course you can. I know you haven't been home for a long time, but I'm sure your family will be happy to see you." I paused and snorted. I wasn't sure I would be welcome at home myself.

"Ngozi, I can't go home." Faith sniffed, her voice recovered from the sobs.

"Why?" I asked, realizing she was serious. "How did you end up at Gambo's camp?"

"I'd gone to see my sister, Fatima, and was on my way back home when a truck stopped beside me and the driver asked for directions. Before I knew it, two men jumped down from the truck, grabbed me, and threw me into the back and held me down."

I wanted to ask if anybody saw, but even if they did, they wouldn't have done anything.

"It happened so fast," said Faith. "They abducted more girls and brought us all to Sambisa. I cried every day for my parents, my brothers and sisters. Kaka told me to forget them, that they were now my new family. After two weeks they assigned me a husband."

I closed my eyes and swallowed. I knew that strategy.

"My . . . my husband raped me repeatedly." Faith paused and wiped tears from her eyes. "Soon after that, my husband went on a mission and never came back. I later heard he died during a raid. Kaka told me they would assign me another husband."

I clasped my hands over my mouth. "Oh, God," I said. My eyes brimmed with tears.

Faith sat on the floor, her arms wrapped around her legs. "My new husband beat me and again I was raped. I told them that if anyone touched me again, I would kill myself. That was when Kaka went to work on me. Before I knew it, they had convinced me that since I wanted to die, it was God's will and I should take as many nonbelievers with me as I could. Gambo had just come back from a trip to the Middle East. He brought back with him a lot of money, weapons, and ideas. 'Put this vest on and press this button at the market,' he had said."

I fidgeted and tapped my lips with my fingers. "What happened?"

Faith nodded. "I agreed to do it. I went to the venue. It was a good target. It was the fish market. There were believers, nonbelievers—and then I saw my brother with my mother. Can you imagine?"

The excitement in Faith's voice was palpable as she relived the experience.

"I couldn't believe my eyes. What was I going to do? Run to them? But I had a problem. Gambo had sent a watcher with me."

"Watcher?" I asked.

"Someone to confirm that I'd blown myself up." Faith chuckled. "He was a coward. As I was thinking of what to do, I saw him board a bike and take off. He left early. He didn't want to be even close when the bomb went off."

"What did you do? You ran away too?"

"Yes! I went into a nearby bush, removed the vest and the wires, and rushed back to the market. By then my mother and brother had moved from where I had seen them. I searched and searched and found them as they were about to enter a taxi."

I smiled. "Your family must have been ecstatic to see you."

"It took some convincing before they believed it was me," said Faith. "They thought I'd been a victim of ritual murder and I was a ghost. They took me home."

There was a flicker of a smile on Faith's face. I sensed the sadness in her voice. I asked quietly, "So what happened?"

"My father wasn't happy; the whole family wasn't glad I came back. They treated me as an outcast and blamed me for getting kidnapped."

"They blamed you? That's rubbish!"

"It got worse," said Faith.

I rubbed the back of my neck and clenched my jaw.

What could be worse than your parents, your family, blaming you for something terrible that happened to you?

"My period was never steady, so I wasn't bothered. But it never came."

I felt a lump in my throat. The groundnuts churned in my stomach. I rubbed my sweaty palms together. The story was going to get worse.

Faith continued. "My tummy didn't show. I was a kid, but I always wore a buba. One day, I was dressing up after taking a shower, and my mother saw me, and she confirmed her suspicions. By then I was advanced. I had the baby."

I clasped my hand over my mouth. Faith had my full attention. I couldn't speak. I remained motionless and waited.

"My family. My own siblings, people I trust, called my child Boko Haram Baby. I tried to tell them it was a different faction, but my father said they were all the same, and it didn't matter. My family was ashamed of me, so you can imagine how people outside treated me."

Faith was now rocking back and forth. I tried to hold her, but she shook her head.

"When Ahmed was six months old, he had a fever."

I'd wanted to ask why she named him Ahmed, whether it was the name of her son's father, but I couldn't bring myself to ask.

"They stopped me from taking him to see a doctor. I loved him so much, and one day he stopped moving."

Tears flowed down Faith's face. Her lips quivered, her whole body trembled. Despite her protests, I wrapped my arms around her. She let me.

"I'm so sorry," I said. Tears rolled down my cheeks too.

"They had to pry little Ahmed's body out of my hands to bury him!" Faith sobbed.

I didn't know what else to say. How do you console someone to whom such a thing had happened?

"Do you know what my father said?" Faith had stopped crying. Her voice was now bitter.

I shook my head.

"He said it was a good thing Ahmed died. It was God's will!" Faith raised her voice as if her father was right there. "'It wasn't God's will, it was your will,' I told him. I'd pointed at him, my mother, my brothers, and sisters. I told them they were no different from the terrorists, twisting God's word to serve their selfish purposes." Faith's voice calmed down. "What did my baby do to them? He was only a baby."

We were quiet for some time, but I had to ask. "How did you end up back in Sambisa?"

"My father couldn't bear any more—the shame and disgrace I'd brought to the family. He threw me out. I had no place to go. So, I went to the village where the terrorists get foodstuff. When they came to buy food, I approached them. They would have killed me on the spot, saying I was an informant. They took me to Gambo. He was mad about the vest I threw away, that it had cost him so much money to get. Kaka intervened and told him to calm down and let me stay. That I would be ready to wear that vest again."

CHAPTER SIXTY-FIVE

"Now you know why I can't go home," said Faith.

I rocked back and forth with my hands clenched into fists. I didn't know how to respond.

"Don't worry, Ngozi, it's my cross to carry. I never wanted to burden you or anybody with my story. Please don't feel sorry for me."

I still didn't know what to say. Maybe when I got home, I'd ask for Auntie Halima's forgiveness and ask her to accommodate Faith.

"Cheer up," said Faith. "We might as well head into town. The earlier we find help, the better."

I got up and pulled Faith up. The groundnuts were a good start. We would need to find food and water once we got into town.

I bent my knees and removed the plywood door. As I straightened, I noticed a thick rope from the corner of my eye. It wasn't there before. It moved and rose from the floor and stood face-to-face with me. I froze and stared into the black beady eyes of a brown snake.

"Does your back hurt? Why are you bent like a stat—"

The snake stared at me. Faith must have seen it too.

"Don't move," whispered Faith.

I watched in horror as the snake's head seemed to expand.

"Tomorrow is too far," whispered Faith.

I knew what she meant. Once bitten, you are dead by the second day. Faith shifted on my left. The snake sensed it and adjusted its head toward Faith, its inky black mouth wide open.

Faith sprang in front of me and dove out the door. It happened so fast. The next thing I knew, the snake was on the ground crawling quickly away from Faith into the thicket.

Faith got up and brushed dry grass and dirt off her clothes.

I rushed over to her. "Are you all right?"

She nodded.

"Thank God you're fine! You saved my life!"

"That was the only way to get it out of the way," said Faith.

I wasn't so sure about that; nothing terrified me as much as snakes. Faith leaned on my shoulder and we left the hut. Within minutes, beads of sweat formed on my forehead. To my surprise, we met another footpath a few feet away from the shed. Littered with newspapers, banana peels, and plastic bags, this was a well-used footpath.

We walked in a single file. I was in front. I sniffed the air, and the unmistakable smell of fried food rushed into my nose.

"Hold on, Faith!" Excited, I took a few steps forward, sniffing the air. "Can you smell that?" I turned to look at Faith. The smile vanished from my face; she was bent over, winded.

"What's wrong?"

Faith grasped my hand. Her's felt cold and clammy. Together we sank to the ground, panting.

"Oh God, the snake bit you. Where?"

She nodded and pointed at her ankle. The same ankle that had twisted two nights ago was now three times the size it had been, swollen with two puncture marks still oozing blood and a greenish liquid.

"Oh God," I whimpered. "Oh God, what am I going to do?"

CHAPTER SIXTY-SIX

Tears streamed down my cheeks. I was on the ground with Faith's head resting on my lap. Should I leave her and go get help? We'd been looking for the past two days. Should I stay and watch her die? What should I do? Then I heard something else.

"Listen!" I cocked my head to the right. Yes, there it was, a male and a female voice. Faith's face was a mask of pain, but she did not cry out. She nodded, and her lips parted in a faint smile.

The voices came closer, the only thing separating us from them were the bushes. Were they friends or foe? A woman's voice broke out into a song in Arabic.

"God is our savior, and only God is God, our guard, and guide. Follow the steps of the prophet. Always extend a helping hand. Generosity never goes on vacation."

"Help! Help," I yelled, but it came out as a whimper.

"Singing," said Faith in a barely audible voice.

Faith's grip on my hand tightened.

I knew what Faith was thinking: *Were they friend or foe?* But we needed help or she wouldn't make it. My mind raced. Our situation was hopeless, but I must make a decision for Faith to survive. I laid Faith's head on the ground and sprang to my feet.

"Help! Help!" I yelled in Hausa.

The singing stopped. The man and a woman took a startled step backward, eyes wide.

"I need help!" I blurted and pointed at where Faith lay. "Please, help us. A snake bit her!"

The woman's hands flew to her mouth in a wave of yellow and black patterned fabric.

The man's eyes narrowed. "Bitten by a snake?"

"Yes, yes," I said and pointed behind the bush.

"Let's see," said the man. He peered over the grass. "Where?"

"Right here! Please help us."

The man took a step forward and looked again. His hand balled up in a fist. His eyes widened. "*Wallahi,* I swear to God!"

"Please," I said.

"Are . . . are you from Akarika Girls?" he asked in a deep voice. It was more of a statement than a question.

"Yes, please help us!" I cried. "I don't want her to die."

He pointed at Faith on the ground. "What happened to her?"

"Snakebite," I told him again.

"A snake?" The man exchanged glances with the woman. "Where's the snake? What's the color?" He asked in rapid succession as they came closer.

"It ran away, it was brownish black," I said.

"How long ago?" the man asked.

"About twenty minutes."

"Do you know what kind of snake it was? That would help with choosing the right anti-venom."

Faith whispered something I didn't hear. I sat on the ground, placed her head on my lap, and lowered my head to listen to what she was saying. It was the same thing she'd whispered just after we saw the snake. It must be the snake's name.

"Tomorrow is too far!" I blurted.

"Oh," said the man. He looked as if he had been punched in the stomach. He and the woman both had a sorry look on their faces.

"She needs medical attention fast. We live close by. Let's get her out of the sun first." The man looked me over. "I can't imagine what you've been through. You've been in the news."

He turned to the woman. They exchanged words in hushed tones. I couldn't make out what they were saying, but I picked up a hint of English and Hausa.

"Come with us," said the woman. "Our home is not far. We'll help you."

I looked at the man, and then at the woman, and a thousand thoughts raced through my mind. We were at their mercy.

"My name is Bala. This is my wife, Kalila." He pointed to the woman. "What are your names?"

I stared at him, not sure what to do. Would our names make any difference in how they treated us? Faith's eyes were on me. I was now our spokesperson. This was the simplest of questions, yet it left me tongue-tied. I could have lied, said another name, a Hausa name, but it was one of those situations when the only thing I could do was tell the truth.

Bala noticed my hesitation. "You don't want to tell us?"

"She's Faith, and I'm . . . I'm Ngozi," I said.

Bala's eyes widened.

I tightened my grip on Faith's arm, heart pounding.

"*Chinekele!* Oh my God!" Bala exclaimed in Igbo. "My sister, what are you doing here?" he continued in rapid Igbo.

I knew the language was Igbo. "I have an Igbo name, but I don't understand the language."

"But you speak Hausa like a native," said Kalila.

"I'm Hausa with an Igbo first name," I said. I knew almost every Igbo native speaker was Christian, but this man's name was Bala. Maybe he was one of those people who learned greetings and a few words in every Nigerian language.

"Don't worry, we understand," said Kalila in English. She pointed at Bala. "My husband is Igbo too, but he has taken the name Bala."

I almost collapsed with relief. Marriage between a northerner and a southerner was not uncommon and showed the strength of character of the people involved.

"Where did the snake bite you?" asked Bala.

Faith pointed at her ankle.

Bala looked, and I noticed a subtle narrowing of his eyebrows. Something was not right.

"Will she be all right?" I asked.

Bala examined the wound. "I can only see a pair of fang marks; good. Less venom. Kalila, give me your scarf."

Kalila handed him a scarf and he tied it above Faith's ankle.

"We have to move you. God willing, everything will be fine," said Bala.

Faith was too tired to move. We helped her up. She put her arms over my shoulder and Kalila's, and we walked.

"Faith, how did you get away?" asked Bala as we made our way down the footpath. Faith began the story, but she was out of breath, I took over, propelled by adrenaline.

"They must have been moving you to another section of the Sambisa forest," said Bala as we walked down the foot path.

I was too tired to say anything out loud. If the government knew where we were, I wondered why nobody had informed the police.

"The government came under a lot of pressure," said Bala. "Dr. Tarbari, the opposition candidate, talked about the abduction all the time in his campaign speeches. The international community demanded answers because nothing was being done. First was the incident at Chibok, three hundred girls kidnapped, and Akarika." Bala sighed. "I guess it's human nature, it's only when things happen to you or someone you know that it means anything to you."

"Why didn't the government do anything when the girls at Chibok were kidnapped?" I asked.

"*Haba*, you know how the government is." He sighed and shook his head. "It's only when something gets out of hand that the government reacts. By then it's usually too late."

Bala's hair was gray at the temples and reminded me of a school principal.

"Kidnapping a whole school of girls got the world's attention," said Kalila. "They knew the girls were taken to Sambisa, but they did nothing. I hope it's the end of this nonsense of doing nothing. I pray for the girls they still have."

"But, why didn't they do anything for us?" I asked. I couldn't let the question go.

"Nobody was interested in saving the children of local farmers, civil servants, and what have you. Maybe the terrain played a part too. See, Sambisa was a game reserve during colonial times but was abandoned decades ago. The lodgings and other infrastructure were already in place, so all the terrorists needed to do was reclaim what they needed from the forest and use it as their base."

A man on a bicycle rode by in the other direction. "Morning, headmaster." He waved and continued.

Bala acknowledged with a glance and a nod. "For a long time now, different criminal elements have used it to hide out. The place is huge and the terrain difficult to penetrate. People always see the north as a savanna, but Sambisa is a hybrid—rain forest and savanna in the same place. The thick cluster of trees and bushes in some areas makes it difficult to see what is underneath. Looking for someone there would seem like looking for the proverbial needle in a haystack. But the government should have done something. We all could have done better for all those girls."

I got worried. Kalila and I were just dragging Faith along. She was gasping for air.

"I think we should stop. Faith's not doing well."

"We're almost there," said Bala.

CHAPTER SIXTY-SEVEN

We emerged from the bush path onto a dirt road. It amazed me how close we were to the village. Less than a fifteen-minute walk. If we hadn't stopped to rest in that hut, we would have gotten to safety with no snakebites. I wished I could turn back time.

"Welcome to Dalsu village," said Bala. "Our home is down the road."

It was a short street, about the length of a football field with houses on both sides. A mixture of mud-brick huts and unpainted cement bungalows, with no rhyme or rhythm to the layout. It seemed like the whole village was that one street. Farther down I could see a building that could be used as a warehouse.

Two naked little boys, full of smiles and squeals, rolled tires bigger than themselves down the road. A few chickens and some goats fed from a pile of garbage on the side. The crackle of a radio suggested there were other people around indoors.

We stopped in front of a bungalow with unpainted cement walls. Next to the house was a blue plastic water tank resting on stones with "500 gallons" written on it in white oil paint.

Bala walked toward the door and brought out a bunch of keys from his pocket.

"Put her down here," he said, pointing at a sofa once we were inside the house. Kalila and I lowered Faith onto the couch.

"Faith, can you hear me?" I asked. She'd shut her eyes when we entered the building.

Faith opened her eyes. "Where are we?"

I smiled. "In Kalila's home. We can trust them."

She attempted a smile. "Trust is a leap of faith. Sometimes you have to take that chance."

I held Faith's hand. She closed her eyes, her chest rising and falling. It worried me that if she slept, she wouldn't wake up.

"I'll get water for you to wash your feet and clean up," said Bala. "Kalila, they will need food and some Panadol for the pain." He entered a curtained-off room.

Bala came back to the living room with a cup of water and some tablets. It took every ounce of control from me not to snatch the water from him.

"Wake Faith up. These will help with the pain," said Bala.

I shook Faith, and she opened her eyes. Bala gave her the medicine, and she swallowed them and emptied the cup.

"I'll get more water," said Bala and disappeared behind the curtain. He came back with a gallon of water and two cups.

I filled Faith's cup. She took the cup hungrily from me and gulped, eyes closed.

I poured some into the second cup and raised it to my

lips. It was the best-tasting water I'd ever had. Some water dripped off my lips and soaked my top as I tried to drink it all at once. I had to slow down. I shivered, goose pimples appearing all over my body.

The cold burn traveled from my mouth down to my stomach, cooling and calming everything in its path.

"Ha, that was good." I refilled the cup and raised it to my lips when I noticed Bala looking at me as if he wanted to see through my top, which was now wet and clung onto my torso.

"We've been married for twenty years," said Bala. "I moved to the north as an English teacher from Anambra State, and I never left. The people welcomed me with open arms. Kalila was my former student. We got married after a long courtship because her father wouldn't let her marry a nonbeliever." Bala laughed. "A Muslim man can marry a Christian or Jewish woman, but not so easy for a Muslim woman to marry whomever she wanted. I converted, and her father relented."

I drank another cup of water while Faith was on her third. *We should stop drinking*, I thought. I wanted to remove the grime of the last few days from my body or at least change. I waited for Bala to leave.

He paused and looked at us. "I'll be back." He disappeared through the same curtain as Kalila.

Faith looked at me and smiled. "Thank you."

Our rescue was anticlimactic. "Thank you too," I said. The realization we had gotten away was beginning to sink in.

"I never knew water tasted so good," said Faith. "Do you think Lami made it to this village?"

I'd forgotten about Lami. I thought of the hyena. "I don't know. I hope she did."

The smell of kerosene, the clang of pots, and the smell of fried onions and tomatoes caused my stomach to rumble uncontrollably. My mouth literally dripped with saliva.

Bala came into the living room through another side door with two buckets of water, a rolled-up crepe bandage, a towel, and a jar of some dark brown ointment in a cylindrical container.

"Soak your feet in the water and wash off the dirt. Kalila will help you clean your wounds. We must leave immediately to get you to safety, to your homes, in case those people come back to look around nearby villages for you."

I scooped up water from the bucket, washed my face, and dried it with the cloth he brought in. Faith did the same.

Kalila walked in, and the smell of food followed her like a shadow. She looked at Faith, surprised. "You look a lot better. Are you sure the color of the snake was brown?" She soaked a piece of cloth in the bucket, wrung it out, got on her haunches, and reached for Faith's foot.

"No, I can do it," protested Faith.

"Don't be silly," said Kalila. "Sit back and get your strength back.

I glanced at Faith and back to Kalila. "It was dark in the shed. The snake could have been any color."

"Must have been the common green snake," said Kalila.

Hope surged through me. "It's not poisonous? Are you sure?"

"It is, just enough to immobilize mice and frogs and give humans aches and pains," said Kalila. "That's why she had the initial reaction after the bite. She would have been doing a lot worse by now if she was bitten by 'tomorrow is too far.'"

Let me see if you broke anything. Kalila wiped Faith's

feet, patted them dry with a piece of cloth, and she dipped her hand into the jar of a dark brown cream and scooped some up. The smell of menthol, shea butter, and something earthy wafted through the air. She massaged it into Faith's feet.

"Oh," moaned Faith. "Feels so good."

The relief on Faith's face was immediate as Kalila worked her magic. She applied the crepe bandage over Faith's swollen ankle and held it in place with a safety pin.

"You're fortunate it was a green snake. Nobody survives a bite from the mamba. I'll bring your food."

CHAPTER SIXTY-EIGHT

Kalila served us a large bowl of steaming white custard and spicy akara balls, made from ground black-eyed peas mixed with diced tomatoes, onions, and peppers. I snatched them one after the other as if someone would take them from me. We each had a spoon and ate from the same bowl. It was the best meal I'd ever had.

Kalila took the plates away after the meal and refused to let us help her wash up. Having satisfied my stomach, I noted my surroundings. On the wall was a wedding picture of a young Kalila and Bala. Under that picture was a photo of two women and a man, maybe in their twenties. Bala caught my eyes.

"Those are our kids. The two girls work in Abuja. The boy works in Lagos."

From the look in his eyes, I knew he was proud of them.

What my mother Matron looked like wouldn't come to me anymore unless I'd just looked at a picture of her. Even the image of my Uncle Thomas too was eroding in my mind's eye. I felt sad. Time was a double-edged sword; it heals but it also steals.

Kalila returned with a bundle of clothes and two pairs of mismatched flip-flops. "It's a good thing I throw nothing away."

Our own clothes were ripped in so many places it would only attract attention.

Kalila gave us two identical black flowing dresses with a hijab to match that reeked of mothballs. They were like what Kaka and Danuwa wore. The thought of them sent a chill down my spine. I dismissed the thought. We were free.

"Good, in case we run into some overzealous character," said Bala.

I fiddled with my new clothes to buy time waiting for Bala to leave. Faith had already slipped out of her own clothes, her bare breasts exposed. Kalila turned and eyed Bala, her face a mask of fury. Bala's eyes were fixed on Faith.

"Oh," said Bala, as if he had come out of a trance, and he excused himself from the room.

I then changed. Kalila did not leave our side until we finished changing. I noticed that her countenance had changed. Stone-faced, no longer smiling.

There was a knock on the door. "Can I come in?" asked Bala.

"Yes," replied Kalila, her voice cold.

"I think we should get going to get you back to your families," said Bala. "We still must shop at Bamoga Market today. That was our destination before we met you." His eyes lingered on Faith, then he frowned. "Emmm . . . but, before we leave, I need to buy kerosene down the road in case we come back late."

Kalila looked at him a little longer, then nodded. Her face still impassive, she watched Bala leave the room.

Bala poked his head through the door. "*Masoyina*, my love, I . . . I think this might be dangerous. You should stay at home. You didn't want to go. I'll bring Bello with me, just in case."

"Hmm, in case of what?" asked Kalila.

I sensed that something was not right. Kalila's attitude had changed. The relief and peace of mind I'd felt since they rescued us faded.

"We'll talk when I come back," said Bala and walked out of the room. Kalila followed him out.

I turned to Faith. "Did you notice anything?"

"Like what?" asked Faith.

"Something is eating Kalila up."

Just then, Kalila barged into the room. She looked flustered. "He's gone, but not for long. You must leave now!"

"What . . . what about your husband?" asked Faith. "Won't he escort us?"

"Why?" I asked.

"Something is not right. We have more than enough kerosene. Here, this is money for the bus."

Stunned, I refused to take it. Which was stupid because we had no money. Kalila stuffed the cash in my palm and squeezed my fingers around it.

"Hurry, you don't have time! They'll soon be back," said Kalila, panic in her voice.

They? I wondered.

She pushed us toward the door. "Listen, your lives are in danger. It all makes sense now."

"What makes sense?" I asked.

"I came home nights ago, and a young, tall girl was here.

She had been wandering the streets, and my husband brought her here. She said a bus driver and his conductor gave her a lift and held her hostage. They would drug her, tie her to a bed, and lock her up in their room when they went to work. The conductor told his neighbors she was his sister and someone from their village had put a madness spell on her over a land dispute. They should ignore whatever she says."

I nodded. "Madness? Nobody would come near her."

"She escaped somehow," continued Kalila. "My husband and his friend offered to take her back to Lamija. She didn't tell us she was one of the Akarika girls. My husband and his friend came back later that night and said she was on her way. Awake in the early hours of the morning, I heard the ferocious feeding sounds of hyenas. Sound travels far at night."

"Joy!" I gasped.

Kalila jerked her head in my direction. "You know her?"

"Yes," I whispered. "We found Joy's clothes in the bush, just before the hyenas tried to get us too."

"You must leave at once," said Kalila. "Make a left at the door and walk fast. Be on the lookout for the first footpath on your right. Follow it to the end, it leads to the bus stop."

"Why . . . why are you helping us?" I stammered.

"I saw the look on his face while you were changing. Something evil lurked behind those eyes. Things you'd only know after you'd been married for a while . . . now go."

I took a step toward the door, stopped, and turned. "He'll beat you when he comes back. Come with us!"

Kalila shrugged, her lips parted in a slight grin. "He doesn't scare me. I can handle him any day. Now leave before he and his stupid friend get here."

Once again adrenalin surged through my veins. The food and the little rest helped. We exited the house and made a left. Faith walked with a slight limp, unaided, and we headed toward the footpath. The street was busier than when we had arrived. Eager to get away, I walked fast. A few people glanced at us, but nobody paid much attention. Most people would know everybody in the village, but so far, we blended in, our faces hidden by the hijab.

"There's the footpath." I pointed ahead at a well-trodden path surrounded by thick elephant grass on both sides. A man pushing a bicycle had just emerged from it.

We stepped onto the footpath. I turned to wait for Faith to catch up and glanced once more at Kalila's house beyond her and smiled. "Freedom."

"God willing," said Faith with a smile. "God willing."

Something behind me made the smile die on her face. I turned. It was too late. I literally walked into Gambo's arms. He engulfed me in an iron embrace as Bala grabbed Faith. I met Bala's eyes and wished I could set him on fire with my eyes.

Bala stared back at me with defiance. "Don't look at me like that. Every day on the radio all I hear is, 'Bring back our girls, bring back our girls.' But after the girls are rescued, what about the local people who don't get helped?"

Bala glared at me waiting for my response. I had none.

He continued. "The terrorists never forget nor forgive. They will come back to extract their pound of flesh." Bala paused. "I listen to BBC. Locals who helped in Iraq and Afghanistan were abandoned by the Americans and other coalition members."

That's not true, I wanted to say. I also watched the news and I saw families relocated to America, Australia, and other countries.

"Please tell them," said Gambo. "They stay in their villas and white houses and talk nonsense."

"Communities around here have picked a side," said Bala and he adjusted his grip on Faith's arm. "They want nothing to do with 'bring back our girls.'"

CHAPTER SIXTY-NINE

Not again. I struggled like a wildcat to free myself. The more I struggled, the more Gambo's grip on me loosened. *Struggle a little longer and I might escape his grasp and dash away. I can run fast.*

"Small girl, stop struggling before you get hurt," said Gambo. His breath, hot on my face, smelled of onions and ginger. His head moved toward me.

Sharp pain exploded inside my head and face followed by twinkling bright light. Gambo had smashed his head into my forehead and nose. The metallic taste of blood flooded my mouth. I looked down, and all I wanted to do was prevent more blood from getting on the borrowed dress.

"I warned you," said Gambo. "You girls never listen to good advice."

He pushed me away from his body but held on to my hand.

Bala secured Faith. I looked around the street, it was getting dark. Little kids stood watching while the adults walked away fast or shooed their children on. People knew what was going on, but they stayed away, terrified.

"Take them to the warehouse," said Gambo. "We can now start our journey tonight or tomorrow morning."

My eyes met Faith's, and I mouthed that we'd be all right. Her eyes widened in horror, alarmed, I thought, by the blood on my face. How did this happen? We'd almost gotten away.

The warehouse was the house we had seen earlier at the end of the street, more in the outskirts of the village. Danladi's truck was parked beside it. We walked up to a metal door with a padlock. Gambo produced a key and, still holding me tight, unlocked it.

We walked in. The air was stale and smelled of urine. A dim bulb hung from the low ceiling. As my eyes adjusted, I noticed that the warehouse was empty except for crying and whimpering girls, guarded by Danladi.

Danladi smiled. "*Iyawo*, why did you run?"

I jerked my head as a figure got up from the floor. It was Aliyu. My eyes widened. I'd thought he was in Cameroon.

"That's an understatement," said Aliyu. "How did you survive the trek through the bush?" He turned to Danladi. "Your wife is dangerous."

Danladi smiled but didn't say anything. What I felt for him was beyond hate. If looks could kill...

"Ah, Gambo," said Bala. "Let me take this one to the back. I won't be long."

Gambo stared at him as if he didn't believe his ears. He exhaled. "As long as she doesn't get away. I have plans for her."

Bala giggled. "She can't run. She twisted her ankle." He dragged Faith with him toward the door.

Gambo waved Danladi over. "Let's talk. Ngozi, sit with the girls." He gestured with his finger. "Aliyu, please watch them better than you did the last time. I wish you had gone on with the others to the border instead of taking a bus back."

Gambo and Danladi hunched together talking while Aliyu's eyes were on the girls and me. I looked at the girls. There were ten of them and I couldn't make them all out. The ones I could see were new faces. Some cried quietly while others stared ahead shell-shocked. We all sat on the floor, and I watched Gambo and Danladi. I wished I had a razor blade or knife. At least I would do damage before they killed me.

Faith had screamed once, and not too long later, Bala brought her back, excused himself, and left. I hoped Kalila killed him when he got home.

Gambo walked toward Faith. "I hope you had a good time with that foolish Bala. I haven't seen any person that likes *toto* so much."

Faith did not look up. She'd glued her eyes to the floor since she came back in from the back of the house with Bala.

"I'm very disappointed in you," said Gambo. "After all we did for you. I forgave you after you threw away a suicide belt worth thousands of dollars and let you live in my compound."

"Look who's talking," I said out loud, disgusted with the whole thing. I'd taunt them until they killed me here.

Gambo looked at me with one eyebrow raised. "You are not afraid?" Gambo walked toward me. "You have caused me so many problems. But you have also made me a lot of money."

"You have a wife, Rakiya," I blurted. "You took the twins Ronke and Lami by force. Who knows how many more women you have abused and killed. Allah will punish you. You'll never get away with this."

Aliyu looked at Danladi with an amused look. "Your wife is strong-headed. I'm glad now you married her and I didn't. Get ready for an early grave."

Gambo laughed. "Ngozi, don't worry about me." You should worry about yourself. You're just an ant. Nobody really cares about what's going on."

"I don't care what happens to me," I said.

"Do you know why we took your school?" asked Gambo. "Do you want to know? I'll tell you: politics."

CHAPTER SEVENTY

"Politics," I whispered. I did not believe I'd heard right.

Gambo paced the room then walked up to Faith. She had assumed the passivity she had when I first met her, like a rediscovered favorite pair of jeans. Gambo grabbed her by the hair and yanked her face up.

"Aieeee!" yelled Faith.

I could see the fear in Faith's eyes; her lips and chin trembled.

"You disappointed me." He pulled out a knife from his belt.

The other girls screamed and moved farther back into a corner.

"No!" I made to get up from the floor.

"Don't," said Aliyu. He pointed a gun at me. "If you move again, I'll shoot one of the girls."

I stopped.

"I haven't finished my story yet," said Gambo. "Business before pleasure." He let go of Faith's neck and continued to pace.

My head ached. I must do something. It was apparent that at some point, he was going to hurt Faith. Even though none of the other girls were bound, they remained frozen with fear.

"In the north, there's Boko Haram terrorizing people. In the south, Niger Delta groups are blowing up oil pipelines and kidnapping expatriates. So, when one of my associates mentioned we can add to the confusion by kidnapping the students at Akarika Girls, I said, Why not?"

"There are hundreds of other schools," I said. "Why Akarika Girls?"

"Good question," said Gambo. "Diversity. Even though there are more Christians than Muslims in the school, all the major ethnic groups of the country were well represented. Hausa, Igbo, Yoruba. A hit on the school would resonate in every part of the country."

I watched Gambo. He had stopped talking and seemed to be thinking. I didn't know what to make of what he'd said.

"We were already working with Zainab," said Gambo. "She was your only friend and needed money. Thanks to poverty, our job was easy."

I stared at him, not believing what he was saying.

"Danladi here," said Gambo and pointed at Danladi, "figured you were at the business center the same day they had gone to upload our propaganda video, and you'd left an e-mail that you needed money. You also left the email address."

I looked at Danladi. Is it at all possible to have more hatred for someone?

"Any luck yet with the e-mail?" asked Gambo.

"No time yet. Busy," said Danladi, giving Gambo a look

that said he should know better. "But it will be straightfor-ward. We'll ask her for ransom."

"So we gave Zainab money for herself and for you to solve the problem you had. In return, you come to school with her," said Gambo.

"Zainab?" I whispered. I felt a fluttering in my stomach. *She has nothing to do with this. He's just dropping names.* "That's a lie," I blurted. "Zainab had nothing to do with me being in school."

"Really?" said Gambo. He threw his head back and laughed.

"I . . . I came because I wanted to be there . . . because I ran away from home." My mind was in turmoil. It couldn't be right. Zainab only asked me once about coming to school with her. But it could be true. I knew Zainab would do anything for money.

"Where did Zainab get money from for you?" asked Gambo.

I remembered I'd used Fatima's money. "I paid with my money. You lie. Zainab got money from her boyfriend, Dan."

Gambo winked and jerked his head toward Danladi.

"Okay, boss, that's enough lies," said Danladi. His eyes darted from Gambo to me. A high-pitched laugh escaped his lips.

"You're a ladies' man," said Aliyu with a chuckle. "Own it."

"Lies," said Danladi with a half-smile on his lips.

"Believe what you want," said Gambo. "Maybe the turn of events worked in our favor. It doesn't matter. I'm waiting for a call that will determine what happens next."

Was it true what Gambo said about Zainab? I had to ask. "Who paid you to kidnap the school?"

Gambo shrugged, picked his nails with the blade, and strolled over to Faith. He grabbed her head again.

My whole body went rigid. "Please, leave Faith alone. Let everybody go." My voice shook. "It's only me you want."

Gambo crinkled his nose. "Why would I want to do such a thing? We already have you and ten more girls. I have nothing to gain from your offer."

I could see Faith. She whimpered and shook. Her eyes were wide. Her nose flared like a rabbit's with every breath she took.

"So, I plan to keep you alive," said Gambo. "Aren't you lucky?" In one swift move, he ran the blade through Faith's neck. Time stood still.

CHAPTER SEVENTY-ONE

"No! I screamed.

A cry rose from the girls behind, and they all backed into a corner. Spots flashed in my vision. I gasped for air. I tried to get off the floor and reach Faith, but something pushed me down and pinned me to the floor. My struggles intensified until I felt something cold jammed into my ear.

"If you don't stop, I'll shoot you," said Aliyu.

I stopped struggling. The cold barrel of a gun was pressed against the back of my ear.

A few yards away, Faith's body twitched, and a gurgle escaped her throat. She'd fallen on her knees and now pitched over to the side, both hands at her neck.

"There's never enough women for the living," growled Gambo. "Yet the spirit world always gets one at short notice." He shook his head. "Release her."

Aliyu released me and I got up, afraid to look at my friend. She was dying. I didn't want to see, but I had to. I turned my head. Faith looked like a bundle of black cloth shoved on the floor. I rushed to her. Her eyes were wide open. One look at the wound and I knew she was beyond help.

"Gambo, this was not necessary," said Danladi.

"I am in charge here," said Gambo. "Don't forget that."

"Faith, Faith," I cried. I knelt beside her. Three times I reached for her and pulled back confused. Would I do more damage if I placed her head on my lap? Her body jerked. My hands hovered over her face and shook like a palm frond during a storm. I stared helplessly as the wound in her neck foamed. Comforting her with words would only be lies. She was no fool.

Faith's body twitched once more and stopped. Tears dripped down my face onto Faith's, rolled down her cheeks, and mixed with her blood.

I leaned down and kissed her forehead. She looked like she was sleeping. A girl who would harm no one, who would turn the other cheek for the sake of peace. I hated Gambo and all the terrorists that destroyed lives in the name of religion.

I looked at Gambo with his knife, guns, and henchmen and I felt impotent. What could I do to make an impact? I looked at the other girls and thought I saw Lami's battered face in there.

Gambo walked toward me, bent down and wiped his blade on Faith's dress, and then sheathed it. Then he looked at me with an amused look on his face.

"Why . . . why?" I stuttered. "Faith would never have harmed you."

Gambo grabbed my blouse and yanked me to my feet. "Who cares!"

I trembled all over. "Please . . . please don't kill me." Deep down inside I wanted to die, but facing death, courage failed me. I never believed I could beg for my life. But there I was, pleading.

Gambo's satellite phone rang. He glanced at it, then at me. He pushed me to the ground and walked toward a corner and pushed the phone to his ear.

CHAPTER SEVENTY-TWO

M alam looked out of the window of his library, hands clasped behind his back. For the past hour, he had paced around his office as he pondered the problem before him. He had always seen himself as a pragmatist. Things that needed to be done must be done. Yet he hesitated. Was he getting too old?

"A smoking gun." The words tumbled out of Malam's lips with deliberate ease. He liked the phrase so much that he had researched its origin. The first use in a story was in "The Adventure of Gloria Scott: A Sherlock Holmes Story," written and published in 1893 by Arthur Conan Doyle. A 'smoking gun' is the most reliable kind of circumstantial evidence. A piece of evidence that relies on inference to connect it to a conclusion of fact.

Malam knew the girl had become a smoking gun. Circumstantial evidence that could collapse a well-laid plan. Malam walked back to the table and picked up his phone. He sighed and pushed a button.

CHAPTER SEVENTY-THREE

Hamza remained awake all night. In the morning he got ready, kissed Ali good-bye, and called Kola.

"I'll be home for the day," said Hamza. "Tired and feeling under the weather."

"Do you need a doctor?" asked Kola. "You know best. Should I come to the house?"

"No, I'll be fine."

"Okay, boss. I'm a phone call away."

Hamza hung up. He had this feeling that something terrible would happen, but he couldn't place his finger on it. Hamza poured himself a cup of coffee and went into his home office and sat behind the big desk. He stared at the pictures on the wall. Apart from Ali's photo on their wedding day and his own, Hamza felt surrounded by ghosts.

A picture of his mother, just the way he remembered her hung on the wall. She had died from breast cancer when he was eight and his brother, Hassan, ten. Father had taken her to the most expensive hospitals in the UK. She fought on until she could fight no more.

Father had been devastated—maybe he was still grieving. She was his soul mate. He had thrown himself into his work and lost himself there. He never remarried.

Hamza's eyes shifted to the next photo frame. He remembered it like it was yesterday. Hamza took a sip of his coffee. He had also been drinking coffee that morning in New York, getting ready for his job at NYU Medical Center. When his cell phone rang, his body stiffened. The screen said "CEO". His father never called just to find out how he was doing. There was always something. He pushed the answer button and placed the phone against his ear.

"Hello, Baba."

"Hamza."

"Yes, sir. Good morning, Baba."

There was a slight pause. "It's afternoon here. Hamza . . . I have bad news and good news. Hassan has died in a car accident. You-"

Hamza felt like the air had been sucked out of the room. His brother, his best friend, dead. "What happened?"

"I just told you . . . car accident." Baba's voice broke. He cleared his throat. "You must come back and continue where he stopped."

"Oh God," Hamza murmured. "I'll buy a ticket and be on the next plane out of—"

"No need. I've sent the plane to get you. Resign your position and come home."

Hamza paused and waited for the good news.

"See you, Hamza, Allah will guide you."

The disconnection tone sounded in Hamza's ear for five minutes before he placed the phone down.

Baba had groomed Hassan from an early age for a life in

politics. He was everything Hamza wasn't. Charismatic, fun-loving, and ambitious. With a degree in political science from the University of Lagos for his first degree, he earned a dual JD and MBA from Harvard.

Hassan had been a managing director at Tarbari and Sons and was getting ready to run for the House of Representatives as a way to dip his feet into politics. Now Father wanted Hamza to continue where Hassan had left off.

Hamza whimpered. Tears stung his eyes. It had been five years, but it still hurt like yesterday.

Father made his money the old way—he inherited it. Hamza's great-grandfather and grandfather had traded along West African countries for ages, and the business activities of their ancestors could be traced back as far as the late 1700s, loading caravans from Kano to these trading destinations, buying and selling.

When the British came on the scene and needed an experienced merchant to deal with, only the Tarbari clan had such clout. The leader of the family then dealt with the British. He became the middleman, procuring raw materials from the interior for export and buying finished European goods to resell to the locals.

Every generation of Tarbari had transferred wealth down. Added to what they inherited. By the twentieth century, wealth was not an issue. What the Tarbaris lacked was political power.

Baba knew Hamza was not cut out for such and placed that responsibility on Hassan. Now he was dead, and that responsibility had become Hamza's.

Hamza shook his head and wiped the tears from his eyes. He could now see the picture of Hassan clearly. He spoke in a whisper. "I won't be the Tarbari that let the ball drop."

CHAPTER SEVENTY-FOUR

"Hello."

As Gambo talked on the phone, I wracked my mind over what to do. I looked at Danladi and all I could feel in my heart was hatred. He was jittery. His eyes moved all over. From the girls to Gambo, to Aliyu and me. Faith's body lay there like something thrown away. What was I going to do?

"Everything will end tonight!" Gambo pointed the phone at Danladi.

I jumped, startled by his loud voice.

"That . . . that was Malam?" asked Danladi.

"Yes! One million wired, just like that!" exclaimed Gambo as he put his phone away.

"Wow! That's a lot of bread. What did he say?"

Gambo chuckled. "Malam wants your wife dead."

Danladi looked confused. "Why?"

I shuddered and glanced from Gambo to Danladi. Did he mean me? My knees trembled. The only people I believed could want me dead included Maryam and Auntie

Halima. But they wouldn't go through all this trouble. "Please-"

"No," said Gambo, cutting me off. "I will not kill you . . . yet." He yanked the hijab off my head.

I gasped, thinking he had hit me again. But I felt no pain. Gambo smiled as I cowered and wiped my tears and blood from my nose with the hijab. He pulled me close to him and I saw the hunger in his eyes.

"Ngozi, Ngozi," said Gambo, pushing his groin against me.

My whole body went rigid. *Oh God, this can't be happening.* I stumbled forward as Gambo tugged at my hand.

Aliyu snickered. "Danladi, Oga has confiscated your wife!"

Gambo pointed at Danladi then the girls. "Danladi, if any of them moves, shoot them. Don't fall for their tricks of wanting to relieve themselves. If they want to piss, shit, or anything, let them do it there. I'll be right back."

Gambo pulled at my hand and headed toward the door. My whole body shook. "Oh God," I mumbled.

"Yes," said Danladi. He stared ahead not blinking. His jaw muscles clenched and unclenched.

Gambo pointed at Aliyu. "Keep your eyes open too." He hauled me out into the open air and I realized how hot and stifling it had been inside the room. I filled my lungs.

Gambo shut the door and looked at the padlock. "Hmm, I don't want to be interrupted." He hooked it into the hole without locking it.

I filled my lungs and wondered what I could have done that would have saved Faith.

"Come," said Gambo. He pulled. I resisted. Then he

yanked my hand forward and dragged my whole body toward him.

I did not even have time to mourn my friend. He dragged me toward the truck. What type of human being was this? He'd committed murder, and the next thing on his mind was rape?

"Don't fight. I don't want to hurt you again. You are worth more alive than dead."

My teeth chattered so much I feared for my tongue. Gambo pinned me against the truck, and pain exploded in my back as the rearview mirror dug into my spine. His hands roamed all over.

I pushed him despite his warning. My effort only excited him more and he slammed my back against the truck. I heard a crack and felt a sharp pain as my back broke the side-view mirror. His sudden rage surprised me.

He wrapped his palms around my throat and squeezed while whispering into my ears. I couldn't make out what he was saying, but I understood that if I didn't get his hands off my neck, he would break his promise.

I grabbed his hands to pull them away from my throat, but he was too strong. He squeezed the life out of me. The light dimmed at the corners of my vision. Then he let go.

Air rushed into my airway as if I'd been underwater and had just broken to the surface to inhale. My vision got brighter as I inhaled. My throat burned.

"Stop resisting. You will only get hurt, and I will still get what I want." His voice was husky and low.

I willed my mind not to fight. But once Gambo's hands touched me again, the repulsion was overwhelming. I pushed back, and like a flash of lightning, he hit me across the face.

"Please . . . please . . ." I sobbed. "Don't." I couldn't let this happen. My skin tightened as if something hideous was crawling over my body. I could not. I inhaled deeply, shoved Gambo back, and drove my knee into his soft parts as hard as I could.

Air rushed out of Gambo. He doubled over, both hands reaching for his groin as he sank to his knees. I looked at him not believing my eyes. I'd thought he was superhuman, but he was just an ordinary man, just evil.

"Bitch!" Gambo groaned and got up to one knee, his face a mask of pain.

"You love to inflict pain and intimidate people," I said, panting. "Can't take what you give?"

"You are dead," growled Gambo, and he lunged for me.

Before I could jump back, he grabbed my wrist in an iron grip. I pulled my hand away, but he held on tight.

"How dare you hit me!" growled Gambo.

I dragged my body back and I tripped. I fell to the ground where Gambo wanted me. I had to get up. Adrenalin rushed through me. I kicked out with both feet as hard as I could.

"I will teach you a lesson you'll never forget," shouted Gambo. He tried to catch my leg with his other hand.

I kicked harder, knowing that if he caught my leg, I was done.

"Uggh!" Gambo moaned. He growled like an animal, and his hands left my wrist as if it were hot coals on his groin.

I'd hit pay dirt. A second direct hit. Panting, I scrambled to my feet and saw what had felled me: a piece of wood. Gambo was still on one knee. I picked up the wood, raised it as high as I could, and smashed it onto Gambo's head. He fell flat on the ground, like a housefly hit in midair with a notebook. I raised the wood again, but Gambo didn't twitch. He lay there dead.

Delirious with relief, I ran. I realized I was still holding the piece of wood. I dropped it and ran faster.

CHAPTER SEVENTY-FIVE

I ran up the moonlit street. I planned to follow the initial route Kalila had mapped out for Faith and me to the bus stop. I whimpered as soon as I remembered Faith but kept on running.

The street had turned into a night market. Roasted corn, pears, and cooked food were sold in makeshift stalls with candlelight and kerosene lamps. I ran on at full speed.

The few people on the road paid little attention as I ran up the street. Some stopped what they were doing and showed more interest but moved on after they figured it was only a girl running. They thought a Nollywood movie was being shot in their village. Where was the footpath? I kept on turning back, expecting Gambo behind me, but I knew he was no more.

I looked for the footpath where Gambo and Bala had attacked us. The thought of Bala had me looking around again. Should I stop and bang on someone's door and ask for help? Bala's words came to mind again: *We don't want to be part of that 'bring back our girls' message.* Were the rest of the villagers of the same thought? I hoped Kalila had poured hot oil on him.

Panic crept into my mind and tried to paralyze me. Where was the footpath? My feet faltered, and I slowed. Had I passed it in my haste?

A woman with a huge basket emerged from the bush and I knew the footpath was there. I picked up speed. Without a second thought, I plunged in, running along the path surrounded by a wall of grass on each side. The sound of crickets and other insects got louder as I ran.

A painful stitch had developed on my left side. I couldn't inhale. I stopped and bent over, my hands on my knees. I took shallow breaths as sweat dripped off my face. After a few puffs, the stitch unhooked.

I cocked my head, expecting someone to spring out of the bushes and grab me. All I heard was the distant blare of a car horn. I listened and detected the distinct whine of car engines as they sped on a highway. I remembered Kalila's instruction keep going straight and do not deviate; the path led straight to the bus stop. I was supposed to take the bus to Bamoga, and at Bamoga catch a bus to Lamija. I sprang to my feet and took off again.

The footpath ended at a bus stop, just as Kalila had said. My heart sank. A bus with a big sign on the back reading "Bamoga" pulled away as I emerged. Three passengers had disembarked from the bus and were picking up their luggage, yams tied together with vines and a huge basket of tomatoes.

"Stop! Stop!" I ran after the bus.

The conductor leaned out of the open door and urged me to run faster. I ran harder, but the bus didn't slow down. The conductor encouraged me using his index fingers in the air, the universal sign to run faster. He smiled and waved.

"Bastard!" I hissed. I stopped and doubled over, hands on my knees, panting. The bus never intended to stop. I watched it disappear down the horizon. Who knew when the next one would show, or if there would be another one.

I glanced toward the footpath; nobody was there. The passengers had disappeared with their luggage. Cars and trucks zipped by in both directions. Each time I heard a car approach, my instinct was to dash into the bush, but I didn't want to miss the bus or any vehicle that stopped.

I glanced around, looking for anything suspicious. I knew I wouldn't be able to relax until I was on the bus. As a girl standing alone without a bag or basket, I knew I would also attract a different predator, men.

Chatter drifted upward from the footpath. My muscles tightened. I stepped back away from the clearing, closer to the bushes for cover. If Bala emerged from the path, I would run. Two women, an older one and a younger one, deep in conversation, came into view. They stopped beside the road and dropped their baskets on the ground without stopping their chatter. I emerged from cover. The older one saw me, paused, and continued talking. Their presence gave me hope. They expected another bus too.

The run exhausted me, and there were no seats. My eyelids got heavier and heavier. The sound of cars was like a lullaby. I sat down and thought of dozing off for a few minutes. An image of me on the ground fast asleep while the bus came and left jerked me awake. I glanced at the bush path again—empty. I nodded off.

I imagined what was going on at the warehouse. Danladi might still wait for Gambo to come back. He would get weary and try to open the door. He'd realize Gambo had locked it and would give it an hour. He didn't want to annoy his boss. By the time he got the courage to break the door, I would be long gone.

"Bamoga! Bamoga, one chance!"

My eyes flew open. I had dozed off.

"Bamoga! Bamoga, one chance."

"Wait, I'm coming!" I yelled in Hausa. The two women were already by the bus and seemed to argue with the conductor.

"Nonsense, I can't leave my daughter behind," said the older woman in a shaky voice. "I'll carry her."

"Madam, the bus is full," said the conductor. "Only one person can go. You people should decide on who will travel."

"No way, we must travel together," said the daughter.

"I'll give you my seat and stand," replied the conductor. "But only if you pay extra."

"I'll pay extra and take the seat!" I yelled. After all, I was at the bus stop before them.

"This does not concern you," said the younger woman. "If I hear your voice again, I'll give you the beating of your life."

I knew cash was king. So I dipped my hand into my pocket and . . . felt nothing. I felt like someone had yanked the rug out from underneath me. I patted myself down. The money Kalila had given me was gone.

The older woman hissed. "She doesn't even have money."

"She wants to get on the bus," said the younger woman.

"Please, please, terrorists are after me," I pleaded. "They will kill me."

The conductor laughed. "Nice try, my sister. Next thing you'll say you're one of the Akarika girls!"

I watched the women get on the bus. The conductor slapped his palm twice against the door, and it drove away.

CHAPTER SEVENTY-SIX

I stood helplessly and watched the bus disappear. The people on the bus did not for a second think of what would become of me. They thought I had a home to get back to, just like I assumed Faith had parents at home who missed her.

Private cars continued to speed by, not slowing down in any form. I didn't know what to do. It was now dark, I'd waited for probably five minutes, and no bus had come. I felt like screaming. Every noise around me sounded like someone after me.

"What am I going to do?" I said out loud, my voice a whisper. I thought of Faith lying on the floor of the warehouse and my body wracked with sobs. She had been reluctant to leave. She did what she was told and kept her head low. But I convinced her that there was hope. She expressed what she wanted, to be left alone. But all the while I was pushing for what I wanted. It was always about me. I'd gotten her killed because of my selfishness. My lips trembled, and fresh tears flowed down my cheeks.

Other people have needs too. I never looked at things

the way Auntie Halima or Maryam would have seen it. When Auntie Halima married my uncle, I was not part of the arrangement. My auntie tolerated me because of my uncle, but once he passed, she saw no reason to continue. I'd gotten so used to fighting for everything, I couldn't put myself in other people's shoes and look at things the way it looked from their position. It might not be in my favor, but it was their choice to make.

An orphan, like a beggar, has no choice. I never showed humility.

We do not all have the same wants. Faith did not want to go home because there was no home to go to. Despite all the challenges she'd had, she was selfless. She came with me and was committed. If she hadn't made the first move and jumped out of that truck, God knows I would have still been on it.

After we jumped off the truck, Ronke drew Aliyu away from us so we could save ourselves. Maybe she did it for her twin sister. Would I have done it? Abandon my friends if the tables were turned?

I thought of Zainab and dismissed all the rubbish Gambo had said. They were trying to sow the seed of doubt in me. I wiped my tears. Mosquitoes buzzed around, crickets and frogs started their nightly collaboration. The sound of the night was in full swing. Even the sound of passing vehicles had dwindled to nothing.

I'd always run from my problems. I would run no more.

CHAPTER SEVENTY-SEVEN

I found the footpath, but it was now dark. I preferred to run through and get it over and done with fast. But I could deviate from the track. Sounds from the village floated toward me, fading in and out depending on the wind's direction. It was reassuring. At least I knew I was headed in the right direction.

Pulse racing, I walked fast, praying not to have the misfortune of stepping on a snake. What were my options once I got to Dalsu? Wait, and in the morning get on a bus and go.

I felt giddy with excitement. I could run away from all the problems here. I remembered the girls trapped in the warehouse and I felt ashamed. If I hadn't lost the money Kalila gave us, I would have been long gone.

People had gone out of their way at significant risk to themselves to help me. Kalila warned us and gave us money. Ronke distracted the terrorists so that we'd have a chance. They had all made selfless choices.

I'd accepted to live with Auntie Halima, afraid to move to my mother's friend's home in the US who had been trying to adopt me since my uncle died. I decided to stay, and my auntie made the decision to antagonize me. Over the years, I'd tried to change her, get her and others to see things my way. But at the end, the only person you can change is yourself. Become the good you want to see in others.

I had to stop running from my problems. Stop trying to change other people. What would Faith do? She wouldn't run. She would help. I walked faster. The sound of the village got closer and closer.

CHAPTER SEVENTY-EIGHT

M y head throbbed from where Gambo had hit me. Apart from mosquitoes, I don't think I'd ever killed anything before, but I felt no remorse for Gambo. I entered the street from the footpath, and the village was almost as I'd left it. People selling their wares and people buying were still there. This time nobody looked my way.

I walked down the street looking into houses through open doors and windows. Families settled down for dinner or sat down chatting. Didn't they know that girls kidnapped by terrorists were down the road? I remembered what Bala had said about people minding their business. Speaking of Bala, his house was ahead. My pulse raced as I approached. Should I look in and see how Kalila was doing? Foolishness.

Candlelight flickered in their home as I passed. I'm sure she was okay. She must know what type of person Bala is, and I didn't think she would have put herself in a situation she couldn't handle. I thought of what they did to Joy—Bala and his friend. They must have abused her and then left her for the hyenas to feed on.

My body relaxed after I'd passed their home. I'd expected Bala to show up and surprise me the way he had surprised Faith and me.

The sound of the town got fainter as I got closer to the warehouse. *Are you sure of what you're doing?* I asked myself again. The truck remained where it was.

I covered my mouth with my hand. Gambo's body lay where he had fallen. Blood glistened in the moonlight on his head and neck. The collar of his camouflage jacket looked damp.

I shuddered and continued toward the door; the padlock was untouched. My fingers trembled as I reached for it. The thought of my safety made me pause. Danladi and the Aliyu had guns. They knew how to use them and might shoot me right away. Danladi had attacked me before, but without their leader, they might hesitate. I should arm myself.

Peer pressure on these men to do things they wouldn't otherwise do was high. Gambo had pissed off Danladi, and that should give him a reason to do something different.

I approached Gambo's body. I would take his gun and brandish it at Danladi and Aliyu. That should give me enough time to talk to Danladi. I'd seen weapons used in movies. Just squeeze the trigger, right? How difficult could it be?

The thought of touching the dead body scared me more than charging into the warehouse. The closest I'd ever come to a dead body was my uncle just before his burial when the immediate family came in to say good-bye.

Gambo's gun was in a black holster by his side. He had fallen close to the tire of the truck, and the holster was pinned between the tire and his leg. I shifted his left leg, unclipped his holster, and took the gun. His pocket bulged with a bundle of naira notes. I stuffed them in my skirt pocket.

I'd never held a gun nor come this close to one in my life. But once it was in my hand, it gave me some authority. A power that when I opened my mouth, people would listen. Back at the door, I unhooked the padlock, opened the staple, and hung the lock back on it. The air smelled of stale sweat and unwashed bodies.

I swallowed. Faith's body was still where it had fallen, but someone had draped a piece of cloth over her. I strolled in, sweat dripping down my forehead. The girls noticed me when I was about halfway in. Whispered conversation among the girls died down as they saw me.

Danladi jumped to his feet. "Ngozi?" His gaze moved behind me. "Where's Gambo?" He shifted his head trying to get a better view behind me.

"He's dead."

"Where is he? Why did he lock me in here for an hour? And take my wife with him? Gambo, show your face."

"He's dead!" I shouted. It seemed like Danladi had had plenty of time to think of how Gambo had treated him.

"How?" asked Aliyu. He raised his gun and pointed it at me.

There was a long pause as Danladi's mind analyzed things. He looked at me, then at the door.

"Aliyu, lower your gun," said Danladi. "I think she's telling the truth. She has Gambo's gun."

"Gambo dead? Let me check." Aliyu made for the door.

"Wait!" said Danladi. He walked toward me, a gun in hand. His eyes were wide, darting from the door to me.

Aliyu exhaled noisily. "What are we going to do?" He glanced around, shaking his head, his finger on the trigger of his gun. "What are we going to do with these girls? The plan was to take them to Cameroon. Should we proceed without Oga?"

His question hung in the air. Sweat poured down my forehead, and I realized my first mistake. I hadn't had a concrete plan coming in. But I had a gun. Nobody was going to Cameroon.

Aliyu whistled. "If Gambo is dead, that money he was talking about, how do . . ." Aliyu's voice trailed off. "We can get it from his bank account," said Aliyu.

"That's my department," said Danladi. "I'll wire it out of his account. We will still take the girls to Cameroon. It's the safest place for us with all the outcry."

CHAPTER SEVENTY-NINE

All the girls talked at once. Some pleaded for their lives. They were an only daughter; they missed their mothers and fathers, brothers and sisters. They all wanted to return to their families. In that brief instant, I thought of Faith and how her family welcomed her when she got home. Would any of these girls have the same experience?

I stared at Danladi, not believing my ears. "You're better than that! You are your own man. God gave you a sound mind for a reason. You cannot follow Gambo like cattle." I pointed at Faith and tears welled in my eyes. "Look at Faith. You know her. She wouldn't hurt a fly, and he killed her in cold blood. Do you believe she deserves what she got?"

"No. It's . . . it's not that straightforward," Danladi stammered.

I heard the doubt in his voice. A crack had formed on his wall, the same uncertainty I'd heard in Auntie Halima's voice. Back then I'd seized the opportunity to save myself. Now I would try to help others.

"He's dead. He cannot control you anymore. Don't

continue with the plan." Tears poured down my cheeks. "He doesn't respect you. Right in front of you, he wanted to abuse me." I saw the flicker of anger in Danladi's eyes. He'd stood there and done nothing while his "wife" was removed to be abused.

Danladi thought for a moment. "It's not that easy. Do you think I can just pack my bag and say I won't do this anymore, I'm leaving? Do you think Gambo would just sit and watch?"

"He's dead!" I screamed.

My words seemed to penetrate Danladi's wall of learned fear.

"But there are others." He looked at Aliyu. "It's not that easy."

"Why not?" I asked. "We will call the police and inform them of what happened. Gambo kidnapped all of us and forced you and Aliyu to do his dirty job, or he would kill your families."

Danladi chuckled. "They won't believe that! Do you know the amount of pressure the police are facing right now? If they show up, they will brand most of us terrorists and culprits." Danladi laughed. "There is the issue of deaths in custody. I don't want to become another person that died in police custody."

"Danladi! Stop listening to this girl," said Aliyu. "Let's decide on what to do. We can take them with us or kill all of them! This police business you are talking about, I don't want to be a part of. You've summarized it already; the police cannot be trusted." Aliyu stabbed a finger in the air. "See what they did to the leader of Boko Haram in 2009. They arrested him at his in-laws', brought him to the police station in Maiduguri, and he died in police custody. When the international community made some noise, what did they say? He died while trying to escape."

Danladi's eyebrows narrowed as he weighed all that I'd said. As he thought of what to do, I put my free hand behind my back and motioned at the girls to flee. I knew that was putting myself in danger. Nothing happened. I'd expected the girls to get up and run. Didn't they see my hand? I didn't want to risk looking back and making Danladi suspicious. That would cost me the trust I'd earned.

"Danladi, with Gambo gone, you're in charge," said Aliyu. "My only fear is if Gambo should resurrect from the dead. He would come after us."

A nervous laugh escaped Danladi's lips. "He's not Jesus." He moved toward me.

Trembling, I took a step back. Was he coming for me? I still had the gun in my hand. *What do I do?*

"What you said is true," said Danladi in a quiet tone.

I shook my head, confused. "Which one?"

"Gambo told me that any day he found me wanting or was not sure of my loyalty, he would sell my sisters into slavery."

"Okay," I said. I gestured with the gun. "Who knew you had sisters. Let's get everybody out then."

Danladi looked down at the gun, then at me. "Do you know how to use that?"

"Point and shoot," I said.

"Can I see it?" asked Danladi.

I hesitated. "Can I see yours?" I knew I couldn't get the girls out without his help. Giving him the gun would show good faith. "Fine." I let go of the gun.

Danladi took the gun and hefted it. "Nice."

"All right," said Aliyu. "I'm on board. Remember that

money is for us to share. But, Danladi, why would anybody pay so much money to have your wife killed?"

"Because she is worth a lot to somebody dead!" said a voice.

The girls screamed and rushed to the corner of the room. I whirled around. Gambo stood by the entrance, blood dripped down his face. He had an AK-47, the type Aliyu delivered to the Fulani herdsmen.

CHAPTER EIGHTY

I shook my head, not believing my eyes. I wanted to run, but my feet refused to move. At that moment I knew my life was about to end. A whimper escaped my lips.

"Gambo!" blurted Danladi. His eyes were wide. He looked at Gambo with disbelief.

"God is great!" said Gambo. "I've come back from the dead. I see you have my gun. Drop it." Gambo blinked as blood dripped from a cut on his head down to his shirt.

Danladi let the gun clatter to the floor.

"Aliyu!" shouted Gambo.

"Yes, sir!" said Aliyu.

Gambo laughed. "You've switched already? Your loyalty is like a leaf, it goes in whatever direction the wind is blowing. I thought it was only Danladi I had to keep an eye on. He was never sure of himself or his beliefs, even when we were at religious school."

"No . . . no, Oga, I thought you were . . ." Aliyu's voice trailed off.

"Dead!" said Gambo. "Danladi's wife meant to kill me. And I see she's already contaminated your minds."

Aliyu pounded his chest. "I'm . . . I'm still loyal," he stammered. Sweat dotted his forehead. His gun hung on his shoulder, useless to him.

"It doesn't matter," said Gambo. "You're dead to me!"

A burst of gunfire shattered the silence. I screamed, crouched, and covered my ears. The girls lay on the floor whimpering and crying.

Aliyu stared at Gambo, eyes wide. Blood oozed from multiple sites on his chest. He fell on his knees and crashed face down on the floor.

Danladi tried to move against Gambo and halted. He raised his hands in the air, his effort stopped by Gambo's gun pointed at him. Danladi's lips trembled as his eyes bore into Gambo's. If only looks could kill.

"Ngozi, you have been a cash cow," said Gambo. "I'd planned to keep you alive and extract more money from the person who wants you dead, but after what you pulled tonight, I'm left with no choice."

I didn't know what to say. I watched Gambo. He swayed back and forth, blinked, and wiped blood from his forehead. Had he lost enough blood to pass out? His gun remained pointed at Danladi.

"Danny boy," said Gambo. "I'm disappointed in you. I listened to how this girl molded you like pounded yam. You bought what she was selling!"

Danladi sighed. "Gambo—"

"Don't Gambo me. This whole thing was your idea, remember? When we were little in religious school. Western education is sacrilege, remember? Now you don't have what it takes to continue. You see blood and find a girl with an e-mail address, and you lose your mind."

My ears had pricked up. This was Danladi's idea?

"Of course, I remember," said Danladi through clenched teeth. "That was the plan when we were kids. I hated the kids that went to regular schools because I wanted to be like them. But I'd moved on, forgotten about it until you came back from Libya a changed person. You talked me into it, and Malam hijacked the organization. The plan wasn't to kill and kidnap. That was all your and Malam's idea. Who is he anyway? He used us to do his dirty work. My plan— we planned to spread the word, course civil disobedience, and get attention. Not kill."

"But we got attention," said Gambo, smiling. "You were joyous with the initial influx of funds, weapons, and training from our supporter, but when he demanded results for the support, you balked. You can't have it both ways."

"Gambo, let these girls go," said Danladi. "We'll iron out our differences."

Gambo laughed. "Something must have softened your head. They've already heard a lot. Too much information is never a good thing." He lowered his voice and laughed. "We should have asked them to cover their ears."

Realization hit me. He was going to kill us all. Gambo threw back his head and laughed like a madman. He stopped abruptly and turned the barrel of the gun toward the girls cowering on the floor.

"Please! No!" the girls shrieked.

I braced myself and waited for the sound of Gambo's gunshots. It didn't come. Instead, I saw Danladi launch himself like a rocket toward Gambo. It happened in an instant—Danladi connecting with Gambo and knocking him to the ground; the gun going off.

Bullets smashed into the wall and I lowered my head. When I looked up, Danladi was on top of Gambo, his face a mask of rage. He punched Gambo once, then twice. He lifted his hand for the third swing when three pops went off in rapid succession. Danladi collapsed on top of Gambo, not moving.

My whole body was shaking. In the corner, the girls cried and moaned. On the floor, Gambo struggled to get Danladi off him. My ears rang. My eyes fixed on Gambo. Blood flowed on the floor. I couldn't move. I remained frozen. A wave of nausea passed through me, the smell of blood, unwashed bodies, and fear overwhelming my system.

Gambo heaved Danladi's body off him. He was covered in blood. He snarled, put the barrel of the gun against Danladi's head, and shot him twice more.

"Oh God," I gasped.

Gambo turned to me and smiled. "Now it's your turn." He pointed the gun at me.

Click. Click.

It was empty. I didn't think. I jumped to my feet and rushed for the door. Behind me, I heard movement as Gambo struggled to get up. The girls remained shocked, frozen where they were as I sailed through the door as if the devil himself was after me.

CHAPTER EIGHTY-ONE

Ears ringing, I burst out of the door and into the night. I'd expected the gunshots would have attracted people to the warehouse, but there was nobody. The villagers had learned that a total lack of curiosity does wonders to their life expectancy.

I saw Gambo's truck and hesitated. He would see me running along the road and would come after me. I could hide beside the truck and escape in the opposite direction he went. There was no doubt in my mind Gambo would kill me once he got his hands on me. As I debated what to do, I heard the door open with a bang and dove to the ground beside the truck. I crawled on my hands and knees to the other side of the vehicle and peeped out.

Gambo hooked in the padlock and clipped it shut, effectively trapping everybody inside. He pulled at it to be doubly sure and looked around. Blood glistened on his face.

"Which way did she go?" Gambo muttered to himself. He took a step forward, stopped, and did a slow three-sixty, looking in every direction. He wiped his face with the back of his hands and came toward the truck.

I held my breath until my lungs burned. I exhaled noisily, convinced Gambo would hear. A chill ran down my spine. The image of him putting a gun on Danladi's head and shooting him was fresh on my mind.

I was a fast runner. This time I didn't hesitate. Like an antelope, I jumped up from my hiding place and ran.

"Ah!" Gambo jumped back, startled.

He hadn't known I was there. I'd given myself away.

The few people on the moonlit street paid little attention when I ran up the road. I passed the path that led to the bus stop and continued going. Some village people stopped what they were doing to watch. I looked behind and Gambo was in pursuit.

They did not take a moment to think about what could be wrong with the situation. I knew Gambo had a knife, but I wasn't sure if he had a gun with bullets. Would he shoot if he had one? These thoughts ran through my mind as I ran for my life.

"*Dakatar da ita*! Stop her!" yelled Gambo.

People watched, not aiding or abetting. *Where do I run to?* I wondered. Panic was paralyzing my logic. Ahead I saw the second footpath I was looking for and without a second thought headed toward it.

I plunged in, running hard. Even though I'd been on the trail only once, my memory of it was as clear as day. A stitch pulled at my side, and I slowed down, gasping for air. I passed grass and trees, which were now just shadows. I had no plan, no ideas. *Just run.*

A sudden sadness overtook me. Just hours before, I'd been on this road with Faith, begging God to spare her from death. He'd saved her, only for Gambo to slit her throat like a chicken. Tears brimmed my eyes, and I wiped them off.

As I ran, the stitch on myside came back. I held on to my side and stumbled along.

The terrain didn't seem familiar anymore. I noticed a dark object to my right and thought briefly to hide behind it. As I got closer, I realized it was the hut where the snake had attacked us. The thought propelled me to continue.

I stole a look over my shoulder. Gambo was close. How did he keep up? I got off the footpath and ran into the bush. Sweat dripped down my face into my eyes, stinging them and blinding me. I repeatedly blinked to clear them.

"Stop there!" yelled Gambo, panting, as though he had the power to command me to stop.

But I froze. Not from Gambo's command but from the smell of decay that hit my nostrils. It was everywhere. It had taken me a shorter time to reach this section of the bush where we had seen a lot of gin traps. The smell was overpowering; hyenas were out there. They had gotten food the last couple of days from this area and were back for more.

"God, help me," I said breathlessly. Doubled over, drenched in sweat, I inhaled and exhaled. Leaving the path and walking into the bushes had been the same mistake I made with Faith yesterday. I was right in the middle of the gin trap minefield.

All I could see around me were shadows. I searched the ground looking for a glint of metal, any sign at all. As Gambo approached, I took one step back, then two. Every step reminded me of a game of Try Your Luck we took part in during church bazaars.

"You . . . you think you can run away from me?" said Gambo, breathless. He was a few feet away from me, bent at the waist, his hands on his knees, panting like the dog he was.

Then I heard the slight jingle of chains. I bent down and saw the unmistakable metal jaws of a gin trap. I knew there were more, and I risked stepping into them. Heart pounding, I walked behind it, bent over with hands on my knees, winded.

"You . . . are . . . tired of running," said Gambo, winded. You thought you were a gazelle, eh?"

Gambo seemed to recover quickly. He stood straight but continued to breathe hard. I said nothing and watched as he walked toward me. He stopped a few steps away from me.

"Well, you might be the gazelle," said Gambo. He slapped his chest with his open palm. "But I am the king of beasts who owns the forest."

I raised one hand. "Please . . . please leave me alone."

"You can't run anymore?" taunted Gambo. "Tired?"

A killer was right in front of me. It took every ounce of will I had not to turn around and run.

Gambo reached for his knife and pulled it out with deliberate ease. "A termite can fly as high as it wants, but it will eventually fall to the ground and a frog will eat it. You are way too much trouble alive. It's time I cut my losses."

The dagger glistened in the moonlight. I followed it with my eyes. It was the same one he slew my friend with.

"Please . . ."

Knife raised, Gambo stopped and watched me. He cocked his head, looked around, then lowered his eyes. Something caught his eyes, and he bent at the waist. "A trap!" He laughed and walked around it. "Nobody stands still with death approaching."

I looked all around me. I must move. Knees shaking, I staggered to the side. "Please don't kill me. I don't want to die." Expecting the worse, I took another step. Death surrounded me.

"Time's up!" With a growl, Gambo lunged at me. I closed my eyes. There was a snap, and Gambo let out a blood-curdling scream and fell to the ground.

"My leg! My leg!"

The distinct metallic tang of fresh blood filled the air, and I knew company would be here soon. I knew the only way out was to retrace my steps as best as I could. The only way out was to walk over him.

"It's an animal trap. Come . . . help me," said Gambo through gritted teeth as the pain ravished his body. He bent down and tried to pry the jaws of the gin trap open. What if he pulled the metal jaws open?

"Come and help me," said Gambo. "I promise I won't hurt you."

I ignored him. Gambo was blocking my way out. I'd have to jump over him.

My heartbeat throbbing in my ears, I walked toward Gambo and leaped. His hand brushed against my feet, but he couldn't get a grip. I landed on my feet. I turned and looked at Gambo and he was up.

He pulled at the chain. "You are dead!" He growled in pain.

The chain was anchored around a small shrub. Gambo could easily remove the chain and walk away with the trap attached to his leg.

I rushed to Gambo and shoved him as hard as I could. As he landed, there was another snap and another. He cried out in pain. His right hand was trapped.

"Please help me," pleaded Gambo. "Forgive and forget."

"Never!" I said. "Now hyenas will come and feast on you. Smell the air? They are already here." I backed away.

"Come back! Don't leave me like this."

I retraced my steps through the bush and back to the

footpath and ran. Gambo's cry and the rattle of chains was like wind behind my back.

CHAPTER EIGHTY-TWO

As the animals that had developed a taste for human flesh feasted on Gambo, I made my way back to the warehouse. There was no other danger I could account for. Gambo and his crew had been eliminated.

I had a confidence in me like I'd dealt with evil and come out triumphant. I was ready to handle anything that came my way. Once again I entered the village. The people hanging around had now dwindled. All eyes were on me as I marched toward the warehouse at the end of the road. It was just as I'd left it. The truck was there and the door to the warehouse was closed.

I opened the door and went in. The girls huddled on one side away from the dead bodies. I didn't look at the bodies.

"Come, let's go," I said. My voice was almost a whisper and I waved the girls closer. This time they didn't hesitate. They rushed towards me and we exited the room, into the fresh night air, hope springing eternal in my heart and the knowledge that God had, indeed, answered this prayer.

THE END

AUTHORS NOTE

Thank you for reading Sambisa Escape. Gaining visibility as an independent author relies mostly on word-of-mouth, if you have the time and inclination, please consider leaving your opinion about "Sambisa Escape," however lengthy or brief.

The story continues, visit the authors website below for more information on the sequel to Sambisa Escape.

www.ifeanyiesimai.com

Thanks!
Ifeanyi

ABOUT THE AUTHOR

Ifeanyi grew up with an inquisitive mind, loved listening to folklore and read across different genres.

Today, he writes stories of his own from his home in New Jersey. When he's not writing or reading, he spends time with his wife, three children, and a bearded dragon.

 facebook.com/ifeanyiesimaiauthor

 twitter.com/IEsimai

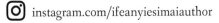 instagram.com/ifeanyiesimaiauthor